THE STORM

Recent Titles by Elisabeth McNeill from Severn House

A BOMBAY AFFAIR
THE SEND-OFF
THE GOLDEN DAYS
UNFORGETTABLE
THE LAST COCKTAIL PARTY

DUSTY LETTERS
MONEY TROUBLES
TURN BACK TIME

THE EDINBURGH MYSTERIES

HOT NEWS
PRESS RELATIONS

THE STORM

Elisabeth McNeill

This first world edition published in Great Britain 2006 by
SEVERN HOUSE PUBLISHERS LTD of
9–15 High Street, Sutton, Surrey SM1 1DF.
This first world edition published in the USA 2006 by
SEVERN HOUSE PUBLISHERS INC of
595 Madison Avenue, New York, N.Y. 10022.

British Library Cataloguing in Publication Data

McNeill, Elisabeth
    The storm
    1. Women disaster victims - Scotland - Eyemouth - Fiction
    2. Fishing villages - Scotland - Fiction
    3. Eyemouth (Scotland) - Social conditions - 19th century - Fiction
    I. Title
    823.9'14 [F]

    ISBN-13: 978-0-7278-6377-5
    ISBN-10: 0-7278-6377-0

Acknowledgements:
Children of the Sea by Peter Aitchison, 2001, Tuckwell Press
An Old Time Fishing Town – Eyemouth by Daniel McIver,
1906, Scotsman Archives, Edinburgh
Berwickshire News, Berwick on Tweed
William Collin, Fantasy Prints, 14 West Street, Berwick on Tweed

All Severn House titles are printed on acid-free paper.

Typeset by Palimpsest Book Production Ltd.,
Polmont, Stirlingshire, Scotland.
Printed and bound in Great Britain by
MPG Books Ltd., Bodmin, Cornwall.

Men have fished out of Eyemouth for over seven hundred years, and their descendants are still doing so today.

Where the Berwickshire River Eye falls into the North Sea it forms a small but deep natural harbour, enclosed on both sides by embracing arms of land.

On its southern side is a green-covered promontory, dominated by an elegant eighteenth-century mansion house, once used by smugglers and later by Customs men.

On the north, across the bay, rears a vast, jagged cliff of grass-topped red sandstone that culminates in a point like the profile of a bulldog. Its flank shows a huge section of fallen-away rock that looks as if a giant has taken a bite out of it.

A short sweep of yellow sand forms a beach beneath the southern promontory, and behind it is the town, a huddle of red-roofed, white-walled houses, hiding from the wind. A tall, thin church spire pierces the sky behind the streets and narrow alleys.

In the spread of open water between the two points a cluster of black rocks rear up like broken alligators' teeth. These are the Hurkars, sinister obstacles between which fishing boats must weave a course before they reach safe harbour – which many of them failed to do on the day of the worst storm in the town's history.

One

Early morning, Friday 14 October 1881

Tangles of her curly yellow hair got into her mouth and woke Rosabelle Scott as she snuggled against Dan's back in the comfort of their bed. She pushed the hair away and laid her cheek on his back, breathing in the scent of him, putting out her tongue and gently licking his skin. The taste of his salty sweat made her whole body quiver, overcome by a wordless, joyous intensity of love.

Was it only a week since they'd been married? They had spent the seven days in uninhibited love-making, and it was so much sweeter to make love in a bed instead of sneaking off to the ruined fort on top of the cliff. They'd done that all summer, but their desire had been made tense by fear of somebody stumbling across them.

She was carrying Dan's baby now but felt no shame at being a pregnant bride. Most of the women in Eyemouth, including her own mother, took their marriage vows pregnant. At least she'd waited till she was nineteen before she fell with Dan Maltman's child, and he was the only man she'd ever been with, or wanted.

He shifted his shoulders like a restive horse when he felt her tongue licking his back.

'Heard the clock?' he asked in a hoarse voice, still full of sleep.

'Aye, it struck five a little while ago,' she told him. The church clock that marked out the time for their town had helped to waken her. 'It smells dry. It's going to be a fine day,' she guessed, sniffing the air, for there was no window in their snug little room to look through.

He sat up abruptly. 'Is it? Then we'll sail.'

3

She propped her head on her hand and smiled at him. 'That's all you want, isn't it? To go to sea. Are you tired of being in bed with me already?'

'Dinna be daft. I could stay here with you for ever, but the boats've not been out for a week and we need money in our pockets. I'll buy you a silken gown if we have a good catch.' He remembered how she'd sighed over the dresses of fine ladies parading along Princes Street in Edinburgh, where they'd spent the day after their wedding.

She sighed and pouted, 'I wish we could stay in bed for ever.'

He laughed and spread himself out on top of her, flattening her slender body beneath his weight. 'So do I, but we have to eat. No fishing, no silk gowns and no eating!'

She locked her arms behind his head and pulled his bristly face down to hers. 'I know something that's better than food and silk gowns,' she whispered, sliding her long legs around his hips and pulling him into her. He groaned as he felt her fingernails digging into the hard muscles of his shoulders.

The clock struck six before they sat up again.

Willie Wave clambered fully clothed out of the pile of rags that was his bed in his son's net shed in the alley called Fouldub, and crawled across the floor on his hands and knees.

When he shoved the door open, dawn was breaking over the North Sea, burnishing the still water with streaks of gold, magenta and green.

It's going to be a fine day. The boats can go out, he thought. Bad weather had kept the Eyemouth fishing fleet in harbour for ten days, and if they stayed in much longer, bairns would be going hungry.

Willie was at least seventy-five years old – his birthday had been forgotten long ago – and no longer able to find a place on any boat; but on fine mornings he forgot his age and imagined that he could go fishing again. All he had to do was find a skipper prepared to take him on.

Unfortunately, he only had one son, Rob, who was under the thumb of a bullying wife, but in his day Willie had been a good skipper with a share in a sturdy boat. He'd lost his mind, though, and Rob, who drank too much, had sold his share of the boat and now sailed as a crewman with Rosabelle's easy-going father, Davy Scott, skipper of the *Myrtle*.

Reaching into his pocket the old man pulled out the tattered woollen fishing cap that he wore to hide his baldness. When he pulled it down over his ears, it made his head look like a black turnip.

He next searched for his seaboots, but they were nowhere to be seen and eventually he remembered that Ella Collin, Rob's termagant wife, had taken them away to sell them.

'I never liked that woman,' he said aloud, and in bare feet gingerly stepped out on to the harbour-side paving stones, surveying the brightening sky as he went.

Suddenly, his happy expression changed and he stood still, staring upwards as a disquieting thought struck him: *Where are the herring gulls?*

There were usually hundreds of them roosting on the pantiled roofs of the houses, patrolling the pier, balancing like acrobats on the tips of the masts of moored boats, with their wicked amber-coloured eyes ever alert for food.

But today there was only one to be seen. The rest of the flock had vanished.

Willie pulled a stinking fish head out of a heap of *fulzie* – rotting guts and mussel shells heaped against the house wall. The stink that came from it gave his alley its unappealing name.

Swinging back his arm, he threw the carcase on to the pathway to tempt the solitary gull that went cruising over his head. To his disquiet, it ignored the bait, and headed on inland, its eyebrow-shaped wings moving with ease. He stared after it, envying its elegance and majesty. Once he too had been able to move with similar insouciance, but no longer.

As the gull flew off, he remembered times in the past when gulls had deserted the town. Though his mind darted about like a distracted spider, some knowledge was part of him, as automatic as breathing. A descendant of generations of fishermen, he knew that when gulls disappeared inland on a fine morning, bad weather was coming, as sure as death.

Slipping on the slime from the fulzie heap, he hurried off towards the head of the pier, muttering aloud, 'The gless. I'll look at the gless.'

The 'gless' was a big barometer on the end of the pier that the local MP had paid to have installed to give warning of bad weather after six Eyemouth fishermen drowned in an unexpected squall forty years before. It was Willie Wave's oracle, and when he skippered his own boat, he would never go out if the mercury level was low. Even now, though he no longer went to sea, he checked it every day.

Reaching up with his gnarled forefinger, he tapped on the long glass tube and watched with astonishment as the silver liquid dropped – down – down – down.

What's happening? he wondered

The level fell a full inch as he watched. He tapped again and it went down even further, registering the lowest reading he'd ever seen.

In disbelief he looked back up at the translucent sky. Early-morning sunshine still sparkled and twinkled on the surface of smooth water, but he was not reassured. He had the evidence of the glass. In spite of the friendly sun, in spite of blue sky above his head, bad weather was coming.

The herring gull spotted Willie Wave's bribe of a fish head but knew better than to stop. Spreading its wings wide, it rose higher in the sky and went soaring inland from where the Hurkars' evil-looking serrated tops marked the passage into the harbour. Breasting the air, it rose in the sky because the black vortex of a storm was roaring at its back. It was heading inland to a stretch of safe water where it would stay till the fury passed.

When Dan Maltman tore himself away from making love to his wife, he went downstairs to look at the dawn, and his already high spirits rose even higher because there was not a cloud to be seen. Raising his arms above his head, he flexed his muscles and felt like a conqueror, capable of taking on the world.

The room where he and Rosabelle were starting married life was an attic on the top of a narrow building. Next door lived Dan's parents – his father, Jimmy 'Dip' Maltman, and his mother, Effie Young, who kept her maiden name because Eyemouth women never changed their names on marriage – with his younger brothers Henry and Robert.

6

The Maltman home was substantial compared to most, for they occupied four rooms, each with a window, which was a great luxury in the overcrowded fishing town. Dan felt blissfully happy. *What man of twenty-one could want more than me?* he thought as he contemplated his world. He was in the pride of his youth and health, his wife was the bonniest girl in Eyemouth, his child was on its way, and he had a place on one of the best boats in the harbour. That was the *Harmony*, skippered by his father, Jimmy Dip. 'Dip' was a nickname that marked him out from several other James Maltmans in a community where fishing families were as intertwined as balls of string. They had sailed together and married each others' relatives for generations.

Most families preferred that their men did not all sail in the same boat, so that, if one went down, someone would be left to look after family dependants. Jimmy Dip and Effie defied custom and all three sons sailed with their father. Effie did not object because she couldn't think of any skipper in the fleet more capable than Jimmy.

Giving a huge yawn, Dan went off to find his father.

In a house at the end of the next alley, Jessie Johnston opened her eyes when the church clock struck six and put her hands palm down on her swelling belly, holding her breath and waiting to see if she needed to vomit as she'd done every morning for weeks. Nothing happened. Today, thank God, she felt fine.

She turned over, pulling at the blanket and uncovering her younger sisters Mary and Fanny, who were sleeping one on each side of her.

'Lie still, you big whale!' groaned sixteen-year-old Mary, and Jessie gave her a sharp push that sent her on to the floor, where two small boys and a little girl were asleep on straw palliasses.

A fight broke out among them and, deciding to feel sick after all, Jessie pulled the blanket over her curly head and moaned, 'I'm going to puke, I'm going to puke!' That worried her next-in-age sister Fanny, who was out of bed in a flash. On previous mornings Jessie had proved that she could make her vomit travel quite a distance.

Once wakened, there was nothing for the youngest children to do but get dressed and go downstairs in search of food. Mary and Fanny stuck it out and climbed back into bed with Jessie, grumbling and saying, 'Move over. It's too early to get up yet.'

Reluctantly she made space for them. 'At least I've only another week to put up with this. Just one more week of sleeping like a herring in a box,' she said and drifted back into sleep, soothed by thoughts of her coming wedding.

How grand she was going to look! From another woman who worked on the fish-gutting gang she'd borrowed a big blue hat with a curly ostrich feather in it. With money saved from her job she'd bought a second-hand satin dress in the same colour. It was too big for her because she was tiny, but her friend Rosabelle, who was clever with her needle, was putting tucks around the hem, taking it in at the waist and cleverly draping the skirt up into a bustle that would distract the eye from Jessie's bulging belly.

Not that being pregnant on her wedding day bothered her any more than it had bothered Rosabelle.

I'm marrying Henry Maltman on Friday – a week from today – and I'll look as grand as a duchess, Jessie thought happily as sleep swept over her.

The clock chimes also woke the Maltman boys' mother, Effie Young, a strongly built woman of thirty-nine with tightly curled light-brown hair that was beginning to show glints of grey, and a broad, high-cheekboned face. When she sat up in bed and saw the lightening sky through her window, she stuck her feet out of the covers, and was down in the kitchen before any of her men stirred.

The weather was fine and money was needed. Henry, her second son, was getting married next week. When Dan married, she and Jimmy paid for the couple's trip to Edinburgh, so it was only fair that Henry receive the same – but she hoped that her youngest son Robert would wait a while before he too took a wife.

Her heart rose when she thought about her sons' marriages. Dan's Rosabelle was pregnant, and so was Henry's Jessie. The promise of grandchildren delighted Effie. If the babies

8

were boys, they would take over the family boat when her husband and sons were too old to go to sea. Jimmy Dip would never have to wander the quay as a penniless beggar like poor old Willie Wake.

Hearing the sound of feet on the wooden stairway, she clattered the kettle on to the fire and shouted out, 'Is that you, Henry? It's going to be a fine day for the fishing. I've baited the lines and they're in the shed. Dan's is there too. Run along and fetch him.'

It was Jimmy Dip who came out of the stair doorway, frowning as he asked, 'Did you bait Dan's line for him again? You've enough to do already and he's married now. His wife should do it.'

She nodded. 'I did it this once because it's Rosabelle's first time and her fingers aren't up to it yet. She's a dab hand at the sewing, tho' no' so good at hook-baiting, but she's from a fishing family and she'll learn. Her mother's one of our best line baiters, and her sister Clara's off wi' the herring boats in Yarmouth right now. Rosabelle'll learn fast enough.'

'It's to be hoped she does. Why did Dan have to go and marry a seamstress?' asked Jimmy in a mock-serious tone, but he was not angry, because he liked the girl.

Eyemouth fishing boats usually carried a crew of six apiece, and each man had to be equipped with two fishing lines. Each line carried a thousand hooks, and it was the duty of the women of his family to bait them with mussels or whelks, which they gathered from the seashore and carried home in creels on their backs.

Pushing the bait on to the fierce metal hooks was painful and very hard on the fingers, but gathering it was worse, because, if many boats were going out to fish, bait became scarce and women competed for the shellfish on the shore. Fist fights often broke out among them.

Rosabelle would normally have been expected to take up traditional fishing women's work when she left school at fourteen, but she escaped that life because of her talent with a needle, which was noticed by her first schoolteacher, Miss Lyall, whose mother owned a dressmaking business in the town.

She persuaded Rosabelle's mother to allow her daughter to

start an apprenticeship with Mrs Lyall, who taught the girl how to make clothes for a clientele of county ladies. Rosabelle had never learned how to bait hooks.

When Effie's kettle began steaming, and breakfast was set on the table, Dan arrived, shouting cheerfully at his father, 'It's a fine day for fishing.'

Jimmy Dip nodded, looked out of the window, and agreed: 'It looks fair, but have you checked the gless?'

Dan laughed and waved an arm at the clear sky. 'Ye dinna need to check it on a day like this. Look out there!'

'I'll check it anyway,' said cautious Jimmy, heading for the door. His sons pulled derisive faces behind his back but walked out with him. Effie watched them go, and smiled to herself, struck by their strength and masculine beauty. It seemed a miracle that she and brown-bearded Jimmy had given life to three black-haired giants.

They were handsome, courteous, confident and cheerful men who, she hoped, would learn the ways of the sea and have good lives.

Before they reached the barometer, however, Willie Wave came running towards them, waving his arms and grimacing wildly. At the sight of the Maltmans he began yelling, 'Dinna gang oot the day! There's gonna be an earthquake!'

Dan thought he was joking and laughed as he said, 'You get dafter every day, Willie.'

But his laughter stopped because a group of solemn-looking fishermen were standing around the barometer, listening to the coastguard, grey-haired David Duncan, who was shaking his head as he said, 'I dinna like it. I dinna like it at a'.'

Dan pushed his way through the crowd to tap on the glass tube. When he saw how low the mercury stood, he turned and said doubtfully to his brother, 'It must be broken.'

Henry joined him, looked at the glass, tapped it, and nodded as well. 'That's what's wrong. It's broken,' he said, but a solemn expression came over their father's face when it was his turn to check.

'I've never seen it so low. I'm no' for goin' oot,' he said firmly.

His sons protested, and other young men in the crowd joined in with them. 'The reading must be wrong.' 'Look out there.' 'It's a fine day. We have to go out,' they choroused. Jessie's father, Robert Johnston of the *Sunshine*, came up to join them, tapped the barometer and also shook his head. 'I'm not for going out either,' he said. The younger protestors were sobered. Like Jimmy Dip, Johnston was well respected.

Dan frowned as he listened to the older men advising them not to sail. He remembered his promise to buy Rosabelle a silk dress to wear at Henry's wedding and didn't want to disappoint her. 'I think we should risk it,' he said loudly. Henry wanted to go out too, because the expense of getting married preyed on his mind. 'Even if the glass is right and a storm is coming, it won't hit us for hours. We can be back before it starts,' he said, and others backed him up.

Two fat brothers, Will and Jim Young, skippers of the *Blossom* and the *Fiery Cross* who had nine small children between them, yelled in chorus, 'That's right!' and Jim said, 'We're for goin'. Our bairns are needin' food.'

Duncan, the coastguard, curled his lip and bit back the remark that if the brothers didn't spend so much time and money in the Ship Inn, their children wouldn't be so skinny and hungry.

'It's money for drink that's worrying you, not bread for your bairns. You'll rue the day if you go,' he snapped; but the young men kept on shouting him down and it looked as if there was going to be a fight, until one of the oldest skippers in the port appeared.

Alex Burgon, master of the *Ariel Gazelle*, cut disdainfully through the squabbling crowd to climb up on to the stone plinth of the barometer. Burgon looked like an Old Testament prophet with a flying mass of wild hair like grey spume flying round his head. The skin of his face was deeply corrugated and marked with ingrained wrinkles, especially around the eyes, etched there by years of staring at seas in all their moods. He was a Revivalist preacher, famous – or infamous – in the town for his terrifying sermons, which shook sinners to the soles of their boots for a few hours but did little to change their way of life in the long term.

Because of his strict religious views and fearlessness in openly rebuking people for too much drinking or adultery, he

11

was not popular. Some of his fellow skippers also disapproved of him because his boat was always shabby and in need of a good coat of paint. They thought the *Ariel Gazelle* let Eyemouth down, because they liked their boats to be as brightly painted and decorated with scrolls and curlicues as fairground carousels. But they knew he was a good seaman, and silently watched as he solemnly checked the glass, tapped it twice to make sure, before turning to say, 'Ye'd be daft to sail today. Ye'll drown if ye do.'

They were arguing again when a fresh group of young men came walking up behind an elegant-looking dandy, carrying a silver-topped walking stick and wearing a tall, shiny silk hat tilted rakishly over one eye. This was fearless Tommy Nisbet, who skippered the *White Star*, a boat that invariably brought in the best catches from fishing trips.

A dandy and a womanizer, with a perpetually pregnant wife, he had a following among the young blades, who admired his style and bravado, especially because he always had plenty of money in his pocket. This was earned not only by fishing but by the smuggling he did on the side. It was said that he was not fussy about what he carried.

'Hey, Nisbet,' yelled someone, spotting this figure. 'Are you for going out? You're no quitter.'

'What's going on?' he asked, squinting under the brim of his shiny hat at the men around the barometer.

Willie Wave shrieked in excitement, 'The gless's doon, Nisbet. There's going to be an earthquake.'

The dandy laughed and his followers laughed with him, but Coastguard Duncan interrupted to say, 'Dinna laugh at Willie. He's no' so daft. A storm's coming and I don't think the boats should go out.'

Nisbet waggled his walking stick at the sky and said scathingly, 'Today? With that sky? An *earthquake*? Damned rot!'

Jimmy Dip interrupted quietly: 'Maybe not an earthquake, but the barometer's very low. I don't think we should sail.'

'I agree,' added Robert Johnston, and Burgon called down from his perch beside the barometer, 'So do I! We'd be mad to sail.'

Nisbet sneered up at him, 'Scared of bad weather, are you?

Don't you trust your Jehovah to take care of you? Even if a storm is coming, we'll be back before it hits us. We can run before the wind – if there *is* a wind.'

His followers laughed and agreed with him, but older, wiser men scanned the young faces with dread. What made them despair was the unwritten Eyemouth law that, if the majority of the fleet was for sailing, everybody else had to go out with them.

Effie and a few other women stood apart from the men, watching and listening but keeping silent. It was not their place to give advice about sailing, but some of them looked scared, for they remembered other times when the mood of the sea had changed and snatched men away.

Nisbet's sarcastic intervention made it a foregone conclusion, however. Though the older men were against sailing, they were in the minority of ten boats against thirty-one. The younger contingent were all for sailing. Even the *Ariel Gazelle* would have to go.

As they walked back from the pier end, Dan tried to cheer his father up by saying, 'Dinna listen to Burgon. All he knows about is the Scriptures.' The other two Maltman brothers nodded in agreement, but Jimmy Dip halted in mid-stride and stared hard at his sons' faces, as if trying to imprint them on his memory.

'That's where ye're wrong. Burgon is one of the best seamen in this port. He's better than Nisbet; he's better than Johnston and he's better than me. I just hope to God he'll not have to prove it today,' he said solemnly.

Two

Word that the fleet was preparing to sail ran round the town like wildfire. By half past seven the harbour side was crowded with jostling spectators, eager to watch the preparations on forty-one boats that were tied up so close together that men could cross the water from one side of the harbour to the other without wetting their feet, by leaping from boat to boat.

In all, forty-six fishing boats were registered out of Eyemouth, but five were down in Yarmouth, following the shoals of herring that moved around the coast during the seasons of the year. The ones that stayed at home fished for haddock and cod, and dealers came from all over the country to buy their catch.

On the quayside, under a bright autumn sun, greetings were being exchanged and good-luck messages shouted out as the pride of the town's men, seaboots slung casually over their shoulders and oilskins under their arms, came out of the houses and inns to clamber down the steel ladders on the quay walls, jumping from deck to deck to reach their own boats.

Some of them were not sober, having drunk their breakfasts in one of the three inns along the quayside – the Ship, the Royal Hotel or the Cross Keys – which opened at six o'clock on sailing mornings.

Jimmy Dip was not an early-morning drinker and he took his farewell of Effie in their own house. When she hugged him, her normally stern face softened and she whispered, 'Good fishing, my dear man.'

As if he was apprehensive, he held her wordlessly for an unusually long time, and laid a kiss on the top of her head. Before he left the house he took extra care to touch the family's lucky stone that hung from a string on the back of the kitchen door.

It had barely closed behind him when she noticed that he'd left his gold fob watch and money purse on the top of the kitchen dresser.

She stared at them in dismay and a strange chill gripped her. It was the first time in their married life that he'd ever done that. *Will I run after him?* she wondered, lifting the purse up, but putting it down again.

Jimmy won't need money in the middle of the sea, she decided. *The purse and watch can stay safe with me till he comes back.*

Next door, Rosabelle was finding the first parting from her husband hard, and fussed round him as he put on his fishing gear, handing him his thick woollen underclothes, long hand-knitted socks and dark-blue jersey with its distinctive pattern that his mother made for all her men. Effie always knitted a line of stylized eyes and initial 'M's around the jersey hems and the tops of their long stockings so that a Maltman's body could be identified if he was swept overboard.

As she watched Dan struggling to pull the jersey over his curly dark head, a chill of fear gripped Rosabelle. It would be small comfort to her if people who found his body knew where he came from; but she drove the idea away.

It won't happen because I love him too much, she told herself. But she was a fisherman's wife now, and every time he went out, she'd feel the same. *I'll have to get used to it*, she thought.

To see him off for the first time she'd proudly dressed herself in the traditional costume of a fishing wife – a dark fustian skirt, white blouse and striped woollen shawl that was crossed across her breasts and knotted at the back. Her head was bare, showing her gloriously blonde, tightly braided and coiled hair.

Respectable middle-class townswomen in Eyemouth would never step outside their houses without bonnets, but fisher-women went bare-headed, though more money went into their households every week than passed through most of the others.

'I'll come with you to the boat,' she said, when he was ready to leave.

He looked down at her bare feet. 'That's good, but put your shoes on first.'

'It's a dry day. I often walk about bare-foot.'

'You might have to step over a net. Have you forgotten that when a bare-foot woman steps over a net it means a poor catch?' he said solemnly.

She laughed. 'You're so superstitious,' she said, but put on her wooden-soled clogs, and kissed him for the last time, because it would embarrass him if she did that in sight of his shipmates. 'Keep safe. I need you,' she whispered.

Jessie's mother Bella Fairbairn, wife of Robert Johnston of the *Sunshine*, was suffering from a hangover. Her head throbbed as if a hammer was beating it out from the inside as she bustled about with Mary and Fanny, getting out fishing lines and finding boots and oilskins for Robert and their oldest son Paul. There was no sign of Jessie, who was still pleading nausea and lying low in bed.

The three younger children of the family tried to help too, but kept getting under their mother's stumbling feet, and she screeched as she swung at them in futile rage.

Little Betsy, aged five and the youngest, was eating a plate of porridge before making her way to school. She grimaced when she tasted it. 'It's too salty,' she complained.

In a second, her mother descended on her with both arms flailing and knocked her off her stool.

'Ye've done it noo. Ye'll bring bad luck on your father and brother . . .' she yelled over the howls of the child.

Robert, on his way out of the door, stopped and frowned: 'What's wrong? What're ye hittin' her for?'

'She said a forbidden word. She said *salt*,' was Bella's reply.

'And now ye've said it too,' said Robert. He was superstitious as well, however, so he took care to say the words *cold iron*, which averted evil, and touch his lucky stone before he left the house. All the way to his boat he pressed his fingernails into the palm of his hands, because that was another way to turn aside bad luck.

In the house behind him, a repentant Bella, who'd promised to stay off the drink till he returned, started to weep. In an attempt at consolation, she found a whisky bottle hidden at the back of the kitchen dresser and took a big swig from it.

* * *

16

In the dining room of Beechwood, one of the most imposing villas that stood high on a ridge overlooking the fishing town, three men sat at a polished breakfast table and commented on the beauty of the day.

The host's long-nosed, twenty-four-year-old daughter Hester fussed over the sideboard, adjusting the spirit lamp to keep the devilled kidneys hot and making sure that their house guest got plenty to eat.

From his seat at the head of the table, the widowed owner of the house, Robert Stanhope, a prosperous licensed grocer and ship's chandler with stores all down the east coast, looked fondly at his plump son Everard and more critically at their spindle-shanked guest Alan Cochrane, the newly inducted minister of the Established Church in the town.

'What a fine day! The fishing fleet will go out, I'm sure. Would you like to see them, Mr Cochrane? It's a grand spectacle,' he said affably.

'I'd like that very much,' said the gaunt young minister. In spite of the early hour, he was already wearing his clerical black with a stiff white dog collar. He had dressed himself in full rig because he was so proud of his new status.

'In that case, let's go down to the harbour. It's only a few minutes walk, but I hope you don't mind if I ask you to change your collar first,' said Mr Stanhope.

Cochrane looked puzzled and disappointed. 'Change my collar, sir. Why?'

'Because fishermen believe it's unlucky to see a clergyman when they're setting out to sea,' said the old man.

Everard, a lawyer who had been up at St Andrews University at the same time as Cochrane, laughed and said, 'Tut tut, Father, you're as bad as they are. Their whole lives are wrapped up in superstition.'

Turning to his friend, he told him, 'You have your work cut out. The fisher people here are quite heathen. There are words they can't say, and dozens of things they can't do. They're not allowed to say *salt*, *pig* or *salmon*, and if a rabbit runs across their path on their way to the boat, they'll turn round and go home. And that's only some of it; there's much more, but it's all illogical nonsense, of course.'

'It may seem like nonsense to you, but it matters to them

17

and they're my good customers, don't forget that,' said his father firmly. He was obviously determined not to take Cochrane to the harbour if he showed his clerical collar.

Unfortunately the fledgling minister had brought no other neckwear with him, and his cheeks flushed much redder than their normal hue as he suggested, 'Perhaps I could wear a scarf, sir?'

Everard laughed again, 'They'll think you're an invalid,' he scoffed.

'It doesn't matter what he looks like so long as he keeps the scarf on,' snapped Stanhope as he rose from the table. Abashed, the two young men hurried behind him.

A silent Hester, who had been listening to the exchange, was standing in the hall and, with a smile, she draped a striped woollen scarf round the guest's neck.

His face expressed relief and thanks, and her hopes rose because she was on the lookout for a suitable husband. Though the new minister was younger than she was, and too willowy and namby-pamby for her taste, he'd make a good enough match; but the men she really admired, and who started funny surgings in her stomach when she saw them clambering over the boats in the harbour, were handsome young fishermen in thick jerseys and thigh-high boots. They were totally unsuitable for someone in her social position, of course.

'Are you coming to the harbour with us, Miss Stanhope?' he asked as she tied the scarf beneath his chin.

She shook her head. 'No, it's not a place for ladies,' she told him.

At ten to eight her father and his two companions reached the harbour wall and found it crowded. A screaming, excited crowd of schoolboys, diverted on their way to school, were running about, eyeing the boats and criticizing the ones that did not belong to their own families. They all longed to be old enough to go to sea.

Most of the fishermen had spent their days of idleness painting and decorating their vessels, but Burgon had done nothing to the *Ariel Gazelle*. Its red-painted hull was peeling so badly that it looked leprous and the spectators tut-tutted in disapproval at the sight of it.

The fishermen's wives were out in force, in family groups

distinguished by their dark skirts and striped shawls. Rosabelle, with her mother Isa and her new mother-in-law Effie, was oblivious to the excitement going on all around her because she looked at nothing and no one but Dan.

As he walked across the deck of the *Harmony*, pulled on ropes, straightened up and pushed the hair out of his eyes, her eyes devoured him.

He's the most handsome man in Eyemouth, and he's mine, she thought. Her whole body throbbed as she remembered their early-morning love-making. Smiling silkily at the memory, she wondered if Isa or Effie guessed at the turmoil of desire inside her. Had they ever felt the same? With the confidence of youth and beauty, she looked at their lined faces and doubted it.

While she was silently adoring her husband, she felt an arm thrust through hers and Jessie's dark head bobbed up beside her shoulder – there was eight inches difference in their height for the newcomer was under five feet tall and Rosabelle was five foot seven – and because Jessie was so tiny her pregnancy looked more advanced than Rosabelle's, though she was five months gone as well.

The older women looked at her with reproach for being late and Jessie pretended to be remorseful as she asked, 'Is Henry on board already?'

The answer was a frown and a nod, because they thought Jessie should have arrived earlier; but the girl sighed and said, 'I'm sorry I missed saying goodbye to him, but I've been awful sick. I nearly fainted when I got out of bed. Oh, I'll be glad when this is over.' As she spoke, she rested her hands on the shelf of her belly.

Effie asked, 'Do you mean the fleet going out? Surely you've seen that before often enough.'

Jessie groaned and said, 'No, not that. I mean this bairn. I'll be glad when *it's* out!'

Isa, whose family conducted a long-established feud with Jessie's, looked over and snapped, 'If you're anything like your mother, you'll be havin' another as quick as winking.'

Jessie looked slyly up at Rosabelle and raised her eyebrows as if to say, *You poor thing, having a mother like her.*

* * *

A few minutes before eight the last stragglers came running out of the pubs and scrambled down the ladders to reach their berths.

When all the crews were aboard, there was much pointing and shouting as ropes were unloosed and the boats began to nose, one by one, out of their moorings.

The crowd held its breath, the church clock struck eight times, and the *Press Home* led the line through the harbour mouth towards the sea.

In the heady atmosphere of excitement Alan Cochrane's head swam. He had never seen anything so basically primeval, and it moved him in a way he could not understand.

Though there were many pretty, or even beautiful, women on the quayside, they did not engage his attention as much as the heroes on the boats, who all looked godly to him, superb as argonauts. When they sailed out, they waved their arms and shouted greetings from the decks, and he was so excited that, as the *Harmony* slid past where he was standing, he raised an arm too and saluted the cheerfully waving Dan.

Cochrane was unusually lanky, nearly six feet tall, and clearly visible over other people's heads. As he waved, the scarf slipped and his clerical collar was revealed. In a second he realized what had happened and grabbed the scarf end, wrapping it tightly back around his neck; but he was not quick enough. Dan saw the tell-tale collar and a look of horror crossed his face.

'Cauld iron, cauld iron!' he yelled, and pointed in an attempt at exorcism.

Men on other boats, and people on the dock, all looked across at Cochrane, who wanted the earth to swallow him up, so accusing were their stares.

'I didn't mean it to show. It was only for a second,' he gabbled to Mr Stanhope, who looked furious as he grabbed his guest's arm and said, 'We'd better get out of here. The women are more ferocious than the men and I don't want them attacking you. Come on!'

At that terrible moment Willie Wave began running along to the end of the pier, waving his arms and shouting at the departing boats, 'Dinna go! Aw dinna go! Ye'll a' droon!'

Three

After the fleet sailed there was plenty of work for the women to do while their men were at sea, and no one had much time to worry about Willie Wake's warning. Besides, they consoled themselves, the sun was shining as brightly as ever. 'He's only a daft old man,' they told each other. Rolling up their sleeves, they cleaned their houses, washed any dirty clothes, which were then hung out to dry in the sun, and set about preparing food for the boats coming back at night. Finally, when all that was over, they shouldered their big wicker creels and headed off for the shore in search of tomorrow's bait.

The thick leather straps of her new creel hurt Rosabelle's shoulders, but she bore the pain in the same celebratory way as a novice nun suffers a penance. Effie saw her grimace as they walked with Jessie towards the shore and said reassuringly, 'In a wee while it'll stop hurtin' and you winna notice it, lass.'

It was noon when they reached the beach. Effie led them past a group of rocks to where they had a stretch of foreshore to themselves. As they turned over rocks and bent over pools in search of their mussel quarry, which was plentiful because there had been little harvesting for the past week, the sun warmed their backs and raised their spirits.

This isn't such bad work after all, thought Rosabelle as she listened to Jessie chattering cheerfully about her wedding. Blithely throwing a handful of mussels into the creel at her feet, she said, 'I'm no' like you, Rosabelle; I dinna want to be married in a church. We're going down to Lamberton Toll to do it.'

The toll house at Lamberton, a few miles south but still on the Scottish side of the border between England and Scotland,

21

was a popular place for fisherfolks' weddings, and also for eloping couples from the south, because the toll keeper there performed civil ceremonies that were legal in Scotland but not in England.

Rosabelle nodded. 'Dan wanted to go to Lamberton too but I chose to be married in church – I don't know why, I just did. It seemed more solemn somehow.'

Jessie gave a meaningful giggle and rolled her roguish eyes. 'I dinna want to be solemn. Nor does Henry . . .'

Rosabelle blushed. She never joined in when other girls nudged each other and giggled about men and love-making. What happened between her and Dan was too sweet and precious for joking.

Jessie saw the blush and giggled again. 'You're as bad as me. You like it too but you just don't want to admit it, do you?'

Rosabelle decided to change the subject and asked, 'Are you going up to Edinburgh after the wedding?' Eyemouth brides didn't have honeymoons. If they were lucky, they got a day out in Edinburgh, travelling by train.

The trip from nearby Burnmouth to the capital's Waverley Station took just over an hour and they always came back the same night. For many women their wedding trip was the only time they ever left their home town.

'Oh aye, we're going to Edinburgh. Neither Henry nor me have ever been there and I'm lookin' forward to it,' said Jessie brightly, prising mussels off the rocks at her feet.

Rosabelle sighed at the memory of her wedding trip. 'You'll enjoy it. Edinburgh's lovely. Princes Street has big gardens and lots of trees, and the shops are full of such bonny things . . .'

With a grimace she wiped her sore hands against the stiff, prickly cloth of her skirt. Her fingertips stung because they were raw and bleeding. She looked at them in dismay and thought of the elegant women in Princes Street who'd gone swishing past her in silken gowns with enormous hats on their heads and long parasols in their hands. The scent that came off them was spicy or lemony, never fishy. She sniffed her sore fingers, but grimaced because all they smelt of was seawrack and mussels.

Effie now joined in the conversation. 'Rosabelle's right. I still mind how grand Edinburgh looked when I went up with Jimmy Dip the day we were married, twenty-five years ago

22

– I've never been back, but I remember everything as if it was yesterday.'

Glancing up from her bent-over position, she compared the girls who were joining her family. Not only did they look different – for Rosabelle was tall, shy and reserved, while Jessie was doll-like and small, with black curly hair and a knowing eye – but they thought differently too.

Jessie appeared to be almost childishly simple, openly sensual and flirtatious with a tendency to raucousness; but that was only to be expected because her mother was worse, especially in drink. Effie privately thought that Jessie's family were too interbred, a common problem in a town where fisherfolk had been marrying other fisherfolk for generations; but the girl was Henry's choice and she seemed to love him, so that was good enough.

Rosabelle's family were more sober-minded and respectable, but she didn't look like any of them. Her mother and father were both dark-haired, square-built and sturdy; her only sister Clara taller and thinner but also black-haired, whereas Dan's wife was like a snow queen with curling yellow hair, blue eyes and very pale skin.

She remembered how a Norwegian boat had been driven ashore in a storm one autumn about twenty years ago and stayed for several weeks while it was being repaired. The skipper of that boat was a tall giant with a bright-yellow beard, who cut a swathe through local women whose husbands were away fishing for herring at Yarmouth. Whispering women always wondered, 'Was he the one who fathered Rosabelle?'

They never dared to say so openly, and Davy Scott ignored the speculations, but Isa, more sensitive to gossip, took care to tell people who admired her lovely daughter that her grandmother had also been blonde.

'That's where her braw hair comes from,' she explained.

When the girls have their babies, *who will they take after?* Effie asked herself, eyeing Jessie's high, round belly, which was much more prominent than Rosabelle's. She wondered exactly how far advanced that pregnancy was, because, as far as she knew, Henry and Jessie had only been walking out for a few weeks before he announced their intention to marry. Yet he'd assured his father that the baby was his . . .

23

It was different with Rosabelle. She and Dan had been sweethearts for at least three years before she'd fallen with child and they'd married.

The three women went on thinking their private thoughts as they prised mussels off the rocks till Effie noticed Rosabelle flinching from the pain of her lacerated and bleeding fingertips. The girl was obviously trying to ignore the pain and pick on, but the older woman saw what was happening and felt pity.

As she straightened up to take the sore hands in her own, she suddenly went rigid and stared over at the sea. 'Oh my God!' she cried in alarm, forgetting everything else.

Jessie and Rosabelle whipped round and saw a huge cloud sweeping towards them, travelling at what seemed like a tremendous speed across the water. It was a threatening purplish blue, the colour of a bruise.

'Look at that!' Effie cried in alarm, pointing at it.

Willie Wake's screamed warning was in all their minds. The sea, which had been gently murmuring over the shingle, suddenly changed its mood and began heaving, crashing and sucking the sand away from beneath their feet. Rain began falling too – not gently, but crashing down in sudden fury.

Without speaking, they pulled their shawls over their heads, shouldered the creels and ran up the beach towards the sea wall. Huge raindrops that pelted down on them stung as hard as falling pebbles.

It was one o'clock and the sky was completely black.

In the town, terrified women rushed out of their houses and stood staring towards the sea from the lee of their walls, cringing in fascinated horror every time another huge wave came crashing over the pier.

The sea was so much part of their heritage that they knew how much worse conditions would be in deep water. Though none of them had ever sailed in a storm themselves, they'd heard the men's stories and chilled in terror at the thought of what they must be going through. The words running through the head of every one of them – mother, daughter or wife – were: 'Keep my man safe. Save him, save him.'

Four

At eight o'clock, when the fishing boats left the harbour dragging their sculls behind them like reluctant children, there had been almost no wind and the air hung heavy as a threat over the bay.

Without a breeze it was hard to reach open sea, so the men had to row a long way before a faint north-westerly wind began to flutter in their sails.

The cod and haddock grounds were twelve miles out and it took twice as long as normal to reach them.

At five minutes past twelve Robert Johnston stood in the wheelhouse of the *Sunshine*, staring out at a sun-dappled expanse of water.

The sea was in his blood; and though he thought he knew all its moods, he could not remember such a strange, brooding stillness. Disquiet filled him as he remembered Willie Wave's shouted warning.

In his heart of hearts he knew they shouldn't have sailed. 'I'll only make one cast of the nets and then head back home,' he said aloud. It didn't matter to him what the other boats did. At least he'd kept his end of the bargain and sailed out with them.

He hoped that Will Young, who skippered the *Blossom*, would have the sense to go back too because his eldest son, eighteen-year-old Paul, was a deckhand on that boat.

When they reached a stretch of still water that looked promising, he shouted out a sharp order and one of his men slung the anchor overboard while the lines were made ready. Fishing was about to start.

From his position in the wheelhouse he could see other boats scattered here and there over the water. Some were so close that he could recognize the faces of men on the decks of the *Blossom, Myrtle, Beautiful Star, Ariel Gazelle, Press Home* and *Forget-Me-Not*. They were too close together for big catches, but there was little chance of moving on because even the faint breeze that brought them this far had now died away. They were becalmed, waiting – for what?

It happened so suddenly that it took him completely by surprise. In an instant, as if a curtain had been dropped, clouds obliterated the sun in front of him. He blinked, whipped round and saw that a terrible blackness shrouded the whole sky. At the same time, the boards beneath his feet began to whip and buckle as if a monster from the depths was rising up and bearing his boat aloft on its shoulders.

As he struggled out of the wheelhouse to help raise the anchor, lashing rain cut through his clothes and he ran back to put on his oilskins. In front of his boat's bows a huge wave rose up like a black wall tipped with white foam. In one terrible second it engulfed the *Sunshine* and the ballast shifted, turning it over . . .

As he hit the water, Johnston knew he must get rid of his thigh-length seaboots because they would weigh him down. Somehow he managed to pull a knife out of his belt and began slashing at his legs, but a whirling surge of sea swept him around like a child's toy and he disappeared for ever.

His son Paul, clinging to the mast on the deck of the *Blossom*, saw his father's boat go down. Tears mingled with sea-water on his face, and his last thought was: 'How am I going to tell my mother about this?'

He did not have long to think about it, for, seconds later, the wind prised his arms off the mast and tossed him into the sea to join his father.

The boats were being stalked by the black storm that had sent the seagulls winging inland and drove down the mercury on the pier-end barometer. They were in the eye of a raging hurricane, the worst ever to hit that part of the coast.

The screeching of the wind was so deafening that the curses and shouted prayers of terrified men were obliterated. Under its banshee-like shrieking, stout canvas sails ripped like pieces of thin silk, and men were swept overboard never to be seen again.

Those who watched their friends disappear lashed themselves to spars and clung on in desperation. But the wicked wind was not easy to satisfy. Like a pagan god it demanded more sacrifices and did not abate, howling on around them till it swamped boat after boat in an orgy of destruction.

Some of their ends were almost elegant, a sudden toppling was followed by a descent like a dancer sinking to the ground. After a few seconds, all that was left on the black water was white spume and an upturned hull splintering under the tearing teeth of the storm.

The first awful squall that engulfed the *Sunshine* also took the *Beautiful Star*, *Industry*, *Fiery Cross*, *Myrtle*, *Guiding Star*, *Florida*, *Lass of Gowrie*, *Six Brothers* and *Margaret and Catherine*.

Out of forty-one boats, ten were gone within fifteen minutes, sunk with all hands – sixty men.

After the first murderous onslaught, the wind paused as if for breath, but only for a brief time. When it started to blow again, it was even more terrifying, but it had given the survivors the opportunity to recover from their first surprise and start bailing out. The time had come to take stock.

Surviving skippers, seeing the devastation around them, had to decide how best to save themselves. Most had the same instinctive reaction – the fishing lines had been snatched away, so there would be no catch today. They had the option of heading for the safety of their harbour and home, or letting the wind blow them down the coast, in the hope of getting out of the worst of it.

One man rejected either course. As usual, Alex Burgon of the *Ariel Gazelle* went against the grain, and while most of the others wrestled to turn their prows in the direction of home, he stood four-square and headed away from land, right into the middle of the raging storm.

The sails of his boat were torn into tatters, but he and his men cobbled them together time and time again, until there was only enough canvas left to make a handkerchief. That was sufficient to catch the wind and drive them on into the maelstrom, however.

As they worked, his crew said their prayers and reconciled themselves to death, but not a man questioned his decision.

Chaos was all around them anyway, and they had nothing to lose by trusting him. They'd sailed with him for years and, even now, in the middle of unspeakable horror, they respected his seamanship.

For himself, Burgon felt strangely exhilarated. Death did not scare him and he braced himself against the howling gale, bare-headed and wild-eyed, loudly singing his favourite hymn. Never were the words 'For those in peril on the sea' more appropriate.

Other skippers watched the *Ariel Gazelle* heading away from them and shook their heads in disbelief. Of the boats that had survived the first terrible onslaught, some were already rudderless, helplessly accepting whatever the storm threw at them. God knew where they would end up. They would either survive or sink with all hands. It was up to chance, and that capricious imp luck, in which they all believed.

One by one they scattered and disappeared into the blackness. No farewell waves were given, not even between brothers, for everyone was too concerned with trying to survive and stay afloat.

In the troughs between the waves of their fishing ground, upturned hulls tossed like broken toys on the water, anonymous because their names were sunk beneath the waves. Broken spars and pieces of flotsam went scudding over the sea.

From the wheel of the *Harmony*, Jimmy Dip saw the devastation after the *Sunshine* went down and grieved because Robert Johnston was his closest friend. It would fall to him to tell Robert's wife and family what had happened.

His whole being was concentrated on getting home: home, home, home – the word echoed and re-echoed in his mind. His determination to see Effie again, and to save his sons, gave him superhuman strength, but he knew it would take every ounce of it to make home before the tide turned, because when that happened, it would be almost impossible to get through the narrow entrance into Eyemouth harbour.

Swinging towards the west, the *Harmony* was caught in a particularly vicious squall and hit sideways on by a mammoth wave that almost tipped it over. Struggling to right the boat, he spotted his son Henry sliding along the almost perpendicular deck, hands clutching ineffectually at nothing, before he disappeared overboard into the sea.

'Henry, my laddie, Henry,' he yelled in anguish, but his son's head only showed for a second in the boiling sea before it vanished.

The wind, howling in what was left of the sails, scudded the boat onwards. There was no chance to try to save the lad, for he was far behind in seconds.

Dan, clinging to the mast, saw his brother being swept to his death and threw back his head to yell an imprecation at heaven. 'God, damn you, God, damn you!' he yelled, and wished with all his heart that he'd backed the older men when they said they did not want to sail.

He could see his father's head bent in grief as he struggled with the wheel. Jimmy Dip was summoning all his strength and clinging to it with bleeding hands while sea-water poured down his face, half-blinding him.

In the howling fury finding a safe course was difficult, but suddenly his heart rose in hope when he saw a dim outline on his left. Was it another boat? Was it a drifting wreck? He strained his eyes and realized that he was looking at the biggest of the Hurkars, guarding the entrance to Eyemouth harbour. Sanctuary was nearer than he realized.

His voice rang out to tell what he'd seen. '*The Hurkars, there's the Hurkars!*' he yelled.

'We'll make it!' the other men shouted back and, as their boat scudded towards the rocks, they could see the beacon on the pier end and the lights shining out from the windows of houses along the harbour side. Home! Thank God, they were nearly home!

Five

As Effie, Rosabelle and Jessie ran for shelter in pelting rain that stung their skin, a line of shrieking children, on their way back to school after the midday break, went careering past pursued by mothers who shouted, 'Get on into the school house. Dinna hang aboot in this. Ye'll get yer deaths.'

Girls ran for shelter, but the little boys pranced around, not caring that the rain was soaking their clothes, till one angry woman stepped into the middle of them and, cuffing their ears, hurried them off to unwanted sanctuary.

In the Ship Inn a handful of men, too old, unwell or idle to go to sea, watched the darkening sky through the rain-streaked window and exclaimed to each other, 'Willie Wave wasnae wrong. It's a storm right enough.' Raising their glasses to their mouths, each of them felt grateful that he wasn't out in the middle of it.

In the town churchyard behind the main square, a sad little family were burying a two-year-old boy who'd died of croup the day before. The bereaved father, Andrew Windram, who should have sailed on the *Lily of the Valley* but gave up the place because of his child's death, held out his open hand and caught the first drops of rain. When he raised his head and saw the approaching storm, his first thought was that his dead bairn had saved him. He knew enough about bad weather to tell that the fury approaching was far from normal.

Ushering his weeping women in front of him, he took them to the Royal Hotel, where they sat in a sad little group, listening to the deluge pouring from the heavens and running like a river down the street. His wife grasped his hand, thinking the same as him; but neither of them spoke their thoughts, for in the funeral party there were other women whose men were out at sea.

Blackness and rain were only the start of trouble. Soon thunder pealed, lightning flashed and a screaming gale whipped through the narrow wynds and courtyards, howling round chimney pots, sending many crashing into the lanes and alleys. Tiles were lifted from roofs and smashed to smithereens at people's feet. Customers cowered in the shops, terrified to step out over the thresholds.

Inside the schoolroom terror reigned when one of the windows was blown clean in, sending the screaming children hiding under their desks from splinters of glass. Worse was to come, because the wind lifted off half the roof and sent it crashing into the small playground. There was no way the teacher could control the children then, and they erupted into the open, pelting flat out to their various homes and howling for their mothers.

Some of them were blown over as they ran, but they crawled on hands and knees and all reached sanctuary.

No one in the town, not even the oldest inhabitant, could remember a storm like it. Creating terror and devastation, the wind roared on inland, blowing down several telegraph poles and effectively cutting Eyemouth off from the outside world. On and on it went, sweeping all before it, tearing up 200-year-old trees by the roots and whipping the roofs off houses. On one large estate, twenty miles from the coast, 30,000 trees were blown down within an hour, and a horse and cart were uplifted by the blast and dropped into a pond.

The fishing town had other worries. By two o'clock the wind dropped enough for strong people to come out and huddle against the harbour wall in silent, fearful groups, staring out to sea.

Instinctively, families grouped together, shoulder to shoulder. Rosabelle was with her mother, Effie and Jessie. Beside them stood Bella Fairbairn, Robert Johnston's wife and mother of Paul, with her sister Euphen, wife of Alex Burgon.

Normally the sisters were distant with each other because of Bella's drinking and Alex's fixation with religion, but the danger hanging over their men made them gravitate towards each other and clasp hands without speaking.

With shawls drawn over their heads, they linked arms and

31

leaned into the wind, anxiously watching the obscured horizon. Other women beside them were weeping loudly, but Effie held up a hand to quieten them.

'Stop greetin' this minute. They're coming back. I'm sure of it,' she said.

Her tone was confident and her face so calm that all nodded in fervent agreement. It was what they wanted to hear.

Because of mist and spume it was difficult to see far out to sea, but suddenly Mr Duncan, the coastguard, who was standing on the pier end with a telescope to his eye, let out a shout and called, 'Someone's out there.'

'Who is it? Who is it?' called the women, and he screwed up his face as he tried to see. 'Ah no, it's a Coldingham boat,' he called back after a bit, and the tension dropped in disappointment.

But Effie was not dejected, 'If they've got back, so will our men!' she cried encouragingly.

Soon Duncan gave another shout, 'Here's another one. Yes! It's the *Onward*. It's one of ours! It's coming past the harbour point. It's in! Thank God, it's in!'

Women belonging to the crew of the *Onward* rushed in a group along the quay and even before the boat tied up they were reaching down to haul the exhausted men ashore.

As the crew stood on dry land they were swamped by other anxious women and besieged by questions – 'Where's the others?' 'What about the *Pilgrim*?' 'Did you see the *Lily of the Valley*?' – 'the *Myrtle*?' – 'the *Beautiful Star*?' – 'the *Good Hope*?'

George Dodd, master of the *Onward*, held up both his hands to stop them. 'I'm sorry. It's hell out there. I saw the *Sunshine* and the *Good Hope* go down. The *Lily of the Valley* as well. The *Myrtle*'s gone too, but I dinna ken aboot the others.'

He was on the verge of tears and exhausted, not prepared to break bad news gently.

Bella rocked on her feet and looked across at a bleak-faced Ella Collin, whose husband Rob sailed as a deckhand on the *Myrtle*. She'd never liked the woman, but now they had something terrible in common.

She felt her sister Euphen putting an arm round her waist and saying gently, 'Come on, dear, we'll go home now.'

She leaned her head on her sister's shoulder and whispered, 'But what about your man?'

'I'll wait for news of him at home,' said Euphen stoically.

Jessie, Rosabelle and Effie, the women of the *Harmony*, did not leave, but kept up their terrible vigil. Though the lightning eventually stopped flashing, the wind still howled furiously and rain poured down in an unceasing torrent. Waves higher than the houses crashed against the pier end, throwing huge sprays of water over the watchers.

Every stitch of their clothing was soaked through, and the wet curls of Rosabelle's hair looked black as the plaits unfurled and plastered themselves all over her head. The baby inside her shifted in discomfort, but she only spread her stance a little wider and never took her eyes off the sea.

Though she heard that her father's ship, the *Myrtle*, was lost, and watched her mother being led away, she stayed on the harbour side, waiting for Dan. She was too frightened to speak, too frightened even to think.

Teeth audibly chattering, Jessie stood beside her. Her round face was white and drawn because she had many people to worry about – not just Henry, but her father on the *Sunshine* and a brother on the *Blossom* as well.

Effie placed herself between the girls and put an arm over each of their shoulders as she said in a reassuring voice, 'You lassies shouldn't be out here in this weather. Your babies'll take bad with it. Go in and make some tea. Our men *are* coming back, I'm sure of it.'

Rosabelle replied, without taking her eyes off the wickedly thrashing sea. 'I'm staying here.'

She felt intense irritation at Effie's mindless optimism – *Has she no imagination? Has she no fear?* she wondered; but when she turned her head to look at the older woman's face she changed her mind. In spite of her apparent cheerfulness, there was stark terror in Effie's eyes. What she was doing and saying was for their benefit.

Jessie accepted the offer of a break from watching. 'I'll brew the tea and come to tell you when it's ready,' she said.

Effie hugged her. 'Good lass. I'll stay here with Rosabelle till then.'

When Jessie ran off towards the Maltman house, which was nearest, the two others held on to each other and Effie draped an end of her shawl over Rosabelle's shoulders.

'Be brave. Dan's comin' back,' she said.

Rosabelle nodded without speaking. She believed that too. God could not be so cruel as to take him away from her. For a moment, she leaned her head on Effie's shoulder and they were standing like that when another shout from the lookout point rang out and they straightened up.

'Someone else is coming in!' yelled Duncan.

Hope rose in their hearts and they tightened their hold on each other as if united strength and desperation would haul the incoming boat over the harbour bar.

'Who is it?' Effie shouted back.

'It's either the *Harmony* or the *Radiant*,' Duncan told her.

'The *Harmony*,' gasped the two waiting women to each other, and the breath caught in their throats till they were on the verge of choking.

After what seemed an eternity, Duncan shouted again, 'It's the *Radiant*!'

'Ah no!' groaned Effie, and Rosabelle too let out her breath in a terrible gasp of disappointment.

But behind them a ragged cheer broke out as other people surged forward to watch the boat battling towards the harbour mouth. It was not out of danger yet, however. On and on it came, sometimes driven sideways by the wind, sometimes almost disappearing beneath the waves.

The crowd watched in horrified silence till a distraught woman started to wail. As if they were afraid that she'd put a curse on the battle, her friends dragged her away, but her voice could be heard trailing off as she disappeared.

The *Radiant* fought hard, but when it was within fifty feet of the harbour mouth, a monstrous wave swamped it and it turned turtle in sight of the watching crowd, who gave vent to a cry of horror that sounded like a terrible *Te Deum*.

Heads could be seen bobbing about in the water. Powerless, and in a terrible, stricken silence, people on the shore watched the crew struggling for life.

A heart-breaking wailing swept the crowd, and a line of desperate older men ran to the beach, trying to wade into the water and reach the survivors; but they were driven back by terrible waves.

A man called George Aitken refused to give up and, pulling off his jacket, began to swim out to reach a man who could be seen struggling towards the shore. When George was about to grab him, the mast from the wrecked boat swept past and carried them both down with it.

'God help them! Oh God help them!' called Mr Duncan in anguish, dropping the telescope from his eye because he did not want to witness their last struggles.

'Whae was it?' quietly asked the man standing beside him.

'Jimmy Windram from the boat, and George Aitken as well,' was the sorrowful reply.

The questioner said nothing, but climbed down from his vantage point and walked across to a crowd of women, seeking two out. Taking them by the arms, he led them away. Other women followed in a mournful procession.

The terrible spectacle they had just witnessed made everyone freeze with horror. Even the wildest schoolboys were silenced by the sight of death being enacted in front of them. The tide was turning fast now and all the watchers realized that, even if a boat managed to get into the bay, there were many hazards to overcome before it could tie up safely in the harbour.

Rosabelle and Effie held hands and whispered prayers – though neither of them had any clear idea of who she was praying to – some capricious god of the sea, or perhaps Neptune with his terrible trident.

'Take someone else's, take anyone, but don't take my Dan,' Rosabelle thought over and over again like a litany.

The stricken silence that fell on the dwindling crowd after the tragic wreck of the *Radiant* was broken again when another boat loomed up in the blackness, battling towards the harbour.

'It's the *Harmony* this time!' yelled Duncan, and Effie could not stop herself giving an exultant yell, 'Yes, yes!'

'Will I fetch Jessie?' Rosabelle asked, but Effie held her back. 'Dinna get her. Let her be. She shouldn't watch this. You ought to go indoors too. It might be too much for you,' she said. It was the first sign that she had any doubts about the men's survival.

Rosabelle took her hand and held it tight. 'I'll stay here with you,' she said.

Only a few tatters of canvas were left of the sail of the approaching boat, but it came plunging bravely over the horizon, urged on by the crowd that started to yell, 'Come on Jimmy Dip, come on!'

Rosabelle's heart was beating so fast that she was afraid she would faint, but she fought to stay strong to justify Effie's confidence in her. She felt as if she was in the middle of a terrible nightmare from which she might waken at any moment and find Dan beside her again.

'He's comin', he's nearly in, he's comin', he's nearly in, he's comin', he's nearly in . . .' Effie muttered over and over again like a madwoman, without taking her eyes off the sea. Her wet face was shining with love. The bond between her and Jimmy Dip had never slackened throughout their years of marriage.

Little by little the distance between the boat and the harbour shrank. Hope ran high in the watchers, but it was not to be. When the *Harmony* was only one hundred yards from the shore, in line with the biggest Hurkars, another terrible wave caught it sideways on and sent it crashing on to the waiting rocks.

Everyone, men and women, shrieked 'Aw, no!' in chorus. Many turned their faces away because they did not want to see what would happen next.

And happen it did. With an ear-splitting sound of splintering timbers, the jagged rocks bit into the boat's side. Men began slipping down into the water, trying vainly to find a handhold, scrabbling for life.

The crowd on land moaned in chorus, every one of them sharing the horror with the struggling men. They gasped even louder, and began to pray aloud when a man was seen climbing up the highest rock. Clinging on with terrible desperation, he raised one arm and waved towards the land.

Across the stretch of water, as if they were tied together by some unseen line, Rosabelle recognized him. His face was screwed up in determination as he grappled for safety; his long arms and hands grasped and stretched, grabbed and missed time and time again.

Unaware that she was moaning in agony, she felt Effie trying to put a hand over her eyes, but roughly threw it off and continued to watch. *This I must see, I must, I must!*

Dan fought hard. Hanging on to the rock with one hand he gestured to the watchers, obviously asking for help that could not come. The sea was too high, he was too far out to reach with a landline, and there was no chance of launching the lifeboat because all its crew were out with the fleet.

Some desperate men did try to shoot a rope out to him so he could hang on to it, but it fell short of the rock and the sea playfully tossed it aside.

Watched by his wife, his mother and the weeping, keening people of the town who had known him since he was born, Dan Maltman, the only survivor of the *Harmony*, was swept to his death. His last gesture was a gallant wave.

He disappeared at once, as if he would not deign to struggle. Till his dark shape reappeared floating in the boiling sea, Rosabelle and Effie stood as still and silent as dead women, so impassive that those around drew away, afraid of them.

Other women were tearing their hair and howling, but they stepped gracefully apart like dancers, turned in different directions and walked sightless through the crowd.

The newly widowed girl went back to her attic room and sat down on the patchwork quilt of the bed where sweet love had been made that morning – so long ago, it seemed.

She stretched out, not caring that her wet clothes were soaking the blankets, turned on her side and inhaled deeply. The smell of Dan was still on the pillows.

'Oh God, he can't be dead. He can't be dead. He can't be dead!' she sat up and screamed aloud. People in the lane outside heard her and shrank in horror.

Six

In Eyemouth people did not lock their doors. Rosabelle did not even have a key for her little home, so she shoved her clothes box against the door and ignored the friends who came knocking.

She listened to them whispering to her – 'Let me in, it's your auntie.' 'Let me in, it's your cousin.' 'Let me in, it's Jessie.' It was hardest to ignore Jessie, who stayed on the landing for a long time, weeping and imploring, 'Let me in, Rosabelle. I've lost my Henry like you've lost Dan. Let me in. Everybody's worried about you . . .'

Her pleading went on for so long that at last Rosabelle was forced to speak. 'Go away. Leave me alone,' she shouted and heard Jessie's feet going off down the narrow stair.

When the knocking started again twenty-four hours later, there was a more imperative note to it. The voice that called out was one that always made Rosabelle jump.

'Open the door. It's Clara. You canna stay in there while mother's mourning for our father. Effie's lost her husband and three sons. Jessie's lost Henry, and a lot of other women are mourning their men today. You're not the only one. Get up and open the door.'

No-nonsense Clara, her sister, a commanding woman of twenty-three, ought to have been in Yarmouth working with the herring fleet and was not expected back till November.

The weeping girl rose from the bed, pushed her hair out of her eyes and opened the door to find her sister, grim and thin in black, standing on the threshold with her arms crossed on her breast.

'I'm ashamed of you!' was the first thing she said.

In a burst of fury, Rosabelle hit her full across the face with an open palm, but Clara did not retaliate. Instead she stepped into the room and asked, 'Did you hear what I was saying?'

Rosabelle turned and threw herself on the bed again, burying her face in the pillow. 'Go away,' she mumbled.

Clara stayed in the middle of the floor, arms still crossed. 'Did you hear me say that our father's lost? I got the news by telegraph in Yarmouth and came up on the train this morning.'

Rosabelle could only think of one thing. 'Dan's gone,' she sobbed.

'And so's our father and Dan's father Jimmy Dip, and Henry and Robert, his brothers. Effie's left without a soul in the world. Our mother's out of her mind with grief too. They need your help . . .'

The answer was a huge convulsive sob, and the girl pushed her face into a pillow already soaked with tears. Filled with pity Clara watched, longing to bend down and hug her sister, but knowing she had to stay strong if Rosabelle was to be shaken out of her paralysing grief.

'I came to tell you that the bodies of the men off the *Harmony* are being brought in. They'll be buried on Monday. Do you want to be there?' she demanded.

Rosabelle sat up and leaped off the bed. 'Dan? Is Dan in? I have to see him. I want to see my Dan.'

Clara put out both hands and pushed her back. 'No, you can't. Dan's in his coffin. They've nailed him down . . .'

In fact Dan Maltman was one of the more presentable corpses, but even then there was no way that the pregnant Rosabelle could look at him. His dark curly hair was his identifying mark, but his face was disfigured and there were terrible gashes and slashes on his body from the cruel Hurkar rocks. When he was fished out of the harbour, he'd been naked except for his woollen socks because the sea tore the clothes off drowning men.

'How do they know it's him?' asked Rosabelle in a dazed voice. Part of her still hoped he'd come back to her.

'By his socks. His mother identified them,' said Clara stonily. Dan had been wrapped in a sheet before Effie was allowed to look at him, but even that stoic woman had recoiled and wept at the state of his corpse.

39

With a moan, Rosabelle fell in a heap on the floor, and her sister's resolve cracked. Stricken-faced, she bent and cuddled the girl.

'Oh you poor lass, you must be starving. Let me find you something to eat. You've got to look after your bairn you know . . .' she cried, cradling the golden head in her arms.

Rosabelle looked up with swollen, stricken eyes. 'Bairn? I dinna care about any bairn. I only want Dan.'

She was filled with a terrible conviction that no matter what happened to her in the future, nothing would ever be as bad as this. Her entire capacity for feeling was used up. She would never feel love again; she would never feel anything again. It was as if every gentle emotion in her had dried up.

For the first time in her life Effie felt powerless. After she was fetched to identify Dan, she went home and sat beside the window of her kitchen, watching as ministers of the various churches in the town went from house to house, knocking on doors and mumbling well-meant words of comfort.

One or two of them came to her door but she did not open it to them. There was nothing they could say that could soften the pain paralysing her.

Every now and again a terrible dull boom erupted into the all-pervading silence and she knew that someone was firing the Napoleonic cannon on top of the cliff into the sea in the hope that the explosions would throw up more bodies of drowned men.

When evening came, she saw groups of men and boys going past her window with spades over their shoulders. Her heart gave a terrible clench when she realized they were going out to bury unidentifiable bits of bodies that had been cast up on the shore.

She was grim-faced next morning when one of Jimmy Dip's cousins came to tell her that the corpses of her husband and her second son had also been found.

'Were they in one piece?' she asked grimly.

The man shook his head. 'I'm sorry . . .' His voice trailed off.

'How did they know it was them then?'

'They knew Henry by his sweater . . .'

'And Jimmy Dip?' She could tell he was keeping something back.

'They got his head.'

'Only his head?'

'Yes.'

She shuddered, and he put a hand on her shoulder as he said, 'At least you can give them and Dan a proper burial.'

'More than I can for Robert,' she said between clenched teeth. Her youngest son was never to be found, though squads of men and boys patrolled the shore scavenging for remains, and over the coming weeks bits of bodies came back to Eyemouth after being washed up as far away as South Shields and the Firth of Forth. Identifying them was a macabre task, because all there was to go on was bloodied scraps – an arm, a leg, a battered torso – but, in a strange way, having that to bury was a kind of consolation for the widows and children. Funerals were celebrations of snatched-away lives.

When the well-meaning cousin left, Effie pulled her shawl off the hook behind the door and wrapped it over her shoulders. She had to see Rosabelle and Jessie.

She found Jessie at home with her family, who were weeping for Robert and Paul.

Effie stood in their squalid kitchen and said, 'I came to tell you that Henry's been found. And Jimmy too. We have to bury them.'

Jessie, face swollen with tears, came across and hugged her. 'Oh my God. And we're burying my dad and Paul on Monday too. Father's body's been brought in and they say he tried to cut off his own leg when he went overboard because his seaboots were weighing him down. Paul was washed up on Spittal sands.'

Effie stood rigid, finding it hard to believe this was actually happening. 'I'm sorry,' she said and turned to leave.

Jessie hung desperately on to her arm. 'Don't leave me. Where are you going?' she implored.

'I'm going to tell Rosabelle. I want to bury them together. They'd like that.'

'I'll come with you,' said Jessie.

41

On their way they passed windows with lamps burning in them as a hopeful signal for men whose bodies had not yet been found. The suspense was taking a terrible toll of the whole town. Some women seemed to have aged twenty years in as many hours.

Rosabelle's attic was empty, so they walked back to her family house where they found Clara trying to persuade her mother and sister to eat. She looked up when the two black figures stepped through the door, and her eyes asked the question that her mouth could not utter. Rosabelle's eyes were wide with terror when she saw her mother-in-law.

'Jimmy and Henry have been found, but not Robert. We'll bury them with Dan on Monday,' Effie said bleakly.

The girl gave a helpless sort of moan and laid her head on the deal table top. Tendrils of her lovely hair fell into her plate, but she did not care.

'I've just been at the post office to ask if there was any message about our father, but there's nothing. It's terrible there because it's crowded with people and every time the machine starts clicking they all rush up to read the message. It's never good news,' said Clara bleakly.

'Poor souls!' said Isa, as if the tragedy that had hit the town was nothing to do with her.

The other women stared at her for a second, and Effie said, 'You too, Isa.'

The answer was a shake of the head. 'Oh Davy's coming back. I'm sure of it.'

'I hope you're right,' said Effie but she was disturbed by Isa's unnatural tranquillity. Davy's boat had been seen to go down – what was his wife hoping for?

She seemed to be in another world and it was difficult to know whether she realized what had happened or not.

In desperation, Clara regarded her weeping sister and catatonic mother. Jessie, weeping too, was sitting on the bench beside her friend Rosabelle, trying to lift her hair out of the soup and cuddling her at the same time. In an instant both Effie and Clara revised their original opinions about Henry's girl. She wasn't as careless as she'd always pretended.

'I can't believe this is really happening,' Clara said to Effie. 'Folk are saying that the town's lost one tenth of its population and half of its working force. Almost every family has lost at least one man. How can we ever get over that? It's going to be like a ghost town.'

'I've lost four men and I'll have to get over it. The first thing to do is arrange a proper burial for them,' said Effie. She knew she sounded hard, but Clara would understand. Someone had to take charge.

On her way back from the undertaker's workshop on Monday morning she passed the Burgon house. She had been friendly with Euphen at school and, on an impulse, she stopped at the door and rapped on it.

The kitchen was immaculate. A fire burned in the hearth and a ginger cat slept on a big armchair beside it. Euphen was standing by the sink, looking out through a window that had a view of the sea.

She turned her head to greet the visitor and cried out with a sob in her voice, 'Oh Effie, I've heard about Jimmy and the boys. It's a tragedy.'

Effie nodded. 'I've been at the undertaker. I'm burying them this afternoon. Is there any news of your Alex and your laddie yet?'

Euphen shook her head. 'Nothing. He was seen sailing into the storm. That's all I know. It's nearly three days now. I've been to see the pastor at the chapel and his friends are praying for him. We'll have a memorial service soon . . .' Her voice trailed off, and she wrung her hands piteously.

They walked towards each other and embraced wordlessly, united by grief. When Euphen collected herself, she said, 'It's worse for you: all of your men are gone.'

'And two of yours; but it's not numbers that matter, is it?' Effie replied.

'What are you going to do?' Euphen asked.

Effie shrugged. 'Carry on, I suppose. There's Rosabelle, Dan's wife, and Henry's Jessie to worry about. They're having bairns soon and that'll keep me from thinking about myself. What about you?'

'My sister Bella isn't coping well and she has that houseful of bairns. I'll find plenty to occupy me there. And I'll help in the chapel – Alex would like that.'

'You're lucky that you can still believe. I told the undertaker that there's to be no praying over my men, no religious service. I couldn't stand it,' said Effie shortly.

Euphen did not argue. She knew there were a lot of families in the town who agreed with her friend.

They were sharing a pot of tea when another knock came to Euphen's door, and when she opened it, a trio of excited men were standing on the step.

'Your man's come back and your laddie too, Euphen,' cried Mr Duncan, the coastguard, without taking time to break the news gently.

She staggered and leaned against the door lintel. 'What did you say?' she dazedly asked.

'Your man's back. The *Ariel Gazelle*'s tying up now,' said a man at Duncan's back. Euphen turned to look at Effie and burst into tears. 'I thought he was dead. I thought I'd lost them,' she sobbed.

The two women walked together to the quayside, with Effie holding Euphen's arm and fighting against her own feelings of envy and longing. *Couldn't the fates let just one of my men come back too?* she thought.

An excited crowd of people were staring down into the harbour and when they saw Euphen, a hubbub of shouting broke out. 'He's here, down here. Come and see him . . . He's back. He's no' drowned after a'.'

Effie let go of her friend's arm and quietly went away as Euphen, transformed and looking like a girl again with her hair flying loose around her face and eyes sparkling, broke into a run.

Her husband's boat was in a terrible state. The sails were gone and only the tatters of a man's shirt flew from the mast. All the decks had been swept clear by the sea; even the wheelhouse had disappeared. It was like a ghost ship, a mythical *Flying Dutchman*.

Euphen stopped at the edge of the sea wall and stood visibly shaking as she counted the heads of the men on the deck of the crippled boat.

One, two, three, four, five, six. They were all there. He'd brought them all back.

She knelt down on the flat stones of the quayside and stared down at her husband and son who were looking up at her with stricken looks on their faces.

'God bless you. Oh God bless you!' she whispered and stretched out both her hands to them.

It was the first time any of the onlookers had ever seen Alex Burgon display tender sentiment, because he too began to weep and wiped his bristly face with the sleeve of his jersey before he climbed up the metal ladder and hugged her close.

They stood with their son in an embrace, not caring that more and more people were crowding round to look at them. When he eventually let go of his wife, Burgon was besieged by other men, who gave him the news of the terrible loss that had hit the town. He shook his head in horror as the names of dead men and lost boats were recited to him.

He'd been away for two and a half days, riding out the storm, while death was gathering in his friends. The magnitude of the disaster seemed impossible and he had to keep asking for more details, questioning them with, 'Are you sure?'

'Aye, we're sure. You'll soon find out how sure we are,' said one sour old man, taking his clay pipe from his mouth and spitting into the sea.

How had he saved himself and his crew? Everyone in the town was asking the question, and it was debated in every bar. How was it that Burgon alone brought his boat and all his men back from the storm?

In the Ship Inn, Willie Wake thought he had the answer. 'He's made a pact wi' the devil,' he suggested.

The other drinkers laughed, but a quiet voice from the back of the crowd said, 'He's a good seaman. He sailed into the storm and stayed out till it passed. The others headed for home and broke up on the rocks. That's how he came through it.'

An old man whose two sons were among those drowned spun round and snapped, 'Ye daft bugger, they were all good seamen. Dinna let anybody else hear you saying that or you could get yourself lynched.'

Rosabelle heard the news of Burgon's return from Clara, who came to her garret room to accompany her to the Maltman burial. She listened stony-faced, and flinched. In her mind's eye she still saw Dan's last desperate wave.

He'd wanted to get home; they all wanted to get home. Only Burgon had the strength of mind to wait. The tears that sprang into her eyes at the least prompting started to flow again, but Clara, determined to get her to Dan's burial or she'd never forgive herself for not attending, hurried her out of the house.

The interment was basic and, contrary to usual custom, women were allowed to stand at the graveside. They were the major mourners, after all. Three deal coffins were lowered into the ground, watched by solemn-faced people, who each scooped up a handful of black earth and threw it on to the coffin lids.

In the traditional costume, with their shawls drawn up over their heads, Rosabelle, Clara and Effie stood bleak-faced, silent and staring like people in a nightmare. Jessie, beside them, made a lot of noise, sobbing and gulping hysterically, and then she had to walk a few paces across to another gaping grave to weep again for her father and brother.

Bella, obviously drunk, swayed at Robert and Paul's grave edge, staring down into it with an uncomprehending expression. Her children held her up as they walked away after the short ceremony was over.

Effie watched the sad little party leave and said to Clara, who she now relied on as a support, 'Jessie'll not be able to cope with her mother and all the others on her own. Somebody'll have to talk to Bella about her drinking.'

'She's not a bad person really,' said Clara in a cool voice.

'No, but she's weak. Jessie's part of my family now, so I'll have to help her. Paul's gone, the sisters next in age are selfish and the others are just bairns, poor wee things. Will you ask Rosabelle to help me?'

A ploy was devised between Effie and Clara to try to snap Rosabelle out of her strange immobility. When she was asked to help with Bella, the girl was surprised by Effie's apparent ability to cast aside her own worries and start taking care of others. It made her all the more sure that Effie could not possibly be feeling the grief that had her in its grip. However, faced with Clara's baleful expression, she agreed to help with Jessie's problem.

Next day they all walked together to the Johnston home

and Bella seemed pleased to see them. 'It's good of you to come when you've got so much trouble of your own,' she cried, jumping up from her chair and hugging them, one after the other.

She smelt strongly of whisky.

Her kitchen was cluttered and dirty, with the smeared dishes of a half-eaten meal littering the table and a sullen fire guttering dully in the hearth.

'Jessie, we've got visitors. Make tea,' Bella called and Jessie came down the narrow stairs, holding on to the bulge of her belly.

'Don't worry about tea. We don't need it,' said Effie, bending down to riddle the fire and coaxing flames to leap up in it.

'Sit down then and talk,' said Bella.

'What can we talk about except this terrible thing that's happened? What can we say that will make it any less terrible?' Rosabelle cried in despair. 'I don't want to talk about what's happened. It was bad enough to come to terms with it on my own.'

But when she saw Effie and Clara finding chairs, she sat down on a little wooden stool next to a flat-topped clothes box. Jessie came across to sit on the box edge beside her. The friends looked at each other, but said nothing more.

Bella, maudlin, leaned across to Effie and pointed at them as she said, 'It's bad enough for you and me, but look at these poor lassies – both of them having bairns soon. What's going to happen to them! Where's the money coming from to feed them? Isn't it cruel? They say one always goes out when another one comes in.'

Rosabelle felt herself chill when she heard Bella moaning those awful words: *One always goes out when another comes in.*

It was a common old wives' saying in their community, and it did often seem that a new birth was followed by a death, or at least could be linked to one by the gossips.

'Did Dan have to die so that I could give birth to his baby? If he did, I hate it. I don't want it. I want Dan back,' she sobbed in distracted grief to Jessie.

She did not bother to listen while Effie tried to bring up the subject of too much drinking with Bella – to no avail, it

47

turned out – and when she eventually managed to get away, Effie held on to her arm and said, 'Let Clara go home on her own. Come back with me. I've something to show you.'

In the Maltman kitchen a wooden box stood open by the big chair that used to be Jimmy Dip's, and Effie rushed over to pull out a diaphanous shawl, which she held out and said, 'I wrapped all my bairns in this. My mother knitted it. I want you to have it for Dan's child.'

Rosabelle flinched, but forced herself to look grateful as Effie shook out the white woollen shawl. It was like a big cobweb. She managed to say, 'It's lovely, and so fine.'

Effie folded it up again and gave it to her. 'Take it now. I've kept it for my first grandchild. I want you to have it.'

'But what if Jessie's bairn arrives first?' Rosabelle asked.

Effie shook her head. 'That doesn't matter. I want Dan's child to have it. He was my first born . . .'

Rosabelle handed it back and said, 'It's lovely, and I'll use it for his baby, but keep it for me, Effie. It might be bad luck to start saving things now. There's still so long to go.'

She could not bear to keep the shawl because she was beginning to realize that she really hated the idea of having the child. She wished it would stay inside her for ever.

Next morning Clara was knocking at the door of the little attic room again and calling, 'Get up. You can't lie in there all day.'

Slowly Rosabelle opened the door and said, 'There's nothing for me to get up for, is there?'

'Don't be stupid. You're not the worst off.'

'Sometimes I hate you, and anyway I don't want to think about other people,' Rosabelle snapped angrily. 'It's all right for you. Your Tom was lucky to be down at Yarmouth, so he didn't go out with the others. You must be one of the few women in this town with her man still alive.'

Clara stepped into the room and sat down on the bed. 'I've something important to tell you. It's about Tom. He's taken against the sea. He lost his uncle and two of his cousins in the storm, and he says he never wants to set foot on a fishing boat again – he's not the only one, mind. Eck Purves that came back on the *Onward* says the same. He's going inland to work on a farm.'

Rosabelle studied her sister's set face. She knew that Clara and Tom had been saving for at least three years because they did not want to marry till Tom had paid up his share of his cousin's boat.

'What about the boat?' she asked.

'It's gone, and the insurance people say they can't afford to pay any money for it – there's been too many claims.' Clara sounded resigned.

'What'll Tom do instead?' Rosabelle asked.

'He wants to go to America. He has a cousin in Boston working as a policeman. He says he can get Tom a place.'

'When's he going?'

'Soon.'

'What'll you do?' was Rosabelle's next question. Clara and Tom had been together since they were at school and, though her sister maintained an implacable exterior, her love for the solemn-faced, unhumorous but reliable Tom was the chief emotion of her life.

'I want to go with him,' said Clara flatly.

They stared at each other till the silence between them was broken by Clara saying, 'That's why you have to get up and start living again. I'm being selfish because I can't go away unless you're able to help our mother. She's acting very strange. She doesn't want to come to terms with what's happened.'

'Why me? I can't help anyone, not even myself! Take Mother to America with you!' The pent-up tears began to flow again, and Rosabelle collapsed like a curled-up baby on the bed.

Clara sat silent till her sister quietened, and said in a matter-of-fact voice, 'She won't go. I've asked her. Dan's dead. So are another one hundred and eighty-eight fishermen. You're carrying his baby. Like it or not, life goes on.'

'I know that only too well,' sobbed Rosabelle.

'So get up,' said Clara.

The draconian treatment worked. Rosabelle was made angry, and being angry she fought back, screaming at her sister, who sat on the bed and accepted the abuse. Eventually, anger dissipated, she dressed herself in her fisherwoman's clothes and went out with Clara to talk to their mother and try to convince her to go to America. They found her in her kitchen with three other women, talking about their bereaved neighbours.

Isa was gabbling as if she could not control her tongue. 'Bella Fairbairn's been drunk since they brought in her man's body. They say she nearly fell into the grave. Tommy Nisbet's Ella's due with her fifth and all of them under ten. How's she going to manage? She's none too bright. Her mother and father were cousins, you see. He was Willie Wake's brother and you know what he's like. Euphen Fairbairn's keeping out of folks' way, like she's ashamed.'

'She's got nothing to be ashamed about,' interrupted Clara.

Her mother nodded. 'Maybe, but folk are talking. They're saying that Burgon should have tried to save some of the other men. They're saying he was only worried about saving himself.'

Rosabelle joined in: 'That's not fair.'

'I know, but you can't stop folk talkin', can you? This has been such a terrible thing. When your father comes back, I'll see what he thinks about it,' said Isa.

The sisters looked at each other in consternation, and Clara said gently, 'Father's not coming back, Mother.'

Isa stopped as if someone had hit her. 'Don't talk nonsense.'

One by one the other women slipped quietly away, leaving the girls with their mother, and it was Rosabelle who brought up the subject of Boston.

'What do you think about Clara and Tom going to America?' she asked.

Isa smiled: 'It's a good idea. Folk do well there, don't they?'

'Would you like to go too?'

Isa laughed. 'Me? What would your father do? Who'd bait his lines if I went away?'

The girls looked at each other helplessly. Was it too cruel to snap her back into reality? Both held their tongues.

'She's out of her mind. I hope she pulls herself together soon,' said Clara when they were out of the house and alone again.

'So you can get away, you mean?' asked Rosabelle icily.

Clara ignored that. 'She'll be better when she starts taking an interest in your baby. What about moving in with her? The house'll be empty if I go, and there's no point you keeping that room.'

Rosabelle stopped in her tracks. 'I won't leave my room.' As far as she was concerned, Dan was still there.

'But you can't stay on alone up there. What'll happen when you go into labour?'

The thought that had been obsessing Rosabelle since she saw Dan drown was again expressed in words. 'I don't want this baby. I don't care if it's never born.'

Clara put an arm over her shoulders and gave her a quick hug. 'My poor wee sister. It's coming whether you want it or not. Things'll be different when it's born.'

'They won't. I'm sure of it. If I could swap this baby for Dan I'd do it in a second,' Rosabelle sobbed.

'If I were you, I wouldn't tell Effie that,' said her sister.

They found Effie scrubbing the floor. She looked up when she saw them and rushed towards Rosabelle, crying out, 'Sit down, lass. How're you feelin'? This terrible thing hasnae upset the bairn, has it?'

Rosabelle sat down and shook her head. She was surprised to see how much Effie had aged in only a few days. There had been a scattering of grey in her hair before, but now a quiff of white was swept back from a face that had acquired a map of wrinkles, especially round her mouth.

But the Effie who rallied them all through the terrible waiting hours of the storm was back and determinedly positive again. 'I've been doing a lot of thinking about how we can organize oursel's. Food's cheap enough and at least we have roofs over our heads. Are you moving in with your mother, Clara? And I was thinking Rosabelle might go to Mrs Lyall and ask for her old job back.' She'd obviously been making frantic plans.

'Clara's going to America,' said Rosabelle stiffly.

Effie, mercifully diverted, stared at the other girl. 'Americky? That's awful far away.'

'Tom says he doesn't want to go to sea again,' Clara explained.

'He'll have to go on the sea to get to Americky,' said Effie with a touch of her old acerbity.

Clara ignored that. 'Tom and I won't be running away from our responsibilities. We've been saving up for a boat, and have enough to leave some money with my mother,' she said.

'That'll help. She'll need it,' said Effie, practicality

returning. Then she dashed over to the tall wooden chest of drawers that stood in a dark corner and pulled open the top drawer. 'Rosabelle and I won't need to worry about money for a while, though. Look at this!' she cried, brandishing a leather purse at the girls.

They said nothing, but sat staring. It was a man's money purse.

Effie was excited. 'It's Jimmy Dip's. On that last morning he sailed, he left it on top of the dresser – and his gold watch too. He'd never left anything like that behind before. I've been thinking about it and I feel he knew something bad was going to happen and left this behind to take care of us – me, and Rosabelle, and wee Jessie.'

She snapped the purse open and poured money on to the table top. There were five golden guineas among coppers and silver coins. 'We'll be all right. Jimmy's lookin' after us,' she said in an exultant voice.

Rosabelle shrank in her seat. When Effie tried to put a guinea in her hand she refused it. 'No, no, keep it. I don't need anything yet,' she cried.

When they left the house, Clara waited till they were out of earshot, and then said, 'The quicker you or Jessie have a bairn the better. Effie needs something to think about or she'll lose her mind too like our mother.'

Not wanting to be with any more grieving women, Clara led her sister into the town and, as they walked past the window of Mrs Lyall's shop, she said lightly, 'That wasn't a bad idea of Effie's about asking for your old job back.'

'Was it?' asked Rosabelle coldly.

'Maybe you're not ready yet, but it's something to bear in mind. Anyway, let's go in and say hello.'

Mrs Lyall, one of the town's biggest gossips, had heard about Dan and came rushing round the counter to hug her ex-apprentice. 'Oh you poor lassie. Only a week married, and having a baby too.'

For the first time in their acquaintance Rosabelle was struck by the peculiar way Mrs Lyall spoke. She had tried hard to sound refined for so long that she'd perfected a speaking style that was performed without moving her upper lip at all. It gave her voice a strangled note and made her look like a rabbit cautiously nibbling a lettuce.

Don't let her say, 'One always goes out when another comes in,' thought Rosabelle. Fortunately she didn't.

The dress shop was opposite the town burying ground and Mrs Lyall pointed excitedly through the window to say, 'There's another funeral over there today. Let's pay our respects. It's Mr Nisbet's. I saw his wife going past a few minutes ago and she's so heavy with child that she can hardly walk. I wonder if that mistress of his from Berwick will have the cheek to come to the interment?'

Clara's interest was captured as she hurried out to see what was going on. 'A mistress in Berwick? How do you know about that?'

'Because my sister lives there and everybody knows about the woman. She's involved with more than one man – they say Nisbet wasn't the only one – and she has a very expensive taste in clothes: silk and lace is more her style than knitted shawls. If we go out on to the step we can watch them coming away from the burying ground. They have to pass here.'

There was not long to wait. In a few minutes a straggling line of mourners, led by Nisbet's weeping wife, walked past. Apart from them walked a smartly dressed woman in a tight-waisted mauve dress with an artfully gathered bustle, and a black hat tilted forward and tied down against the breeze with a black gauze scarf that also acted as a veil.

'That's her, the hussy,' hissed Mrs Lyall gleefully. 'Just look at that gown. Five pounds if it cost a penny.'

As the mystery woman prepared to get into a little trap drawn up at the burying-ground gate, she was the most dashing person any of them had ever seen, even better than the fashionable ladies of Edinburgh's Princes Street. Compared to Nisbet's wife in her mourning clothes, his mistress was like a bird of paradise against a crow. *I don't blame him for preferring her*, thought Rosabelle.

Walking away from Nisbet's open grave, the woman, who called herself Rachelle de Roquefort, felt such deep-seated sorrow that her heart ached inside her ribcage. She'd loved him because, with him, she was able to be herself, to stop pretending, to forget the plans and schemes that otherwise continually occupied her. Now he was dead, where would she go? What would she do? One thing was certain: she would survive. She'd always been alone . . . he'd been her one interlude of frivolity. Only because of him had she come to this benighted part of the world.

She stiffened her back and stood straighter as she walked past the mourning party, noticing how they avoided looking directly at the stranger, gathering round the widow as if they were protecting her from this dangerous woman. Rachelle poked out her chin, defying them, hoping that Nisbet had left some money for his wife. She herself had never taken any from him.

Climbing into the trap, with the heavy folds of her skirt gathered in her gloved right hand, she noticed the three other women watching her from the opposite side of the street. One of them, whose hands were being clasped by the other two, was all in black, but surely she was too young to be a widow? Some drowned man's daughter perhaps. Though she herself was grieving, Rachelle's powers of observation were sharp and she noted that the youngest girl was a beauty, with the sort of tall, elegant figure that could make any clothes – even dreadful mourning – look good.

'I could make use of that girl,' she thought as the trap driver took up the reins. When it drove past the three watching women, her eye caught Rosabelle's, as she meant it to do, and the girl was unable to tell whether Nisbet's mistress was frightening or fascinating.

Seven

While the people of Eyemouth mourned their dead, they did not know that their tragedy had touched the hearts of the entire country. They were not mourning alone.

For a whole week, the *Scotsman* of Edinburgh ran dozens of column inches about the tragedy, listing the names of the lost boats and 189 fishermen from the fishing ports of Berwickshire who had gone down with them. It told its readers that, when all the casualties were totalled up, Eyemouth alone had lost 129 men who left behind eighty new widows and 260 orphans, as well as several unborn, but already fatherless, babies.

The newspaper predicted that it would take the town at least two generations to recover – if it ever did.

These reports, and others like them in newspapers from John o'Groats to deepest Devon, shocked readers and touched hearts so much that even people who had never heard of the stricken town before began thinking of ways of helping the bereaved.

Civic dignitaries, from the Lord Provost of London to mayors and provosts of smaller towns, launched charitable funds. Money poured in, not only from the well-off but from the poor as well. By 22nd October – a week after the storm – the sum stood at the astonishing amount of £30,000, and was still growing.

This astonishing generosity caused a problem. People of influence in Eyemouth debated what was to be done with such a fortune. How was it to be distributed? Who by – and most of all, who to?

While they were discussing the problem, money continued to stream in. By the end of October over £50,000 had been sent to ease the situation of the widowed and orphaned of

Eyemouth. It lay in the town bank, undistributed, because no one knew what to do with it.

'Isn't it fortunate, Mr Cochrane, that you've arrived here at such a time?' said Hester Stanhope to her brother's friend the Rev. Cochrane when they met in the upper town.

'Fortunate, Miss Stanhope?' he asked in a puzzled tone. To be in Eyemouth and witness to such a tragedy was anything but fortunate as far as he was concerned. It was proving very harrowing, because when he went from house to house attempting to find words of consolation, he felt tongue-tied and ineffectual. The magnitude of what had happened affected him so deeply that he was beginning to question the belief that had guided him into the ministry in the first place.

'I'm finding it very hard,' he told Hester.

She looked surprised, and he stumbled on: 'You see, when I go round the houses of people who have lost their men, most of them are quite polite to me, but some women slam the door in my face.'

She sniffed: 'They are rough people, no manners!'

This was no consolation to him. 'I don't think it's just that. I'm sure some of them remember how one of the fishermen shouted "Cauld iron" at me on the morning they sailed . . . He saw my clerical collar, you see . . . Maybe the women think I'm responsible.'

'Don't be silly,' she said shortly.

'But your father said that to catch sight of a clergyman was very bad luck for fishermen.'

'Father has worked among those people so long he's almost as superstitious as they are. Most are a heathen lot and it's going to be a hard task for you to bring them to God.' She patted his arm as if he was a nervous child, but he was not reassured. He wished he could find out if the man who shouted out at the sight of him had survived, or was one of the casualties of the storm.

He shied away from thinking about it. Hester guessed nothing of what was going through his mind as she walked by his side, smiling at him in a coquettish way.

'It can't be easy for you being a bachelor, with no one to share your thoughts. Aren't you lonely?' she asked.

He felt himself shrink away from her. 'I'm very busy settling in at the moment.'

'You'll have to find yourself a wife, Mr Cochrane, or every single woman in the town will be chasing you.'

He knew he must marry eventually, because unmarried ministers were often regarded with suspicion; but he was in no hurry. 'I can't afford a wife at the moment. You see, I support my mother, who is a widow in poor health, and my stipend is not large,' he told her. His church looked imposing, but the congregation was small and careful with money.

'In that case, you must find a rich wife,' she said with a light laugh.

As the only daughter of a rich and well-established man, she was a good match, and they both knew it. The Paisley shawl draped over her shoulders was richly coloured and sumptuous, the flower-trimmed bonnet obviously new. But though smartly dressed, she was plain in appearance, thin as a rail and white-faced, with a sharp nose and a jutting-out chin that would give her the profile of a witch when she grew older.

When they passed women of her acquaintance, she bobbed her head and greeted them as if she already owned him. He wanted to take to his heels and run because there was something about her archness that frightened and repelled him.

Unaware of his dark thoughts, she put on a serious expression again and resumed their earlier conversation. 'Yes, as I was saying: it's very fortunate that you've come here now. You can be a power for *good*.'

'But I don't know what to do for the best, or what to say to these poor people. I don't feel fortunate to be here. They need someone more effective,' he said in an outburst of honesty.

She dismissed his fears with a wave of her gloved hand. 'When I said it's fortunate, I meant that the Town Council is lucky to have someone level-headed and caring like you to sit on the committee that will see to the paying out of the relief-fund money.'

This was news to him. 'Me? On a relief-fund committee? What committee?' he enquired.

She laughed lightly. 'Don't you know yet? My father was offered the position but he refused it because he knows too many of the people who will be making claims, and he suggested your name. As a stranger to the town, you'll be impartial, and they won't be able to influence you. He told me this morning. I thought I might meet you on your walk and congratulate you.'

Cochrane's face took on an even more solemn expression. 'It's a very big responsibility, Miss Stanhope. There's a lot of money in the fund.'

'Indeed there is. It's up to fifty thousand pounds by now. Isn't that astonishing? I was so touched when I heard that Her Majesty the Queen sent a hundred pounds. Wasn't that generous of her! Perhaps one of the first things the committee should do is suggest that people who get money should write to Buckingham Palace and thank her. It would be nice to show that they are grateful.'

Grateful seemed an inappropriate word, he thought, and he was certainly not concerned about sending letters of thanks to Queen Victoria. The stricken people of the town had more pressing problems.

Hester was still talking about the Queen, however. 'When I think of her taking up her pen and sending money to our town, I am filled with admiration and gratitude. It's so kind! And as well as the Queen, the Berwickshire landowners have also been very generous – a gentleman with an estate near Duns actually sent two hundred pounds!'

'And I heard that a railway signalman sent a pound and a letter saying he was sorry it couldn't be more,' Cochrane interjected, because that struck him as commendable as the largesse of the rich.

She leaned on her parasol and looked at him, getting an inkling of what he was thinking. 'Yes, even the poorest have sent money. That's all the more reason you have to be careful about giving it out when you become a trustee. You have a responsibility to the people who contributed, especially the less well-off. Be careful, Mr Cochrane; don't let yourself be exploited, and don't let your kind heart rule your head. Getting too much all at once can be corrupting for some people.'

He looked at her, wondering what she was telling him. 'No one has tried to exploit me. In fact, as I told you, most of the houses I call at won't even let me in,' he said.

'They'll let you in fast enough when they find out how

much money you have in your power,' she warned with a steely look in her eye.

'But all the committee has to do is divide the money up and hand it out to genuine cases. It's only a matter of mathematics. There's eighty widows and about two hundred and seventy fatherless children in Eyemouth. If we give them each a lump sum, they'll be able to make a new start in life,' he said.

Hester was so horrified she stopped dead in the middle of the street and gasped, '*A lump sum!* Impossible! Nothing of the kind. These women are not to be trusted. If they got a lot of money all at once, they'd only waste it. Money donated like that can't be frittered away.'

'But it's their money. It's been sent for them. I'm sure they won't all fritter it away,' he protested.

She was genuinely shocked. 'Have you any idea of the sort of people you will be dealing with? Some of them drink, you know. They're not *ladies*, and they have no idea how to manage money. They're not even proper Christians. They hardly ever go to church. Most of the dead men's funerals haven't been properly conducted! No services – just put in the ground!'

Cochrane shook his head. 'That's their business, but the money was donated to help the women and their children restart their lives. A committee can't hold on to it.'

'But they must. The capital has to be safeguarded. Let's say that if ten thousand pounds is allocated to relatives of victims of the storm in the other fishing villages, that leaves over forty thousand pounds for Eyemouth alone. If that was to be handed out all at once, each claimant would receive over one hundred and fourteen pounds, *which – is – quite – impossible,*' said Hester, stressing the last words in a slow and definite tone. Her certainties terrified him.

'How many committee members are there?' he asked.

'Father said between ten and twelve,' she replied.

He sighed in relief, glad that he wouldn't have a large share of responsibility for handing the money over.

In fact, he had hardly any responsibility at all. On the committee with him were two big landowners, the local Member of Parliament, the bank manager, and representatives of every church or mission in the district – five clergymen in all, though ninety of the dead men had not belonged to any church, and scorned religion.

Moreover, even those registered as church members were only occasional attenders at services.

But all the clergy were automatically put on the committee and graded themselves in importance by the size of their congregations. The most popular religious establishment in town was the Evangelical Union, which had lost thirty-two of its members in the storm. The United Presbyterian Church had lost twenty-six, the Free Church twenty-seven, the Methodists sixteen and Alan Cochrane's Established Church half a dozen, which put him lowest in the pecking order.

Alex Burgon clicked his tongue when he heard about the clerical predominance of the relief-fund committee. 'Trouble, trouble,' he predicted, and took himself off to consult with his friend, shrewd old Donald McIntyre, manager of Eyemouth's Commercial Bank.

'You'll have to fight for fairness, Donald, or some of those ministers will be giving money to their cronies and keeping it away from folk they don't approve of,' he said.

'They won't get past me because all the money is in my bank and I'm determined to keep an eye on where it goes. Like you, I'm worried about impartiality. They'd never let a fisherman on the committee, but we need someone with links to the community. I'm going to propose co-opting Coastguard Duncan, because he knew all the dead men,' said McIntyre.

Burgon nodded. 'Aye, Duncan's fair-minded. But there should be outside help from someone who has no ties within the district. Ask the MP what he thinks.'

The MP consulted friends in Edinburgh and, after a few days, word got round that an official, with the title of Inspector of the Poor, had been appointed to supervise the paying out of the donated fortune.

The town was agog with curiosity on the day that this important man was due to arrive.

A group of black-clad ministers and Mr McIntyre, the banker, were waiting on the platform of Burnmouth station when Steven Anderson, a sturdy, good-looking fellow of thirty, with curly brown hair and a luxuriant moustache, alighted from the Edinburgh train.

When they shook hands, McIntyre's first impression of the new man was favourable, for his physique was strong, his handclasp firm and his eyes bright and frank. As they walked in a group to the station entrance, Anderson seemed very confident and asked sensible questions about what urgent measures needed to be taken to ease the situation of the poorest widows and children.

It was nearly November and the cold days were upon them. 'Are the local winters very bitter? Do the bereaved families need assistance with fuel and food?' he asked.

The questions were sensible, and he listened, quietly nodding, to the answers.

'Have you set up a soup kitchen yet?' was his next query.

'A soup kitchen?' asked McIntyre in surprise.

Anderson nodded. 'It will be absolutely necessary, sir. I have been working among cholera victims in Edinburgh and the city's soup kitchens were much appreciated there. In fact, I may say that they saved many lives. I'm sure we can take the necessary money from the fund . . .'

'There is no need for such a thing as a soup kitchen in Eyemouth,' said McIntyre stiffly. He hardly dared imagine the reaction of the town's proud women to such a suggestion.

Anderson paid no heed to his objection. 'A soup kitchen is essential. A plate of hot soup keeps body and soul together, especially for the children. I have seen their little faces light up when they smell good broth!'

'Sir, our town is not an impoverished slum. Till disaster struck it was a prosperous community where people took pride in their homes and their families. All they need is tiding over till they re-establish themselves. They would be insulted if we tried to feed them all together like cattle.' McIntyre's face reddened as he spoke.

Anderson recognized that he had overstepped some sort of line, but seemed disappointed not to be instrumental in setting up a soup kitchen. McIntyre hoped that no one suggested his idea to the fishing widows, who prided themselves on the way they fed their families.

A charabanc drawn by a pair of horses was waiting in the

station yard to carry the new arrival and his reception committee the two miles back to Eyemouth. As he stood back to allow the others to go in first, Mr McIntyre had the opportunity to study Anderson more closely.

The man's skin was clear and healthy, the heavy moustache exceptionally silky, but there was something odd about his head. What was it?

Then McIntyre remembered a boy who had gone to school with him – a boy with the same sort of head – who was a total dunce. His head was out of proportion to the rest of his body and the skull was much broader and heavier at the bottom than at the top.

Anderson's head was the same. The depth of his chin and the disproportionate wideness of his jawbone gave him the look of the truly stupid. Caught unawares, waiting to take his seat in the charabanc, he had the puzzled expression of a baffled bullock.

The committee had taken rooms for him in the Royal Hotel and he was to set up an office on the ground floor of the Town Hall on the other side of the road from the hotel. The Town Hall was a fine building with a full-sailed fishing boat carved out of red sandstone over a pillared front door, and it was also next door to the bank, which would be convenient when it came to handing out the money.

As he stepped out of the charabanc and his imposing working premises were pointed out, Anderson's eyes shone and he could barely conceal his delight.

McIntyre lingered behind when the others left and said to him, 'If there's anything I can do to help you settle into the town, you must ask me, but I suppose you will have had experience of this sort of thing before.'

'In a way, but not for such a big sum of money, though I've always worked with the poor and my father was a workhouse supervisor. Till last week I distributed alms to poor families in Edinburgh's Old Town. I was appointed to this position because my superior was a friend of your Member of Parliament and he suggested my name.'

McIntyre nodded. 'This isn't alms distribution exactly. I hope the committee will set up a fair system to distribute the money sent by well-wishers for the bereaved people here.

Eyemouth folk are very proud and self-reliant. They won't like taking anything that seems like charity handouts on a long-term basis.'

Anderson looked surprised. 'But if they're hungry they'll need it.'

'I know,' said McIntyre sadly, 'but they ought to be helped to get back on their feet, to regenerate the town. This has to be handled carefully.'

Anderson did not appear to get the point. He rubbed his hands together and said, 'I'll manage them. The people I had to deal with in Edinburgh were often very difficult – degenerates sometimes. You learn to sort them out.'

McIntyre felt himself chill. 'There's no question of sorting people out here and you will certainly not be dealing with degenerates. This is a small town and everybody knows everybody else. Everyone must be given their fair share. Your task is to distribute the money fairly and without bias.'

There was a desk in the room with a pile of writing paper on it and Anderson walked up to carefully straighten the white sheets. 'I've been told there's a lot of money involved,' he said in what he hoped was a casual tone. He did not want to show how much the magnitude of his new task awed him.

'Indeed there is – more than fifty-three thousand pounds now. It's a fortune and a considerable responsibility. It's lying in my bank vault at the moment,' said the banker.

Anderson beamed at him. 'And it'll stay there, sir. Don't worry. I won't be handing it out to all and sundry.' McIntyre could not decide whether the man was obtusely avoiding the issue or was too stupid to understand.

On his second night in town Anderson received an invitation to dinner from Mr Stanhope and his daughter. The dining room of Beechwood, with its gleaming furniture and highly polished silver, impressed the man from Edinburgh, whose background was impoverished. Growing up in the workhouse with a bullying father was very hard.

Since stepping off the train from Edinburgh a new future had opened up in front of him. As far as he was concerned, it was going to take a considerable time to distribute the relief fund because he was not prepared to return to his lowly position in the capital too soon.

He swelled up with importance as he looked around the Stanhope dining room, with its glittering chandelier and sparkling crystal glasses. In a long mirror above the fireplace he caught sight of his reflection and pulled himself up to his considerable height, straightening his shoulders.

I was born to live like this, he thought, and turned to smile at Hester, who was looking elegant in a claret-coloured gown from Mrs Lyall's establishment.

She smiled back, registering the newcomer's sturdy physique and glorious moustache. *This is a manly man – not a long narrow beanstalk in a clerical collar*, she thought, mentally discarding Alan Cochrane, who watched the preening couple with secret amusement and an enormous sense of relief.

Eight

Five chimes of the church clock still woke Effie every morning. The habit of a lifetime was hard to break.

When she opened her eyes there was always a few seconds of forgetfulness as she put out a hand to wake Jimmy. But he was not there any more and she felt her whole body clench in pain. In the middle of her chest there was an aching hole where her heart should have been. It seemed to throb like an open wound. She hoped it was the beginning of an illness that would kill her.

She lay against her pillow, staring at the black square of the window. Running through her mind was a memory of the disaster seventeen days ago when the sea had snatched up her men like a hungry dragon and swallowed them down for ever. Why had it devoured them all at once? Couldn't she have been left with one?

There was nothing to get up for; she had no work to do – no mussels to gather, no lines to bait, no one to cook for, no voices to listen to – only empty rooms full of the memory of dead men.

Hot tears trickled down her cheeks and she wanted to scream out in agony but stayed silent for fear of waking the neighbours.

Wearily she climbed out of the bed and went stiffly down to the kitchen. Her body seemed to have been aged and weakened by grief. A faint flush of light was filling the sky when she went outside to fetch a shovel of coal for the fire.

As soon as it was burning brightly she sank into Jimmy's empty chair and put her head in her hands. She could hear the sea lapping softly and deceitfully against the harbour wall only a few yards away.

'There's nobody about. I could drown myself now without anybody trying to stop me,' she said aloud.

She had a mental vision of her body floating in the water with her nightgown floating out around her. Would that be a good way of joining Jimmy and the boys? She was not frightened of dying, but she did not want to be disenchanted. What if her fears were right and there was no heaven, no afterlife, nothing but blackness?

Another reason for living was the responsibility she felt for her sons' legacies – Henry's Jessie and Dan's Rosabelle. They were suffering the same pain as she was. Every time she met Jessie she grieved to see the once-pretty face puffy and swollen with weeping; but Rosabelle was even more frightening, because she seemed to have lost all animation. After the first terrible few days she no longer shed tears. The once-friendly, trusting girl had turned into a woman made of ice.

Though both girls had mothers of their own, she felt they'd been left in her care, especially because Bella was drinking to drown her sorrow and Rosabelle's mother Isa, almost demented by grief, was rapidly losing contact with reality.

Though she was not a qualified nurse or midwife, Effie helped friends when they were in labour because she had a vast amount of knowledge passed down to her by her own mother, who had also assisted in the delivery of local babies.

She sat up straighter in her chair and told herself that she had to stay alive long enough to guide her grandchildren into the world. She wanted to hold their little bodies in her hands, to hear their first mewling cries. She had to stay alive for that moment.

Afterwards she could drown herself.

She gave herself a shake like a dog and was rising to brew some tea when she saw a hunched black shape pass her window.

Looking closer, she recognized old Willie Wake staggering along like a scarecrow in his ragged clothes.

Poor old man, he must be hungry and cold, she thought and, rapping on the glass, gestured to him and called, 'Come in, Willie, come in.'

He unlatched her door and stood on the threshold, staring at her. 'What do ye want, Effie?' he croaked.

'Would you like a cup of tea?' she asked.

'I would,' he said solemnly and stepped up to the table, where he stood like an obedient child.

'Sit down by the fire then and I'll brew it. I was just making a pot for myself,' she told him.

He sat and held his arthritic hands out to the flames. 'That's a braw fire, Effie,' he told her.

'Aye, it draws well,' she agreed, wondering how long it was since the poor old soul had enjoyed any comfort. He looked dirtier, more ragged and thinner than ever before.

When she handed him a steaming cup, he looked up at her with rheumy eyes and suddenly asked, 'And whit are ye goin' to dae noo, Effie?' He seemed perfectly sensible, not the demented old man he'd been for the past few years.

She answered him in an equally serious tone, as if he was a confidant: 'I don't know what I'm going to do, Willie. Earlier this morning I thought about drowning myself.'

He sipped his tea and solemnly considered this. She wondered if she'd done right in talking to him so frankly. Would he dodge the issue? Would he go off on one of his fantastic ravings and make her feel foolish?

He thought for a few moments, and what he did say was: 'Well, they say that drowning's no' a bad death, but ye canna do it yet, Effie. A lot of folk need your help.'

'My help! What can I do? I can't even help myself!' Her voice was hopeless.

'Ye've aye been a strong person, ever since ye were a bairn. The town needs somebody strong to give it life again. Dinna let strangers take us over and try to change us. I dinna like the look of that fellow that's come doon frae Edinbury to run us. The dead men wouldnae like that either. I'm too old and too dottled to help – but you can do it, Effie.'

She looked at him with surprise and respect. 'I don't know what you mean,' she said.

'Have ye seen that new man? The yin wi' the big moustache. Folk'll have to stand thegether and fight him, or this town will lose its pride. He'll make us into beggars if he has his way,' he said.

She was astonished by the return to the sharpness that the old man had once shown, and remembered his insistence that the boats should not sail into the storm. If only they'd listened to him. Perhaps she ought to pay heed to him now.

'I haven't seen the new man yet. What's he come from Edinburgh to do?' she asked.

'To give out the relief money. Mind what I'm saying, Effie: dinna let him turn us into paupers.' He rose creakily from his seat, turned towards the window and stared out. Then he looked at her with his old vacant smile and said, 'It's going to be fair weather. I'll just go along and see if the gless is up. Then the boats'll be able to fish again. Life goes on, Effie.'

That evening a group of dejected men met in the bar of the Ship Inn overlooking the harbour.

They turned up in ones and twos, bought their drinks and talked in subdued tones about their dead friends. There didn't seem to be any reason for them gathering, but within half an hour all the survivors of the storm who were fit enough to walk were there, as well as men who had not gone out on the terrible day.

Even Alex Burgon, who normally avoided drinking, was among them, and it was he who raised the question that had brought them together.

'When do we sail again?' he asked.

Johnny Maltman, one of the lucky ones whose boat had been washed up at South Shields with only two crewmen lost, grimaced. 'You're in an awful hurry. For myself I won't care if I never go to sea again, but maybe you didnae have it as bad out there as the rest of us.'

A few of his friends muttered in agreement. Some men – and especially women – in the town resented Burgon for coming back with all his men.

He stared his critic out. 'I had it very bad and you know it.'

'And what brought you through then?'

'I prayed.' He was not a man to boast about his seamanship and genuinely believed that prayer had saved him.

Some others muttered, but whether in sympathy or disbelief was not obvious. Burgon saw that they had to be kept to the point, and said sharply, 'We have to go back out as soon as we can. If our town's going to survive, the boats must sail again. If we give up, Eyemouth is finished.'

One or two men said they intended to leave the sea and

find other work, but admitted it was not a prospect that pleased them. Fishing and the sea were all they knew.

A crewman looked down into his ale mug and said, 'I've got to find work soon to feed my bairns.'

'Exactly,' snapped Burgon, 'and you're not the only one. The whole town needs money, especially the widows and orphans. We can't sit around waiting for charity handouts. It's not our way. We're not beggars. I propose that we sail as soon as our boats are repaired and divide the first catch so that everybody gets a share.'

One of the Hood family, which had lost two men in the disaster, looked up in surprise. 'Divide the catch? Why? Can't each man look after his ain folk?'

'No!' said Burgon. 'We've lost too many men. It's our duty to take care of the people they left behind – whether they belong to our own families or not. We must pool our catch so that they all get something.'

A younger Hood sneered. 'Will the widows do the same for us when the fund money that everybody's talkin' about is handed oot?'

A noisy discussion broke out and someone else asked, 'Have you seen the big fellow that's come down from Edinburgh to handle the money? He's got a grand opinion of himself, walking round the town as if he owns it.'

Burgon pulled a face. 'The women can't wait for handouts. Where's your pride? Eyemouth has always taken care of its widows and orphans in the past. This time there's just more of them. The fund money's charity and taking charity is bad for folks' self-respect. They'll not feel so bad about taking from us – it'll be like taking it from a community chest or something.'

Someone in the crowd agreed with him and said, 'It'll be a long time before the relief money's divided up anyway. They'll all be arguing the toss with each other about who's to get what for weeks. Burgon's right. We must look after our ain folk.'

'But McIntyre the bank manager told me today that there's over fifty thousand pounds to be given out,' said Johnny Fairbairn.

The magnitude of the sum shocked everybody. Each man was working out in his head how many boats could be bought with the money. A good fishing boat cost around £450 – so the entire fleet could be replaced and there would still be money left over.

Burgon scowled when he heard the mutterings. 'Dinna imagine that the men in charge of the money are going to give it away to the town without a quibble. Think about who they are – that Inspector of the Poor brought down from Edinburgh, Members of Parliament and ministers, bankers, property owners and landlords. There's no fishermen on the committee. That money's going to cause more trouble than it cures, and we shouldn't rely on it,' he shouted.

'I don't like it either,' said a voice from the back of the room, 'but the wives and bairns of the men who died have no money coming in, and if kind folk have sent money for them, I don't see why they shouldn't have it.'

'As long as they don't have to go on bended knee for it,' said someone else.

A man sitting on a stool near the door spoke up. 'We need to get one of oor ain folk on the relief-fund committee.'

'Mr Duncan, the coastguard, has been appointed,' said Will Hope, host of the Ship Inn, who had written off all the dues that dead men had left on the slate in his bar as his contribution to helping the bereaved.

The gathering nodded in approval of Duncan, and they were all talking again when Willie Wave's voice rang out.

'There ought to be a woman to speak up for her kind,' he said, and a silence fell as the other men thought of the wives, mothers, sisters and daughters of the dead men, many of whom were their blood relations.

'I don't see that committee asking a fisherwoman for advice. If they take a woman on, it'll be some titled lady, or a landowner's wife,' said Will Hope.

'But none of them would have any idea about who is in need,' said another man.

'What about Jimmy Dip's Effie,' shouted Willie Wake again.

'That's not a bad idea. She's a sensible woman and she'll know what to do,' said Hope.

'Effie's the best one,' they all agreed, but without much hope, for they knew how unlikely it was that local dignitaries would listen to the opinions of a fishwife.

Before the meeting broke up, however, one big decision was made: the Eyemouth fleet was going to sail again, and as soon as possible.

Two days later, at eight o'clock in the morning, twenty boats sailed out to fish for haddock. Some were still only half patched up after the battering they'd had from the storm, but all defiantly flew coloured pennants from their masts and men on the decks waved to the watchers on the shore as they left the harbour.

The first boat out was Alex Burgon's *Ariel Gazelle*.

Two hours after the fleet sailed, Steven Anderson, in a dark-coloured suit and a stiffly starched collar, sat at his work table in a large room on the ground floor of the Town Hall, surveying the solemn faces of the relief-fund committee members, who were all looking at him with attentive respect.

His heart was bursting with pride and he thought to himself, *Only a week ago who could have predicted how important I am today!*

Before him lay sheets of paper inscribed with lines of figures, and carefully worked out calculations. The amount of money he had to deal with awed him.

'Good morning, gentlemen. This is a very solemn task that we are about to undertake. I have to tell you that today the Eyemouth Disaster Relief Fund stands at fifty-three thousand, three hundred and seventy-five pounds.'

The expressions on the faces of his listeners told him that they were impressed too. Only Mr McIntyre from the bank looked unflustered, but he knew the figure already, and anyway he was used to handling large amounts of other people's money.

Anderson went on, 'This magnificent sum has been donated by members of the public, the aristocracy and even royalty. Our first duty is to decide how it will be distributed to deserving cases.'

Mr McIntyre was the first to speak up. 'Surely everybody who lost a man is deserving?'

This intervention flustered Anderson. 'There has to be some order. We must decide our priorities.' He turned over his papers till he found a particular sheet and said, 'I have here the names of each man who drowned, and the places they came from – mostly Eyemouth, I see. Some of them were married but others were not. I think we have to leave the unmarried cases to the last.'

McIntyre coughed and Anderson could see he was going to be troublesome. 'But several of the unmarried men had children. And others had mothers and sisters depending on them. The households into which they took their money will be hard hit. It's not only widows we must worry about. It's everybody in need.'

This banker is going to be a damned nuisance, thought Anderson.

Mr Pearson, minister of the Free Church of Scotland and a man known for his narrow-minded and puritanical opinions, chipped in: 'I suggest we first give money to people who were legitimately married with legitimate children . . . It's not our place to be encouraging immorality. There's enough of that in this town already.'

Anderson favoured him with an understanding glance. 'I quite agree, Mr Pearson. Though I have recently arrived here, some of the things I've heard shock me. It's only proper that we take people's way of life into consideration.'

There was a screeching sound as one of the audience pulled his chair along the wooden floor and everyone turned to look at him. Alan Cochrane, the youngest cleric, whom Anderson had dismissed as unimportant when he first cast his eye over him, stood up and blushed scarlet as he began to speak.

'I've not been living here long either, but it seems to me that most fishing-family couples marry outside the Church. Their marriages are irregular, but the children are still legitimate, aren't they?'

At first Anderson thought Cochrane was backing him up. 'Quite right, Mr Cochrane. The marriages are irregular, and I've been told that none of the wives take their husbands' names. Even among the lowest people of Edinburgh there's not so much open flaunting of propriety. We'll have to be very careful about who claims money in case we are cheated.'

Cochrane's flush deepened. 'I think anyone who is recognized by the community as being the wife or helpmate of a casualty of the storm is entitled to be a beneficiary of the fund,' he managed to say.

There was a flash in Mr McIntyre's eye as he said, 'I agree. And any child that a man recognized as his is entitled to its share as well. The fishing community has its own customs and traditions, Mr Anderson, and we will have to observe them.'

The clerics banded together in disapproval but the well-to-do gentlemen and landowners leaned back in their chairs, dissociating themselves from the discussion. They were used to scandals, but their own scandals. The sort of thing that went on among the fisherfolk was as much a mystery to them as the goings-on of an aboriginal tribe.

Piqued at the way the proceedings were diverging from his intentions, Anderson rapped on the top of the table to re-establish control.

'I've drafted a handbill asking any wife and mother with a legitimate claim to come before me to put her case. But before we pay anything out, we must decide how much each woman and child will receive.'

Various sums popped up in the minds of his audience.

Alan Cochrane was about to suggest a hundred pounds each when a well-off gentleman farmer said, 'How about five pounds a head to start with?'

Anderson shook his head firmly. He was determined to hand out the money in small sums – that way it would take longer, and might even ensure him a job for life. 'My dear sir, that's far too much. You haven't had my experience in dealing with the indigent poor. They'd have five pounds wasted in a week. This is not our money; we are only the *custodians* of it. And besides, the fund will have to go on paying people for years. We must not allow them to imagine they can have five pounds a week for ever.'

Cochrane felt it necessary to protest: 'But they're not indigent poor – not like people in city slums . . .' His voice trailed off, and he hated himself for feeling intimidated when Anderson glared at him like a fist-fighter.

The Reverend Pearson chipped in: 'Perhaps they are not so debased, but we must be careful not to spoil them with too much money. Being exposed to such unexpected largesse all at once could be very bad for them,' he said solemnly.

'It will weaken their spirit,' chipped in the Methodist minister, while his colleague from the Baptist chapel added, 'Many of the women drink too much already.'

'Yes, I've been told that several of them have very dissolute habits. Getting their hands on money could lead them into bad ways,' said Anderson, who had heard Hester Stanhope on the subject at her father's dinner party.

Mr McIntyre broke in with, 'I don't know if you're aware that on average every man who died took home five or six pounds from a fishing trip; but if you think five pounds each is too much for the widows, what should we pay them?'

Anderson had prepared an answer for that. 'I worked out that we can pay every legitimately married widow the sum of five shillings a week, until such time as she dies or remarries. That means we won't be making heavy inroads into the fund capital,' he intoned.

Mr Duncan, the coastguard, cleared his throat and asked, 'But what is the capital for?'

Anderson gave him a pitying look. 'Many of those women are very young, and I believe that some men also left unborn children. Widows could live into their eighties, another sixty years at least for some of them, and there has to be enough money to cover that. We must be cautious.'

Duncan was not easily put off. 'As Mr McIntyre said, considerable sums of money – at least five pounds for every man – usually came into these women's homes each week. They are used to handling it, and are no more wasteful than well-to-do women.'

'And the street sweeper in this town is paid one pound a week. Five shillings is a shameful pittance,' added McIntyre angrily.

Anderson glared. 'Five shillings a week would be welcomed by many poor families in Edinburgh. Though you say at least five pounds was earned by every man on a fishing trip, they didn't go out every day, did they? These women will have to accept that their days of prosperity are over. Disasters happen and people must adjust their lives to them. It's God's will.'

The assembled ministers murmured in solemn agreement. Only Cochrane among them sat silent.

'There were few weeks that they didn't bring in at least

one catch,' Duncan said, because he was not prepared to be put off so easily.

A landowner who paid five pounds a year to his domestic servants was growing bored with the arguments. 'I think five shillings a week is a generous payment for the widows,' he said.

Anderson seized this advantage offered to him. 'That's agreed, then. As well as the widows' five shillings, each orphaned boy will be paid two shillings and sixpence a week until he reaches the age of fourteen, and every orphaned girl will receive the same amount to the age of fifteen. Do you wish to say something, Mr Duncan?'

Duncan's face was reddening as he looked from one man to the next. 'But these are families that have been used to good money and the relief fund was contributed for *them*. How are they going to get out of poverty and start again on such pitiful money? It will only keep them in basic food.'

The Methodist minister shook his head. 'As Mr Anderson has already said, bad things happen, Mr Duncan. Good times don't last for ever. They have to realize that.'

Mr McIntyre looked sad as he said, 'Five shillings a week for the widows and half a crown for the bairns isn't going to make much of a hole in the money that's lying in my vault. I suggest the money be put on deposit, where it will earn interest.'

'Of course. Don't worry, Mr McIntyre; it will be safely invested outwith the town – preferably with some big bank in Edinburgh – because it has to last for a very long time,' said Anderson piously, thereby earning McIntyre's loathing.

'The beneficiaries certainly won't die young of overeating,' he snapped back.

As soon as the meeting broke up, Coastguard Duncan hurried off in search of Effie and found her helping Rosabelle's mother along the harbour wall, grasping the other woman by the arm and saying, 'Come on home, Isa. There's no boats comin' in yet.'

Between them they delivered Isa back to Rosabelle, who was looking more pregnant every day, and then Duncan said, 'I need you to help me, Effie. The relief committee have just decided how much is to be paid out to the women.'

'How much?' she asked.

'Five shillings a week for a widow and half a crown for each bairn till they go to work.'

Effie gasped. 'That's not very generous!' She didn't want to seem grasping, but she'd heard how much money had been sent to Eyemouth.

Duncan nodded grimly. 'I think so too. I told that big galoot Anderson how much our men were bringing in, but he didn't seem to believe me. I don't think he's ever handled more than a couple of pounds a week himself.'

Effie shrugged. 'How are they going to distribute the money?'

'He's sending out handbills telling people to apply to him for it.'

'I can think of a lot of people who are too proud to do that, and anyway, most of them can't read,' she said sharply. In fact she could read – one of the few fisherwomen with that ability – but she was also very proud. Duncan knew that too.

'It's their money, Effie; they have to apply. You and I must make them, or they'll get nothing. Anybody that's lost a man must get their share.' Duncan was urgent in his appeal. He hated to think of the people he knew and respected being denied their rights.

She appreciated his fervour. 'How can I help?' she asked.

'You know all the women. Go round and tell them what they must do. Make them see they're not begging. It's money given for them, and it's their money that's paying wages for that man Anderson and keeping him in the Royal Hotel. He should be working for them, not against them, as he seems to think.'

Effie smiled faintly. 'That'll stiffen their spines a wee bit. Who can claim? Everybody who's lost a man, I suppose. Like Rosabelle and wee Jessie?'

Duncan frowned. 'Rosabelle of course, but Anderson said something about *legitimately married* women that worried me a bit . . . He doesn't know much about the way things are here.'

Effie shook her head. 'He'll find out there's more common-law marriages than church ones. Jimmy Dip and I took our vows at Lamberton Toll. Is that legitimate? And what about

Jessie? She's carrying Henry's bairn, but they didn't have time to get married and I know there's other girls in the same state.'

'How many?' asked Duncan.

'At least six or seven, and a few have bairns without any kind of marriage, though everyone knows who the father was. You're a local man; you know how things are around here. There's no shame in it,' said Effie.

'There's no shame in it for us – but I'm not sure about Mr Anderson,' said Duncan ominously.

'So what do you want me to do?' asked Effie.

'I want you to tell everybody who lost a man – husband, father, son or lover – that they've got to put in a claim. Everybody, married or not. Kind people sent them that money and I'm sure they didn't mean it to be handed out with strings attached, or to lie mouldering in a bank for sixty years,' said Duncan.

Nine

It's good to have something useful to do, thought Effie as she hurried through the town, telling women to claim their share of the fund money.

They listened to her, and eventually even the proudest agreed to do as she said. 'It's our money. People sent it for us. It'll be ungracious if we don't claim it,' she told them.

Her last and hardest task was in Rosabelle's family house. Isa, hardly recognizable because her hair was uncombed and her blouse heavily stained, was there with her two daughters. Even Clara's scolding could not get her to wash herself or change her clothes. She shook her head, saying, 'Ask for relief? But I dinna need to ask for money. My man's coming back tonight. He's out fishing right now.'

Rosabelle, face rigid, said to her mother, 'Father's dead. We tell you that every day,' but Isa only walked away.

Effie turned to the girl and said softly, 'At least you'll claim your money, won't you? Maybe you can get your mother's at the same time.'

Rosabelle smiled and said, 'Yes, I'll try.' But something told Effie she would do nothing of the kind.

In a way, like her mother, Rosabelle was denying what had happened. Asking for money because of Dan's death would be a sort of acknowledgement that he was never coming back. She was very confused and unwilling to think about the future, restricting her expectations to each day and even each hour.

She ate hardly anything and when she allowed herself time to think, she always went back to the terrible sight of Dan drowning within sight of the harbour.

Did he see me standing on the pier end? she wondered in anguish. *Was it to me that he gave that last wave?*

She asked herself those two questions over and over again, and they tore at her heart.

During daylight hours she could no longer bear to stay in her garret room and, to stop herself brooding, walked the town, going from house to house where other women were mourning, always ending up in her family home, where her once sensible and fastidious mother was losing contact with reality.

The sisters, Clara and Rosabelle, watched with despair as she walked up and down the alley by their house, muttering to herself. Clara groaned and said to Rosabelle, 'I'm ashamed at what's happened to her. She used to be so clean and tidy. Remember how she hated dirt and her washing line was always the whitest in the town.'

Rosabelle nodded, noticing that worry lines were marking each side of Clara's mouth. She was certainly deeply concerned about their mother, but something else was on her mind. Perhaps it was money. She had given up well-paid work in Yarmouth and there was nothing at home for her.

'Are you going back to the herring soon?' she asked.

Clara shook her head. 'No. Mother needs me. I'll stay here till the boats come back.'

'It'll be better for you when Tom's home again,' Rosabelle said.

'I don't think he's coming with them. He's found out about sailings to America from Liverpool. He's set on going to Boston.'

'And what about you?'

The question hung in the air between them for a few moments before Clara spoke.

'I want to go with him. I love him. There's never been anyone else and there never will be. If I let him go without me, I'll never see him again . . .' Clara usually hated to show emotion, but her lips were quivering.

Rosabelle closed her eyes. She knew only too well what it meant to adore a man. She knew what love felt like. The sun rose and fell with Dan as far as she was concerned, and though their time together had been so very short, she was grateful that they'd had it.

Clara lowered her voice so their mother couldn't hear. 'She's the problem. She can't be left on her own. Last night she got up and went wandering out looking for our father. She could fall into the harbour. I feel cruel having to tell her all the time that he's not coming back, but she refuses to believe me. And money's a problem too. The insurance company won't pay out on father's boat either because there've been too many claims.'

Rosabelle looked scared. Her family had never had to worry about money before because their father was a good earner. Clara seized her arm. 'Thank God the boats are due back today. Burgon's Euphen says her man's going to share the catch with the dead men's families. You'll be able to eat fish at least,' she said.

Rosabelle gathered herself together with an effort and told her sister, 'You want to go with Tom, don't you? Go. I'll take care of our mother.'

Clara stared bleak-faced at her. 'But won't you want to get away from here too? There's nothing to keep you now.'

'I can't. I'm having Dan's bairn soon and I can't think of anything but that.'

'You don't sound as if you're looking forward to it,' said Clara.

'I'm not. People keep telling me that one goes out when another comes in, but if I could exchange the baby for Dan, I'd do it. I'll have it because I have to, but I don't think I'll ever love it.'

Clara groaned. 'Oh, don't say that. How can I go away and leave you and our mother when you're both in such a bad way?'

'I'm not in a bad way! I'm luckier than most. After the baby comes, Mrs Lyall will give me work and Effie's good to me. I'm well capable of looking after myself and Mother too. I'll handle her and see that she doesn't starve. Write to Tom and tell him you'll meet him in Liverpool next month. Go! If you don't, you'll always blame us,' said Rosabelle.

Clara shook her head. She realized that though Isa was the one who was showing most signs of mental distraction, Rosabelle's state was almost as bad. She grasped her sister by the shoulders and stared into her face. 'You're not up to it yet, Rosie,' she said softly. She hadn't called her by that baby name for years.

But Rosabelle's love for her sister made her persist. 'I am. I'll take care of our mother. I'll even move in with her,' she said.

They hugged each other as if they were sheltering from danger, but Clara was crying. 'I can't go. I have to stay here. I'll never blame you. You're pregnant and even if you get relief money, that's not enough for you and our mother to live on,' she sobbed.

'What is all this about money?' Rosabelle wondered. 'There are so many worse things to worry about – like facing the rest of your life without your man. But if it's money for us that's stopping you, I'll make sure we get what's due to us from the relief fund,' she promised, because she saw it worried Clara.

At Bella's, Effie found Jessie trying to cope with the demands of her sisters and brothers while her mother lay drunk and snoring in the kitchen box bed.

'Oh Jessie, sit down. Let me help you,' she exclaimed, and led the wan-looking girl to a chair.

'I'm dead beat,' said Jessie. 'The bairn's been kicking inside me all night and my mother's spent all our money on drink so there's nothing to eat in the house.'

Effie's patience snapped. 'This is ridiculous,' she cried as she went over to the bed and roughly shook Bella, but it was like trying to rouse a corpse.

In exasperation she turned to Jessie and said, 'Get your shawl and come with me to that relief-fund man to claim the money that's due to you and the bairns. Then you'll be able to buy food – and make sure you hide what's left from your mother.'

Steven Anderson was sitting in his Town Hall office, eagerly awaiting the first applicants for disaster relief.

He smoothed down his bushy hair and ran his fingers through his moustache. It made him look strong and manly, he thought. He'd felt that way since he arrived in Eyemouth – strong, manly and very important.

In Edinburgh he was only a minor official, always deferring to his superiors, always trying to save them money. Now he was the man with the power. Eyemouth was a smaller area of influence than the capital, but he didn't mind that. He was an important man here.

While he waited for the expected procession of pleading women, he laid a hand on his locked metal cashbox, filled that morning with money from the bank because Mr McIntyre had provided a float of twenty pounds for the first-day rush. Knowing he had control over so much money made Anderson feel godlike.

To keep himself occupied, he sorted his papers and opened the desk drawer to count the postage stamps he kept there. Tomorrow he would send a money order to his widowed mother and consumptive sister. They would be delighted and amazed to receive five pounds – more than they had ever had at once before.

He imagined their reactions. His mother, who doted on him, would sing his praises – *so clever, so talented, so capable, so handsome . . .* His sarcastic sister, who usually scorned him as an unimaginative dolt, would be forced to admit surprise and gratitude. She wouldn't be able to jeer at him for stupidity any longer.

He breathed out and expanded his chest, feeling himself filling the chair like a king on a throne. At last there was a tap on the door, and when he shouted out 'Enter!' a maid he had recruited from the hotel stuck her head round and said shortly, 'There's some folk here for you, mister.'

'Mister *Anderson*,' he prompted. 'Show them in.' He was annoyed because he'd tried to coach the maid in the proper way of introducing callers, but she refused to follow his instructions.

She flung the door back and said cheerfully, 'He's here. In ye go then, Effie.'

Two women in fishwives' clothes entered. The one who stepped in first was middle-aged and greying. Because she looked baleful, he avoided meeting her eyes, concentrating instead on her companion, a very pretty, dark-haired girl with curly hair and a pert, rosy mouth. She was heavily pregnant and seemed gratifyingly scared of him.

The older woman put her hands on her hips and said, 'Are you the Inspector of the Poor?'

'Yes, I am.'

'The one who hands out the relief money?'

'Yes.'

'Then I've brought you an applicant. This is Jessie and she's carrying my son's bairn. I'm applying too because my man was drowned as well.' Effie felt she could not harry other women into accepting charity if she was not prepared to do the same.

Anderson smiled at the girl and said, 'Would you like to sit down? There's a chair behind you.'

Jessie sat but the older woman did not. She stepped up to the table and leaned forward on it, making Anderson instinctively draw his money box closer.

'She's your son's widow then Mrs . . .?' he said.

Effie shook her head. 'My name's Effie Young. My son was Henry Maltman and she's Jessie Johnston.'

He shook his head in pretend amazement, although he knew by now that Eyemouth women kept their maiden names; but he did not see any good reason for condoning that practice. If he could do anything to change it, he would.

'Young, Maltman and Johnston,' he said, writing the names down.

Effie watched the moving pen. 'Mr Duncan says that Jessie's entitled to five shillings a week,' she said.

'Of course. Has she brought her marriage lines?' he asked.

That threw the woman off her stride, he was glad to see. 'They didn't have time to get married. The wedding was fixed for the Friday after Henry drowned,' she told him.

He screwed up his face in disapproval and eyed the pregnant girl. Judging by the bulge of her belly, she was six or seven months gone. They'd had plenty of time to legitimize the situation.

'I'm afraid that I'm not empowered to hand out money to unmarried women,' he said firmly.

'But she was pledged to Henry. The wedding was fixed for the Friday after he was drowned,' protested Effie.

Anderson looked down at the papers in front of him, and then switched his stare to Jessie. 'In which church were the banns called?' he asked.

'In no church. We were going to Lamberton Toll,' she whispered.

'An irregular wedding?'

Effie intervened. 'If that's what you want to call it, but it's a wedding right enough. They get marriage papers,' she said.

'But they didn't do it, did they?' he snapped. He was growing very tired of Effie's attitude. She looked as if she might reach over the table and throttle him at any moment.

'They meant to,' she insisted.

He leaned back in his chair. 'That doesn't change the situation. She's not a wife and I'm only allowed to hand out money to the wives of the victims. I have to be careful to guard against fraud.'

She leaned even nearer to him. 'I expect you're not suggesting that we're trying to cheat you?'

Her grey eyes were fixed on his and he could see frank loathing in them. He quailed. When he was appointed to this post, people in Edinburgh had warned him about the ferocity of fishwives, and now he could well believe what they said.

'Of course not, but it is my responsibility to distribute the money correctly. I have to abide by the rules,' he said.

She stepped back and took Jessie by the arm. 'Everybody in the town knows they were getting married. Look at her. She's having a bairn.'

Anderson's eyes skidded over Jessie's protuberant belly. 'But how am I to know it's his child? It could be anybody's,' he said.

Effie let out an exclamation of outrage. 'I'm his mother. Before he died, he told me she was carrying his child. If you're suggesting anything else, you're giving the girl a bad name. She's entitled to her money the same as the other women.'

Anderson wished the girl had come to present her case alone, because she looked as if she would be easy to bully; but her mother-in-law, if she could be called that, was a different proposition.

'I'm not empowered to hand out money left, right and centre,' he said slowly and firmly, crossing his hands on the money box. Effie was furious but powerless, which made her feel worse. 'It's not your money! It was given to help folk like Jessie,' she snapped.

Anderson pursed his mouth. 'I doubt it. She's unmarried

and pregnant. As I've said, I'd be irresponsible if I went about handing out money to any waif off the street.'

Effie felt herself go cold. She saw there was no point arguing with this man. Taking Jessie by the hand, she turned and walked to the door without taking leave of him. If she'd been forced to speak, it would have been to utter a curse.

Instead of going home they went to the bank further along the main street, where Effie asked to speak to Mr McIntyre, who appeared and ushered them into his office. He knew her because she and Jimmy Dip were among the most respected members of the fishing community.

When he heard her story, his face darkened. 'I'm afraid Mr Anderson doesn't know much about our local ways,' he said.

'Maybe not, but Jessie must get her due, and so must the other lassies who are carrying dead men's bairns, though they haven't got wedding rings on their fingers. You're on the relief committee and you're a local man, so you'll know how awful it is for us to go pleading for money,' said Effie fiercely. Her own grief was sublimated in the grievance she felt for her friends and neighbours.

McIntyre looked at her with admiration. 'They have a good woman fighting for them if you're on their side. Let me know about every application he turns down or quibbles over. I might not be able to get money out of him, but I'll certainly try if you tell me the claim is justified. Go home now, and I'll have a word with Mr Anderson this afternoon.'

By the time he went to the Town Hall, however, Hester Stanhope, who was stalking Anderson as a possible husband, had looked in on him and heard the story of his encounter with Jessie and Effie. To his relief she took his side and agreed he'd acted properly.

'You're right to regard the money as being in your trust. It mustn't be given away to undeserving people. I know about that Jessie. She's a flirtatious little thing and her mother's a notorious drunk who falls over in the street. She's been incapable ever since the disaster. You'll be getting her in here asking for her five shillings a week too, but any money going into that household will be out again very quickly. It's a pity that it can't be refused to people like that,' she told him.

Neither of them acknowledged that if Bella did spend the relief money on drink, most of it would go into Mr Stanhope's till.

Bolstered by Hester's support, Anderson was prepared to stand his ground against McIntyre until the bank manager said that, unless a more reasonable attitude was taken to claims, he would write a letter to the *Scotsman*, telling contributors to the fund how grudgingly their money was being distributed.

Cowed and afraid of critical publicity, Anderson agreed to a compromise. Till her baby was born, Jessie would receive half a crown a week, and when it came, another half crown would be added.

'It's better than nothing,' Jessie said when McIntyre sent a messenger to tell her of his partial victory.

Word soon got round that anyone who experienced problems with the relief fund should go to see Effie. They arrived in ones and twos, their shawls over the heads, and poured out their troubles.

'I went to see that Anderson man and he as good as told me I'm a trollop,' said Lucy, an indignant lass from the Windram family, all of whose women were known to be very upright. Like Jessie, Lucy was pregnant by the man she intended to marry – but he was dead.

Back to the Town Hall went Effie with her, and Anderson flinched when she walked into his office again. Because of what had happened with Jessie, however, he reluctantly made Lucy the same kind of pay-out.

'I canna understand why he's acting like that. It's not as if it's his own money he's handin' oot,' said Lucy when they left.

'I've a feeling that he's beginning to think it is,' said Effie darkly.

Later that night Lucy returned, bringing with her a small, frail woman in a tattered shawl. She was Mary Lee, the wife of George Aitken, who had been drowned trying to save the struggling survivor off the *Radiant*.

Mary, his wife, was one of the few childless women in Eyemouth, for all her pregnancies had ended in miscarriages, and she could often be seen staring at the mothers of newborn babies with a kind of hopeless longing.

She was weeping when she sat down in Effie's warm kitchen. 'It's about my Geordie. You'll remember how he drowned on disaster day. I heard I could claim from the disaster fund for him, so I went to see the man at the Town Hall. I havenae much, you see. George was bringing in some money from stacking boxes and mending boats. We've no savings because his lungs have been giving him trouble and he couldna go to sea. The doctor said he was suffering from consumption. That didna stop him trying to save a drowning man, though.'

Her voice trailed off and Effie said, 'Your George was a hero. What he did was very brave and it cost him his life. Be proud of him for trying to save Jimmy Windram.'

'That's true. But the sea was too strong for them both,' chipped in Lucy. Jimmy Windram was her father.

Mary dried her eyes and continued with her story. 'I dinna like asking for money, but I went up to the Royal Hotel today because I've no money left for food, and that man said he couldn't give me anything because George wasn't working on a boat. He said the fund is only for fishermen's families.'

Effie felt red rage rise in her. 'That's not fair!' she exclaimed.

'I thought so too, but he said something about having a responsibility to the people who sent the money,' said Aitken's wife.

'Rubbish! That's what he said to Jessie as well. I'll see about it,' spat Effie.

Grabbing her shawl, she set out in the gathering darkness for the Royal Hotel and found Anderson eating his supper alone in the dining room.

She didn't waste time with preliminaries. 'I hear you'll not pay a widow's pittance to George Aitken's wife. He was as much a victim of the storm as any other man. She should get her money. She's no children and he was all she had in the world.'

He put down his knife and fork and stared at her as if she'd gone mad.

'Mrs Maltman—' he began.

'I've already told you my name's Young,' she snapped.

He grimaced as if she'd said something stupid. 'Then Mrs *Young* – I am only empowered to give money to fishermen's widows and children, not to anybody else.'

'Do you know what happened that day? You weren't here, were you? Have you heard what George Aitken did? He sacrificed himself trying to save another man.'

'He was not a fisherman. She's not a fisherman's widow. There's no money for her,' he said.

For an instant she contemplated grabbing the knife off his plate and prodding him in the chest, but thought better of it and stormed out.

Her next call, on Coastguard Duncan, met a friendlier response and he arranged a meeting of the full committee, or as many of them as could be got together at short notice. George Aitken's wife's case was put to Anderson and he explained his reasons for refusing it.

Unknown to him, Aitken was known to be very anti-religious, a man who scorned churches and churchmen, and none of the ministers on the committee were prepared to consider him as a worthy candidate for what they called 'Christian charity'.

In a show of hands Duncan and McIntyre were outvoted. Alone among the clergymen, Alan Cochrane refrained from voting, but later he privately castigated himself for not casting his vote against the majority.

Already he was worrying about what was happening in Eyemouth, and that night he began what was to become his principal secret obsession: writing an account of the disaster and everything that was going on after it.

'*Is it true that giving out money too readily will sap the fortitude of the people of this town?*' he wrote in his elegant copperplate hand:

I don't know what to believe, but I feel very strongly that it is wrong to make people suffer for something that was not their fault, when a partial remedy is at hand. Surely a little gentle consideration and generosity can be applied. Unfortunately I'm afraid that gentleness and consideration are not among Mr Anderson's strong suits.

On her way home after failing in Mary Lee's case, Effie shed scalding tears of fury and did not bother to hide her face when she bumped into Alex Burgon in one of the narrow wynds near her home. He was carrying a bucket and a mop.

In an attempt to divert him from noticing her swollen eyes, she smiled and asked, 'Have you been doing some cleaning-up?'

He shook his head. 'Not exactly. It's the boat. Some folk have taken to tipping the fulzie heap over my decks when it's tied up at the harbour side.'

She was astonished. 'Why would anybody do that?'

He shrugged. 'Probably because some folk are angry at me for bringing it back safe from the storm. They're angry at the town's losses and canna help themselves.'

Effie looked sad. She often heard murmurings against Burgon from resentful widows. 'They're wrong. I tell them so,' she protested.

Burgon shouldered his mop. 'Time'll cure the problem. It cures everything eventually. You've been greetin', haven't you? Time'll soften your sorrow too,' he said.

She shook her head. 'I'm not crying for myself. I'm crying for Mary Lee' – and she told him the story of her abortive trip to see Anderson about Aitken's wife.

He grimaced. 'There's times I wish that those folk outside had never sent us all that money. It'll cause more trouble than it cures. This town has always looked after our ain widows and orphans in the past. Tell Mary Lee that she'll get her five shillings a week because I'll collect it for her from the other skippers.'

His sympathy hardened Effie's determination not to let Anderson off with paying one penny less out of the fund than he should. She could see how jealously he was guarding the money and thought that, even if he was not helping himself to it, he was deriving a strange satisfaction in making it diffi-cult for the women to get their due.

Next morning she sought out Rosabelle and asked, 'Have you claimed your widow's money yet?'

'Clara went to collect our mother's,' said the girl guard-edly.

'I didn't ask about your mother's money. I asked if you're getting Dan's?'

'I don't like begging,' was the short reply.

'It's not begging. It's Dan's money. It's for his wife and bairn. You must go and get it,' Effie scolded.

'I will, I will,' said Rosabelle, putting her off.

'See that you do,' threatened Effie.

For almost a week Rosabelle didn't go to the Town Hall, however, and when Effie tackled her again, asking, 'Have you got your money yet?', she was forced to admit that she had not yet applied.

She reeled back in shock when Effie's temper burst out like a thunderbolt. Seizing Rosabelle's arm, she shook her fiercely and shouted, 'I go back and forward to that awful man trying to get money for other folk – some of whom might not be fully entitled to it, though I'd never let that on to him – and you, who have a right, don't claim your money! Shame on you. What do you intend to live on? Your mother's five shillings a week won't keep both of you. What'll happen when Clara goes away and the baby comes? You'll need money then.'

Surprised at the change in the normally placid Effie, Rosabelle promised to make her claim.

On the morning she put on her shawl to go to the relief-fund office there was a sickening feeling in her stomach. It galled her to have to ask for money from charity, especially because it was dispensed by a man who went striding through the streets of her town as if he owned it. She did not want to be included among the intimidated women who bade him good day in respectful voices, because they were afraid of his power to withhold their money. Already there were rumours about widows who consoled themselves by sleeping with other men having their relief payments refused for 'immorality'.

Steven Anderson was alone in his office, adding up columns of figures, when she knocked on the door. Annoyed by his overbearing attitude, the hotel maid had given up announcing his visitors, so he called out 'Come in' in a loud voice, and was frowning when he raised his eyes to see who was entering.

Then something very strange happened to him. He felt as if there was a small explosion inside his head and he had to grip the corner of his table to stop himself falling out of his chair. His eyes swam. He wondered if he was going to faint. Had the fried eggs he ate for breakfast upset his stomach? His heart was racing and the palms of his hands and his forehead felt wet.

When he put a shaky hand up to wipe his brow, the girl in the doorway said, 'I'm sorry. Did I surprise you? Are you all right?'

'I'm quite all right,' he assured her, trying to gather himself together and partially succeeding. When his eyes were no longer blurring, he managed to lean his hands on the desk for support and ask what she'd come for.

'My name is Rosabelle Scott and I was married to Dan Maltman, who drowned in the storm. I've come to claim my share of the disaster money,' she said in a flat tone. She hated having to do it.

He looked hard at her: tall, thin, yellow-haired, with porcelain-white skin that contrasted with the darkness of her clothing. His eyes ran down her and he saw that this was another pregnant petitioner whose belly stuck out beneath the waistband of her skirt.

Somehow that made him more confident. She was as bad as the rest of them. He looked at the bulge and then back at her face before he asked, 'Do you have a marriage certificate?'

Though he'd already noted her unusual height, she seemed to grow even taller, straightening herself like a guardsman on parade, when he asked his question.

'I've brought my marriage lines,' she said coldly.

'Show them to me please.'

Effie and Jessie had warned her about this. She reached into the deep pocket at the side of her skirt and brought out the precious sheet of paper.

'Here,' she said, laying it on the table.

He spread it out with flattened palms and ran his eye along the lines very slowly, using the time for collecting himself.

With a kind of wild relief he saw that the date of the marriage was only one week before the disaster.

'The seventh of October of this year,' he read aloud. She did not flinch or look away, although the bulge in her belly had been there for many more weeks.

91

'At least you were married in a church,' he said softly, as if talking to himself.

She stared him out.

The women of this town are a libertine lot. They must be easy meat. Is there a single virtuous woman among them? he thought. He looked at her again and saw that her eyes were green, as green – and as cold – as the sea. Some pretty fisher-girls and handsome women had come through his door, but this one was a real beauty. She awed him as well as attracting him more than anyone he'd ever seen.

'Your papers are quite in order,' he said, opening his ledger to inscribe her name, which he remembered from the marriage lines. 'You are Rosabelle Scott, widow of Daniel Maltman. That's right, isn't it?' he said, drawing the money box towards him.

She murmured, 'Yes.' How final it seemed to be called 'widow of Daniel Maltman . . .'

'Rosabelle is an unusual name,' he said as he finished writing it down.

'I was named after my grandfather's boat,' she said shortly, and he could think of nothing to say to that, so became businesslike again.

'You are entitled to the sum of five shillings a week, Mrs Maltman,' he said, inscribing the figure in one of the columns of his account book.

'Scott,' she said, but he did not seem to hear her, for he took a key off his watch fob and unlocked the money box. She could sense the satisfaction he felt in doing this small task.

Carefully he counted out five silver shilling pieces and laid them in front of her. She scooped up the coins and put them in her pocket without looking at them.

Her hands, he noticed, were long-fingered and white, not chapped and chilblained like most local women's hands. 'Aren't you going to count it?' he asked, desperate to keep her in his office for as long as possible.

'No, I saw there were five,' she said stonily.

'Don't forget that when your child is born, you will receive another two shillings and sixpence a week for it,' he told her in a cordial tone.

Her level gaze met his and he reeled at its directness. Was there invitation in it? he wondered. Then she turned on her heel and left.

She was barely out of the door when Hester, who had taken to spending much more time than usual in the good vantage point of her father's grocery emporium on the other side of the street, came hurrying across the cobbles.

'I saw you've had another of those Maltman women in,' she said.

'She said her name was Scott,' he replied.

Hester sneered. 'She was married to the Maltman boy, the one called Dan, son of that Effie Young who's giving you so much trouble. That girl had another just-in-time wedding, and people were surprised when she married back into the fishing community because she worked as a dressmaker for Mrs Lyall. She looks too fine for mussel-gathering and line-baiting – but Dan Maltman was a handsome man. I suppose that's what did it.'

Steven Anderson said nothing but thought that, no matter how handsome Dan Maltman had been, the girl he married was even more so. Though she was unsuitable for a man in his position, she haunted him and he lusted after her as he had never lusted after a woman before.

Though he'd only been in the town for a short time, he'd half-decided to propose to Hester Stanhope, for such a marriage would advance him in society and in fortune.

He had no doubt that Hester would accept him and almost wished he'd never seen the tall, fair-haired girl. As Hester talked away, he was barely able to pretend he was listening to her, for his entire mind was concentrated on ways of seeing the fishergirl again.

Ten

The winter was bleak in every way. Grey skies lowered overhead. The sea thundered mercilessly like a waiting assassin outside the harbour wall, its muted roar filling everyone's ears. The town turned within itself and its people felt like injured animals, hiding from danger, waiting to either recover or die.

They walked slowly, as if grief was weighing them down. Sorrow and grieving filled the houses; money was short and there was nothing to spare for anything but necessities. Children's treats – even the cheapest liquorice strips – were rarely bought from the little sweet shop beside the sheds where record catches were once auctioned.

Tired-looking women walked the shore, no longer looking for bait but gathering driftwood for their kitchen fires. Sometimes they picked up spars from the swamped boats on which their men had died and took them home to burn. Once or twice they found seaboots or oilskins washed up on the shingle, but never picked them up for fear of finding body parts inside them.

The Yarmouth herring fleet came back to a low-key welcome, not the normal happy jubilation. They arrived without Tom, who sent Clara a telegram from Liverpool, telling her he'd wait in the city for four days before boarding his ship for America. If she didn't join him, he would understand.

Clara read his telegram to her sister.

'What are you going to do?' Rosabelle asked. Their mother was rocking herself to and fro in the chair by the fire, apparently oblivious.

'I can't go. She's not any better. In fact she's worse. She still thinks father's coming back,' said Clara.

They found it hard to bear when Isa nagged her daughters

about going out to fetch bait for the men's lines, or wasted food by cooking big meals for the boats coming back. Though they told her time and time again that the man she was cooking for was dead, she seemed to accept what they said at first, but within a short time was back in her land of make-believe.

The strain made Clara drawn and white-faced, but she couldn't bring herself to ask poor, grieving Rosabelle to shoulder the burden of their mother alone.

'You must think I'm useless,' said Rosabelle when she saw Clara reading Tom's telegram for a second time.

'Of course I don't,' protested Clara.

'Then why don't you go with Tom? I've already told you I can manage,' was the angry reply.

'But you're just a lassie. You're not able to manage on your own. I have to keep nagging you to go out and try to start living again, don't I?' Clara insisted.

'And are you so clever and capable? There's only a few years between us. I'll survive. I have my five shillings a week and mother has the same. Effie's a big help too. She'll see me through the delivery. You wouldn't be much help then, would you?'

It used to be a joke in their family how squeamish Clara was. She didn't even like watching their cat have kittens.

'I'd feel guilty leaving you with Mother,' she said.

'Go. She won't notice you've left,' snapped the younger sister without mincing her words.

It was necessary to sound hard, but in fact Rosabelle's feelings were very confused. Without Clara she would feel alone and unprotected. Though her sister treated her in a high-handed way and was often very bossy, there was a strong link between them. If she went away, Rosabelle would have nobody. Her mother was a broken reed; Jessie was friendly, but they did not share the same likes and dislikes; Effie was strong and reliable but a bit frightening – and of course the biggest gaping hole in her life was Dan.

She dreaded Clara leaving, but in a way it was necessary to be free of her because she felt very old compared to her sister now. Suffering had aged her. Part of her did not care if Clara suffered too because she herself was so sad, but deep inside she knew it would be selfish to keep her sister at home.

95

Clara loved Tom deeply, and it was true when she said she'd probably never see him again if he sailed for Boston without her.

I've had my happiness, I've had my life. I'll always have loving memories of Dan. If Clara stays here she'll grow old and sour with no good memories at all, Rosabelle thought.

So she shouted angrily at her sister, '*Go!* Get away from here. I'll be better off without you nagging me all the time.' She gave Clara a sharp push and saw from the expression on her sister's face that she'd scored her victory.

They rose before dawn next morning. After their tea, Clara kissed her mother, who did not seem to understand where she was going, and they set out to walk to Burnmouth station, covering most of the distance without talking, for both of them were sunk in their private thoughts.

At the top of the first steep hill, Clara stopped, put down her carpet bag and looked back towards her home town, where trickles of smoke were beginning to rise from the clustered chimneys; then turned and stared out over a glassy sea.

'I'll miss it, oh how I'll miss this place,' she said with a catch in her voice.

'Don't be silly! You'll be better off in Boston,' said Rosabelle, thinking how happy she'd be to get away from Eyemouth and the ever-present cruel sea. It terrified her.

At the station they had only a few minutes to wait for the train that would carry Clara south. Dry-eyed and still inarticulate, they embraced on the platform, but when Clara leaned out of the window to wave a final goodbye, she was weeping bitterly and Rosabelle's tears began to flow then too. Waving wildly she ran along the platform, trying to catch her sister's hand for a last loving touch, but the train gathered speed and steamed away.

Sobbing like a child, uncaring who was watching, she crouched against the back wall of the platform, mourning because she was sure she would never see her sister again.

When she finally gathered herself together and walked out of the station, she wondered if the child she was carrying in her belly would fill the gap in her life. Would she love it when it was born? She hoped so, because she didn't love it yet. In fact, she resented it.

She was walking down the hill from the ridge where Clara took her last sight of home when she saw a man coming up towards her. As he drew nearer, she realized it was the relief man. Her face closed up when she recognized him, but he was too near for her to make a detour.

Steven Anderson was proud of his fine physique and very keen on exercise. Every morning, when he got out of bed, he swung a set of wooden Indian clubs to expand his chest and broaden his shoulders, bathed in cold water and took a brisk walk before breakfast. He never varied his programme, or the route of his constitutional.

Eyemouth suited him, because the sharp, cold wind that came off the sea filled his lungs with salty air and made him feel he was suffering discomfort in the commendable cause of maintaining good health.

When he saw the muffled figure on the road before him, he first thought it was only one of the ordinary fishing women wrapped up in her dark shawl; but as the distance between them lessened, he recognized the tall, slim girl who haunted his thoughts.

His heart gave a jump in his chest, and he remembered the direct way she'd stared at him. *It's her. Did she deliberately come on this road where I walk every day to meet me?* he wondered.

It was a struggle to collect himself, but when they drew abreast of each other, he managed to say in a cheerful tone, 'You're out early, Mrs – er – Scott.' He wondered if he should have taken the risk and called her Rosabelle.

She nodded, but only said, 'Yes.'

'It's very cold,' he ventured.

'Yes,' she said again.

He lingered, willing her to pause too. 'Hurrying home?' he asked desperately.

Politeness made her reply. 'I've been to see my sister off at Burnmouth station.'

'On the early train? To Berwick?' It was all he could think of on the spur of the moment.

'She's going to America,' said Rosabelle stonily.

That stopped him. Nodding slightly, she stepped round him and hurried on down the hill. He turned and watched her, thinking, *America?* Was she thinking of going there too, when her baby was born? He'd have to move fast.

Even the few words they exchanged sharpened his fascination with her. The cold had brightened her pale cheeks, and pale curls of blonde hair escaped the folds of the shawl to cluster round her face and make her look like the Botticelli Venus he'd seen illustrated in a book about art.

The Venus had been naked: she would look magnificent naked.

When she finally reached the sanctuary of her mother's kitchen, Rosabelle leaned her back against the closed door and allowed bitter, angry tears to run down her cheeks. She was crying for Clara, bravely setting out for a new life, but most of all she was crying for herself, stranded alone here in unending hopelessness and misery.

She hated Eyemouth; she hated the sea that was forever within earshot. Never again, even on the brightest summer day, would she look out at it and feel that it was beautiful. It was impossible to forget the way it had swallowed up Dan. Every time she raised her head and saw the Hurkars, those black stumps of evil, she remembered watching him drown, and the terrible wave of anger and grief swept over her again, carrying her life away as inexorably as the sea had taken his.

Thank heavens, Isa was still asleep in the box bed beside the hearth as Rosabelle moved around cutting bread and boiling the kettle, trying to be quiet and not wake her. But when the church clock rang out eight times, she sat up, clutching the quilt to her chest and blinking.

'Was that eight o'clock?' she asked.

'Yes, eight.'

'Why did you let me sleep in? Your father's lines aren't baited! Has his boat left? Are they fishing today?'

Every day it was the same; every day she had to be told. 'His boat's sunk. He's dead. And Dan's dead too.' Rosabelle spoke sharply because she was tired of breaking the news gently.

Isa's shoulders slumped. 'Oh aye, of course they are. You poor lassie. How're you feeling? Have you any pains yet?'

'Not yet.' There was still over six weeks to go before the

baby was due and she didn't want to think about it. When it started, she'd fetch Effie. Isa wouldn't be much help.

She put her hands on her belly and felt the child inside her slowly turning as if it too was waking up. She wondered how Jessie was.

When she gave her mother a cup of tea, she said, 'Stay in bed. It's cold out. I'm going to see Jessie.'

She left the house, remembering to lock the door and pocket the key in case Isa tried to get out and go wandering around as she had taken to doing at every opportunity.

The Johnston home was in its usual chaos, with children milling around, grabbing something to eat before going to school. Bella, looking raddled, was screaming and lashing out in all directions, but they only ducked under her arms and did what they wanted.

Jessie was sitting at the table with a cup in front of her and grimaced when she saw Rosabelle.

'Come in, if you can stand the din,' she said.

'Clara went off to America this morning,' Rosabelle said, sitting down heavily.

'Lucky Clara,' said Jessie.

'She says she'll write and send money as soon as she can. Letters aren't much good to me because I can't read,' said Rosabelle.

'Neither can I. The money'll come in handy, though,' was Jessie's comment.

'Poor Clara felt bad about leaving our mother,' Rosabelle sighed.

'I certainly wouldn't mind getting rid of mine,' Jessie replied.

Bella could be seen ducking into a deep cupboard off the kitchen and her daughter nodded at her back saying, 'There she goes. That's her away for the first nip of the day. By dinner time she'll be incapable. That man Anderson who gives out the money was scolding her for drunkenness the other day. Miss Stanhope has been telling him how much my mother drinks. She should mind her own damned business, if you ask me.'

'So should he,' said Rosabelle.

'He's threatening to cut her money if she doesn't sober up,' Jessie told her.

'He can't do that!'

'He can. He took five shillings a week away from one of the Purves women because she's been sleeping with Tommy Drysdale. He said it was immoral. My God, when you think what Drysdale's like, she should be paid to sleep with him. She must be desperate to get a man in her bed – that's what I think.'

Rosabelle didn't care about the Purves woman but was filled with indignation against Anderson. 'He's no right to tell any of us how to live. If your mother wants to drink, and if Mary Purves wants another man in her bed, that's no business of his.'

'He thinks it is, and that crowd of ministers on the committee back him up. They'll have us living like nuns if they have their way – all for five bob a week.'

'I met him on the high road this morning when I was coming back from seeing Clara off at Burnmouth,' said Rosabelle.

'You met the relief-money man?' asked Jessie curiously.

'Yes, he stopped and tried to talk to me.'

'What did he say?'

'He asked where I'd been and when my baby's due.'

Jessie's eyes were sharp. 'Maybe he has a fancy for you.'

Rosabelle's face flushed. 'If he has, he's wasting his time.'

'Don't be silly. You could make good use of him. You're a bonny woman and you could have him running around like a wee dog.' Jessie was a pragmatist.

'I'd never do that. I don't want anybody but Dan.'

Jessie groaned and patted her own belly. 'Dinna be daft. You've the rest of your life to live. If you can take advantage of men, you should. They'd be quick to take advantage of you if they could. As soon as I've got rid of this, and back on my feet again, I'm looking out for somebody.'

'You wouldn't!' Rosabelle gasped at such effrontery.

'Just you watch. I'm not going to stay at home greeting and scraping by on five bob a week,' said Jessie, lumbering to her feet. There was a determined light in her eye and for an instant Rosabelle saw what she would be like when her first youthfulness was gone. Her friend was growing up fast.

'Come on, I want out of here. I'm not going to sit and

watch my mother drink herself silly. I had some funny pains in my back this morning. I'm going to ask Effie how long she thinks I've got to go,' said Jessie.

Effie was busy as usual, sorting out a heap of clothes in the middle of her kitchen floor. She held up a pair of heavy seaboots when she saw the girls coming through the door and said, 'I dinna ken which of them owned these boots, but they're in a good state. I'm going to take them and these oilskins to Berwick to sell them to that man who buys second-hand fishermen's gear.' She was fired with the febrile nervous energy that never seemed to leave her now.

Jessie put her fists on her hips and scowled. 'You mean Finharty's? He's a cheapjack. He'll pay you next to nothing.'

Effie looked up from the clothes. 'Next to nothing's better than nothing – and besides I want all this out of the house. Every time I see their oilskins, their boots and these big jerseys my heart pains me. Come with me and help me carry them. I'll give you both a share,' she said bleakly.

At the mention of money Jessie forgot her pains and perked up. A trip to Berwick on the carter's van appealed to her too, but Rosabelle stared at the heap of clothes on the floor, wondering if there was anything of Dan's there. She still had a sweater and some thick socks of his, and slept with them in her bed at night. She wasn't prepared to sell them – ever.

'Have you anything to sell?' Effie asked, but she shook her head.

'Everything went down with him,' she said and thought it wasn't a lie. He'd taken her heart, her life, her better feelings, her hopes for the future – everything.

Berwick was bustling because it was Wednesday: market day. The three women in their fisherwomen's clothes walked along Marygate, staring at the colourful goods heaped on stalls that lined both sides of the roadway. The ancient Town Hall, with its great sweep of stairs, towered over them. It was the biggest and most imposing building any of them had ever seen. As far as they were concerned, Buckingham Palace couldn't be any finer.

Finharty's in Bridge Street was easy to find and they dragged their bundles in, depositing them on the deal counter beneath the eyes of a high-busted woman in a grey dress, who stared at them disdainfully.

'What's this?' she asked.

'It's fishing gear that belonged to our men. It's all in a good state, hardly used,' said Effie.

'Mr Finharty,' the woman called over her shoulder, and a finicky-looking little man came bustling in from fitting rooms at the back to look at Effie's offering.

'Three oilskins, three pairs of seaboots, four jerseys and five pairs of socks,' he said, turning them over.

'The socks and the jerseys have never been worn,' said Effie.

'Even then, they can't be described as new. I'm afraid it's impossible to give you very much. We've been offered far too much stuff in the last few weeks . . . everybody's selling . . .' His voice trailed off, and Effie stared at him balefully.

'That's because so many men drowned, and their families need the money,' she said flatly.

'True, true,' he agreed, but didn't ask if she was among the bereaved. This was business and he didn't want anybody trying to waken his sympathy.

He turned over the goods again, and finally said, 'The most I can offer is five shillings.'

Effie's face stiffened, but she said, 'All right,' and pushed the pathetic bundles towards him.

Outside the shop she handed a half crown to each of the girls and said, 'There, take that. It's not much. I don't need it because I've still got the money in Jimmy Dip's purse and I'm keeping that for emergencies. Five bob isn't much for gear that cost at least six pounds, but I couldn't stand to see it around any longer.'

Jessie took the money, then bent over and groaned. 'There's that pain again. I think I'll have to go home.'

Effie looked anxious. 'I'll come with you,' she said.

Rosabelle was disappointed, because she wanted to wander round the market stalls, and Effie saw the expression on her face, so she said, 'Don't you bother coming, lass. It's probably a false alarm. Have a look round and spend some of that money. It'll cheer you up. I'll take Jessie back and look in on your mother to make sure she's all right when I'm going past your house. Give me your key.'

There was no argument from Rosabelle, who walked up the hill with them to the carter's van and waved as they rode away. The town was bustling and full of people. English soldiers in red uniform jackets mingled with smartly dressed people and farmers' families in from the country for the day. Women laden down with baskets and parcels bumped into her as she walked along, and apologized when they saw her bulging belly.

She wandered back to the end of Marygate and turned down towards the harbour, past a big hotel where carriages were drawn up at the wide front door. Coming down the steps was a woman in a dark-blue gown with a big skirt and a colourful shawl draped over her shoulders. Her hat was decorated with wax cabbage roses. Though Rosabelle had only seen her once before, she recognized Tommy Nisbet's mistress.

The elegantly dressed woman didn't look as if grief was weighing her down, because she was smiling at her escort and laying grey-gloved fingers lightly on his arm. Obviously she shared Jessie's view of life, thought Rosabelle, not realizing Rachelle's talent for hiding her true feelings.

To her disappointment, Rosabelle felt very aimless wandering through the town alone, so by early afternoon she was back in Eyemouth, where she found her mother excited and fluttering with news, which, amazingly, she'd been able to retain in her head.

'Wee Jessie's gone into labour. Effie thought the bairn was going to come in the carrier's cart! She said to tell you as soon as you came back.'

'Where is Jessie now?'

'At Effie's. Her mother's house isnae the kind of place you'd want to bring a bairn into. There's enough of them there already.'

A little knot of women were standing outside Effie's door listening to Jessie's yells, which chilled Rosabelle's blood when she heard them.

Oh, I don't want to have a baby if I'm going to suffer like that! she thought as she pushed her way through the crowd and ran up the stairs to where Jessie was lying on the bed with her face sunk into a pillow, biting at it with her strong teeth.

'Aw my God, aw my God!' she shrieked between bites.

Round-eyed with horror, Rosabelle looked at Effie, who was standing at the end of the bed and calmly rolling up strips of linen.

'Is she dying?' she whispered.

'Not a bit of it. Everything's perfectly normal. It's coming away fine. You go down and boil a kettle for me. It'll not be long; she's very lucky.'

'Lucky!' Rosabelle flinched when Jessie started howling again. 'Is that lucky?'

'Believe me it is,' said Effie.

Within an hour Jessie was delivered of a girl. In what seemed no time at all, she was sitting up in bed with the tightly swaddled child in her arms, beaming as if nothing had happened at people who came to see her.

'It wasnae due for another month, but I'm awful glad it's over,' she told her visitors.

Effie said nothing, but she could tell that the baby was full term, if not over, for it was large, well nourished and fully developed, with a fine head of light-brown hair. It didn't look like either Henry or Jessie.

The new mother was bursting with pride as she held the baby to her bulging breasts, and announced, 'I'm going to call her Henrietta after her father . . .'

Eleven

Although it didn't seem possible, the weather grew bleaker and life harder. Fishing was poor and the boats took no chances, staying moored by the harbour wall while men lounged on the dockside, smoking their clay pipes and muttering to each other.

Alex Burgon was still treated like a pariah. His wife Euphen also suffered when women who used to be her friends turned their heads away if she met them on the street. Her only friends were Effie, and her sister Bella; but Bella was drinking more heavily than ever.

When Euphen tried to speak to her husband about the attitude of the other women, he refused to accept that there was a problem. 'They're acting that way because they're mourning their men. They'll stop blaming us in time,' he said calmly.

So Euphen went to her sister's house to pour out her woes, but found little sympathy there either.

'What are you moaning about?' asked Bella, who was belligerently drunk. 'At least you've got your man and your son. The rest of us have lost everything. You dinna hae to go up to the Town Hall and ask that bastard for five shillin's a week. You dinna hae to listen to him telling you to stop drinking and clean up your house. He thinks he's God, that one.'

Despairing of finding understanding or sympathy, Euphen took a brush from the corner and started to sweep her sister's dirty floor. She washed the dishes too and put a pot of potatoes on to the fire.

'What else will the bairns have for their tea?' she asked when she finished doing that.

Bella looked up with bleary eyes. 'Whatever there is in the larder. They'll find something.'

'Oh Bella,' sighed Euphen, 'you have to try harder. Your

big girls will be leaving home soon, but you've still got to care for the wee ones.'

'Mary's walking out with some lad off the *Highland Lassie* in South Shields. He's one of the other Johnstons. I think Fanny's going to be harder to suit – but she doesn't seem too worried. Her and Jessie can take care of the wee ones.' Bella did not seem to care what happened to her children.

Euphen sighed: 'Fanny's only seventeen.'

'That's old enough to get married. I got married at that age. Because she's over fifteen I dinna get any money for her from the fund, but she's still eating as much as ever. Jessie's got her five bob a week now and another half crown for the new bairn, but she's living more wi' Effie than here. I'm not good enough for her any more.'

Looking around at the squalor, Euphen did not blame Jessie.

She put a hand on her sister's shoulder and said softly, 'You have to stop drinking. It was bad enough when Robert was alive, but then you only overdid it occasionally. Now it's all the time, and Alex heard that you've been hanging around the pubs cadging drink off the men.'

Alex had heard worse than that, but she could not bring herself to accuse her sister of it, though she was terrified that, if Bella was found to be selling herself to men for drink, the puritanical relief committee would cut off her money altogether. It had happened to another woman already.

Bella groaned. 'Dinna worry, Euphen. I've been thinking that I ought to do something about the wee ones. They're too much for me. That man Anderson told me the other day that they could be sent to an orphanage. He said they'd be better off there. They'd get a start in life at least.'

'You're not going to send them away?' Euphen was shocked.

'I might. I'm no good for them here.'

Effie, Jessie and Rosabelle were in Effie's kitchen admiring Henrietta in her cradle – the same one that Effie's sons occupied when they were small – when Euphen appeared at the door in an agitated state.

'Can I come in, Effie?' she asked. Since the resentment against her husband had grown, she was nervous and tentative about going into other women's houses without invitation.

'Of course. Come in and look at Henry's daughter. Isn't she bonny?' said Effie, pulling out a chair for the visitor.

Euphen bent over the cradle and when she stood up there were tears in her eyes. Effie wondered if she was affected because she'd never had a daughter, or because she was suffering from the whispering against her and Alex in the town.

'Sit down and have some tea,' she said gently.

Euphen turned to Jessie and asked anxiously, 'You'll be keeping the bairn?'

'Keeping her? Of course,' was the prompt reply. Jessie was a doting mother.

'You'll not let your mother send your wee brothers and sister away either?' asked Euphen with a sob.

Jessie's face changed and she looked guiltily at Effie. 'What's she been saying to you?' she demanded.

'She said that the relief man suggested she send the wee ones to an orphanage.'

Jessie looked at Effie and said, 'She was going on to me about that too, but she was drunk at the time so I didn't take her seriously. Anderson told her that there's been an offer from a man called Mr Quarrier to take our orphans into his children's home in Bridge of Weir. He'll see they get a proper schooling and good food, and when they're old enough he finds them work or sends them off to Canada . . .'

A surge of outrage filled Effie. She stood up from her chair so abruptly that it fell over backwards, bounced off the cradle and wakened the baby.

'I've had about enough of that man's meddling. No child from Eyemouth is going into any orphanage. We can look after our own,' she snapped.

'That's what I think, and I know Alex'll think the same. We'd look after Bella's bairns ourselves rather than let her send them away,' said Euphen.

Next morning Effie was back at the Town Hall as soon as the town clock struck nine. 'I've come about Quarrier's Home,' she said abruptly when Anderson let her into his office.

'Oh yes, I received a letter from Mr William Quarrier with the kind offer of taking any fatherless children from Eyemouth into his children's home at Bridge of Weir. He was very affected by what he read about the disaster in the newspapers and wants to help. He's a good, kind man,' said Anderson.

'I've no doubt of that, but I think you should write back to tell him that Eyemouth won't be sending any bairns to his orphanage – or any other home,' said Effie bleakly.

He eyed her with unhidden dislike. 'I don't think it is your place to say whether any children will go to Quarrier's Home or not, Mrs Maltman,' he said.

'Young – Effie Young – is my name, and it *is* my business,' she snapped.

'We'll see about that,' he said, getting up and opening the door to show her out.

As soon as she left, he sat down and wrote to William Quarrier, inviting him to come to Eyemouth to discuss what should be done for the children of the dead fishermen; then he went round the town soliciting support from other committee members.

He was so eloquent on the subject that he persuaded them all to agree with him. Eyemouth's children, he said, would have a better future and a more Christian upbringing in Bridge of Weir than they could hope for in the ghost town with only a gaggle of dissolute women to bring them up.

Hester Stanhope and the wives of the ministers of local churches were enlisted to go round the bereaved mothers to explain William Quarrier's offer. Being polite and, in some cases, awed by their social superiors, the fisherwomen heard them out and then met together on street corners or in each others' kitchens to discuss the proposal. Effie and Euphen went round the town too, but they were arguing against the Quarrier proposal.

A week after Anderson's letter was sent off, William Quarrier himself descended from the train at Burnmouth and rode in a cab to Eyemouth. Word went round that he would address the bereaved families in the big dining room of the Royal Hotel that night.

Even Bella, almost sober for once, turned up. In company with other women dressed in their traditional clothes, she stared at the table where the man from Glasgow sat with Steven Anderson.

Quarrier was a kind-faced man in his mid-fifties, soberly dressed and unassuming. When he addressed the meeting he spoke with a strong Glasgow accent.

'I want to help you all,' he said. 'The scale of the loss you suffered here in October has really touched my heart. It is going to be difficult for you to bring up so many children without the help and support of your husbands. My children's home at Bridge of Weir could be a haven for them. I started it five years ago and already we have fifty children living there, all studying hard and bettering themselves. When they are old enough, I'll find them work.

'A lady I know is already placing some in Canada, where they will have a chance in the New World. I was very poor and orphaned when I was a boy, so I know how hard it can be. I want to help your children survive this tragic time in their lives.'

His sincerity was obvious and the audience listened intently. Some of the women wept and were visibly swayed by what he said.

'Would anyone like to ask me questions?' he invited.

Hands went up all over the room. One woman asked whether she would be allowed to see her children again if she sent them to Bridge of Weir.

'Of *course*,' he told her.

Others enquired about how the children would be looked after – who would take care of them? What if they fell sick? And how about religion? What sect or church did Mr Quarrier adhere to?

He answered everybody with tact and care. Doubters were soothed.

When it looked as if some women were prepared to accept his offer, Anderson made the mistake of standing up and saying, 'That seems to be decided then. Tomorrow Mr Quarrier will take custody of any children whose mothers are prepared to give them up. Let us have their names now and, believe me, you'll be doing the best thing.'

At that point Effie Young rose to her feet in the back row. A silence fell when her voice rang out. 'Hold on a minute, Mr Anderson,' she said.

Her eyes were burning and her high-cheekboned face was

grim. She looked more like a Slavic warrior queen than a Scottish fishwife. The other women turned towards her as if she was exuding some strange magnetic force.

'Hold on a minute, Mr Anderson,' she said again, even more loudly.

The Reverend Alan Cochrane, sitting among the other committee members in the front row of the audience, turned in his seat too and felt his heart clench at the sight of her.

She threw out her hands and said to the gathering, 'Wait! Think a bit. This is Eyemouth. This town has always looked after its own people. We've had losses before and we have taken care of the survivors. None of our children have ever been given away to strangers. It's the way we are. We don't send our bairns away. They're our future.

'If this town is ever to live again, we need children. The men who died would despise us if we gave up our responsibilities. We can manage. We *will* manage. I plead with you not to send one single Eyemouth child to an orphanage!'

She spoke with such passion that some women burst into shamed weeping, sinking their heads into their hands. A wife of the Young family, who had lost her husband and eldest son, stood up and shouted too: 'Effie's right. We've got to keep our bairns. It would be bitter cruel to send them away.'

Cochrane felt a kind of jubilation rise in him as he listened. He realized that, though he'd initially gone along with Anderson, he had secret reservations about the wisdom of sending the children away, and now he was entirely won over to Effie's point of view.

She stood still as a statue, holding out her hands, and everybody in the room stayed silent as she cast her eye over the meeting. She looked at one face after another, and women who'd been considering accepting Quarrier's offer shrank in their seats.

'Who agrees with me that we must keep our bairns?' she asked eventually.

Every woman, even the poorest, backed her up. In the hubbub of their voices she walked down to the table and spoke directly to William Quarrier.

'Please do not think we are ungrateful, Mr Quarrier. We know you have our good at heart, but Eyemouth folk are very proud. We don't send our bairns away. Thank you, sir, for your kind intentions, but no thank you.'

He stepped out from behind the table and came round to shake her hand.

'I respect your reasons. It is an honour to meet you,' he said.

That night Alan Cochrane wrote another entry in his diary:

The Eyemouth women are keeping their children. They have turned down the offer of sending them to an orphanage. It may not be the best thing for the children, but it is very noble and I applaud them for it, though I do not dare to say so to my fellow committee members.

Twelve

L ittle by little Steven Anderson was establishing himself with the clergymen of the town. By adopting a pious manner and agreeing with everything they said he succeeded in winning them over, though he was not sure about Cochrane, but dismissed him as weak and ineffectual anyway.

Soon he felt safe enough to treat the lanky minister as an object of mockery and it gratified him to see how his tentative sallies were enjoyed by the others. The majority of the relief committee were now on Anderson's side.

He first tried out his power by removing, without consultation with the rest of the committee, the five shillings a week from two disaster widows who were rumoured to be sleeping with other women's husbands. He also imposed a similar penalty on Bella Fairbairn, who refused to stop drinking, and worse, was rumoured to be augmenting her income by selling herself to men in the alley behind the Ship Inn.

His source of information about the goings-on in the town was Hester Stanhope, who carried gossip to him.

When he told Bella that there was no money for her, she looked as if she'd been slapped in the face.

'Ye canna do that tae me,' she gasped.

'Oh yes I can,' he said, crossing his hands on the desk.

'But it's my money . . .'

'It's in the discretion of the fund distributors who receives relief. You are leading a dissolute life and until you change your ways, your payment will be withdrawn.'

'But what will I live on?' she whimpered.

He leaned across the desk to her and his eyes sparkled like a hound on the scent. 'Where are you finding the money for all the drink you pour down your throat at the moment?'

'I'm not . . .' she stammered.

'You are. And you've been seen at the back of the Ship with your skirts around your waist. You're the mother of young children and should be ashamed. If you're not careful, I'll turn the law on you. Prostitution is an offence. What would your children think if they were told about the way their mother is behaving?'

The thought of her children finding out terrified her. 'I'll stop. It was only once . . . I'd no money to buy food for the bairns . . . They're aye hungry . . .' she moaned.

He sighed in a long-suffering way and handed her a florin. 'Buy food with that. If you stay sober, and out of trouble, I'll give you more next week. And don't think you can sneak drink behind my back. I'll hear if you step out of line.'

Bella's first stop after leaving his office was the Ship Inn, where she leaned weeping on the bar and poured out her story. She was bought a consoling whisky by one of the regulars, and all agreed that the man from Edinburgh was taking too much on himself.

Willie Wake, who called in every noon for a free pint of ale from the kind-hearted landlord, shook his head and said, 'It's time that lad was stopped. Somebody should do it.'

'Do what?' asked another man.

'Put a stop to him. Push him in the harbour on a dark night. It wouldnae be the first time a pest's been got rid of in that way,' said the old man.

They all laughed.

Fortified by the whisky, Bella went home, where she found Mary and Fanny gossiping in the kitchen and making no effort to clean it up. Dirty dishes covered the table and the ash from the fire was falling on to the hearth.

She stood with her hands on her hips and cursed them roundly: 'Ye manky wee bitches. Ye should be out earning some money not hanging about here eating my food and warming your arses at my fire!'

Fanny, the more spirited of the two, turned on her mother. 'Where can we get work? They're not taking on fish gutters any more because the catch is so poor. What do you suggest we do? Walk the streets in Berwick?'

This was close to the bone for Bella, who was mortally afraid that her children would hear about her misbehaviour.

Instead of answering, she started attacking the girls, swinging her heavy arms and sending them flying across the little room. They were both huddled weeping in a corner when a furious Jessie came running down the stairs, clutching her baby to her breast.

'What the hell is going on here?' she asked.

'I want those idle wee bitches out o' my house. All they do is eat food they canna pay for,' yelled Bella, still swinging at the girls.

Jessie jumped between them and shouted, 'Stop it. What can they do? There's no work. They can't even get taken on as maids because nobody thinks fishergirls are good enough to work in a house. We're only good for gutting herring and baiting lines. Let them alone. You're their mother. It's up to you to feed them and not drink the money you get from the fund.'

'Then they'll have to go out and beg for bread, because that bastard Anderson's taken my fund money off me,' yelled Bella.

Everybody stopped screaming and weeping when they heard this and looked at their mother with frank terror in their eyes.

'He can't,' said Jessie.

'He can and he has. I've only got seven and sixpence a week for the wee ones and that doesna keep us all in food.'

Something told Jessie not to enquire why her mother's money had been withdrawn. She hugged her baby closer and said, 'This is a terrible state for us to come to. You spend every penny you get on whisky. Don't deny it. I hide my money at Effie's rather than leave it here because I know you'd help yourself to that too if you got your hands on it.'

Bella reddened even more, and she was about to yell back when her daughter's grimness stopped her. Instead she put her hands over her ravaged face, pressing the broken-veined cheeks under her fingers, and groaned, 'Aw Jessie, you're right. I'm a disgrace. I know it. Euphen's aye at me, and so's Effie, but I canna help myself. Whisky makes everything easier. When I drink, I forget. I want to stop, I really do, but I can't, I just can't.'

Jessie was unforgiving. 'You can. You must. All it takes is keeping the stopper in the bottle. And don't tell me it's the storm that's done it. You were nipping away before that.'

Mary and Fanny still huddling at the back of the room, watching the encounter, were moved by the pathetic way their mother collapsed and moved towards her. Mary hugged her while she defended her to Jessie: 'She wasnae so bad before the disaster though, was she?'

'Maybe not, but our troubles are worse now than they were then. Father and Paul were earning good money, but now we've nothing. The wee ones are ragged. Their clothes are too thin to keep them warm. Unless they beg from the neighbours they don't get enough to eat. They might have been better off in Quarrier's Home after all,' said Jessie bitterly.

'You're awful hard,' sobbed their mother.

'And I'm going to get harder. I've my own daughter to think about now, and I'll not let her go about like a tramp begging for scraps like your bairns do. I'm going to do something to get us out of this.' And with that Jessie stormed out of the house, not sure where she was going, but determined to do something – anything – to make their situation better.

Walking fast she hurried down the harbour wall, not caring where she went, and in a few minutes found herself in St Ella's Square, outside Stanhope's High Class Victuallers and Licensed Grocers.

Three big windows showed her that the shop was full of delicious things to eat and drink: cheeses; mounds of yellow butter on marble slabs; candied fruits and green strips of angelica in wooden boxes; massive hams hanging from brass hooks; japanned tins of Indian tea; boxes of biscuits with pictures of flowers on the lids; crystallized violets on top of dark chocolates; pyramids of wine bottles; and almond-encrusted Dundee cakes. A mouth-watering smell of coffee mingling with the scent of sweet wine wafted out every time the door opened to let a customer in or out.

Hester Stanhope, in a dark gown with long sleeves and a high neck, was walking about in front of the counter, speaking to favoured customers and overseeing the work of aproned men and women who were doing the serving. She didn't serve herself, nor did her father when he was in the shop; but their sharp eyes missed nothing.

On impulse, Jessie pushed open the door and went inside.

The heady aromas of cheeses, brown sugar, candied nuts and Orange Pekoe tea made her head swim. Stanhope's specialized in serving the carriage trade, and only rarely, even in times of prosperity, did frugal fisherwomen buy luxury items from the shop. Most of their food purchases came from handcarts or little shops set up in the front rooms of houses in the town, but they appreciated the quality of the big grocery store, which was patronized by all the well-to-do people of the district.

Hester watched the fishergirl, with a baby wrapped in her shawl, gazing around the shop as if she was in a fairy grotto.

'Are you looking for something special?' she asked sharply, thinking the quicker she got this one off the premises the better. She was not the sort of customer Stanhope's encouraged.

'You've got a grand place here. I was wondering if you need any help,' said Jessie, dimpling in her most enchanting way; but that cut no ice with Hester.

'Help? What sort of help would we need from you?' she asked.

'Behind the counter or sweeping the floors – anything really. I have two sisters looking for work, and I need some myself. We're strong and we're willing.'

'I'm afraid we are fully staffed at the moment,' said Hester primly. Jessie's fetching smile annoyed her more than a scowl would have.

Then Jessie had an inspiration. 'You must have an awful lot of washing to do. Who launders the aprons for you?' she said, nodding at the immaculate white coats and stiff aprons worn by all the counter assistants.

Hester hesitated. Laundry was a problem, especially in winter, and even more especially today because one of the women who washed for the shop was ill and not able to do as much as usual. But in her opinion fisherwomen were slatterns; and this girl probably has no idea of how clean shop aprons have to be, she thought.

She was shaking her head in refusal as her father came out of his glassed-in office at the far end of the shop to find out what was going on.

When he first spotted Jessie coming into his establishment,

he'd bristled with suspicion, because shoplifters often carried babies in shawls to mask their pilfering. Seeing her approach Hester, he decided to intervene.

'What's this?' he asked, striding across and towering over the two women, because although he was sixty, he was still tall and straight. His Dundreary whiskers started high up on his cheeks and spread out in carefully combed grey profusion around his chin. His eyes were also grey and very hard.

'This girl is looking for work, but I've told her we have no vacancies,' said Hester.

'I could take in your washing,' offered Jessie, who had noticed Hester's hesitation when the subject of aprons was raised.

As she made this suggestion, she raised her dark head and twinkled at the old man. She was an accomplished twinkler who could make her eyes dance with exciting promise any time she chose. He caught their direct beam and it woke something in him that he thought had died.

What a pretty girl! Some of those fisherwomen are very bonny when they're young, he thought. It felt good that she did not think him too old to flash her eyes at him like that.

'Give her a chance, Hester. The fishing folk are having it hard right now. She can wash some of the aprons, perhaps?' he said.

Hester said reluctantly, 'I could try her out on them, I suppose. But I'd want them to be washed and ironed in our own washhouse. We have to consider hygiene, you know.'

She glared at Jessie and told her, 'I'll pay you a shilling for every two dozen aprons and a penny each for every overall jacket you do, provided they're perfect, which I doubt.'

Jessie pretended not to mind the insult. She dropped her long eyelashes and said, 'Me and my sisters'll wash them any place you like, Miss Stanhope, and you'll be pleased with our work.'

'Let her try. Give her some this evening and see how she gets on,' said the old man, walking back to his eyrie. He felt at least ten years younger than he had done half an hour before.

Jessie had never washed and starched white aprons or jackets in her life. Fishing people were immaculately clean in themselves, and on fine days pristine underwear, shirts, sheets and pillowcases danced in the breeze along washing lines strung across the narrow wynds between their houses; but most of their clothes were not the sort that needed starching. The only time starch packets and Reckitt's blue sachets came out for them was when the men needed stiff shirts and neckcloths for special occasions like funerals.

Rushing back into her mother's house, she shouted upstairs to her sisters, 'I've got work for us.'

They came clattering down, round-eyed with amazement at her swift success.

'What sort of work?' asked Fanny.

'Up at the Stanhope's big house in the top town.'

The girls gaped in astonishment. 'As maids?'

'No, as washerwomen. We've to wash the uniforms the workers in the shop wear. We've got to get them as white as snow and so stiff that they'll stand up by themselves. There's a washhouse up there apparently, and it has a boiler and flat irons and mangles – all that sort of thing. We collect the aprons and things tonight, do them straight away, and if we make a good job of it, we'll get more tomorrow.'

The girls groaned at the thought of working through the night, but their mother's outburst had scared them, and this was a way of making their own money.

Jessie rushed off to Effie's with her baby and asked, 'Will you keep the wee one for me? I've got work. Me and Fanny and Mary are going to earn ourselves some money.'

Effie held the child tenderly, looking down into its little face. 'What are you doing?' she asked.

'Washing the aprons for Stanhope's shop. We've to collect them tonight and have them clean by the morning.'

'That'll be hard work. They're aye spotless. Sometimes they change their peenies three times a day,' said Effie.

'They can change them every hour as far as I'm concerned. Me and the girls are going to wash them. Miss Stanhope's trying us out,' Jessie exulted.

'What's she paying you?' asked Effie.

'A shilling for two dozen aprons, but it's her soap.'

'That's a ha'penny each. She's getting you cheap.'

'I don't care. It's money and we can ask for more if she

likes what we do. How much starch do you put in an apron, Effie?'

'I don't know, but old Lizzie Bartram that lives behind the bank used to wash for the butcher. She'll know. Go and ask her.'

Waving her hand, Jessie ran off. She felt as if she'd been liberated, even if it was only to stand with her arms up to the elbows in a washing sink.

With the help of old Mrs Bartram, who went along to show them what to do, the girls worked till midnight, then spread the aprons out on drying racks beside the boiler fire. As they dried, they crackled with starch. Mary slept the night on the washhouse floor and in the morning was delighted to find the aprons dry enough to be ironed.

When the others came back at five o'clock, they heated a series of flat irons on the top of the boiler and set to work. By nine in the morning, two dozen immaculate aprons and five jackets were neatly folded, wrapped in brown paper, and delivered back to the shop. Hester shook them out and found nothing to criticize. Grudgingly she paid Jessie one shilling and fourpence and told her to return in the evening for the next supply.

Their routine began. Jessie and her sisters spent their evenings and early mornings labouring in Beechwood's washhouse, while Henrietta was looked after by Effie.

Thirteen

As Rosabelle was making her slow way towards Effie's house, she saw Jessie running off into town and envied her fleetness of foot and lithe slimness.

Even during her pregnancy Jessie had never been really fat and recovered her old shape within a month of Henrietta's birth, but Rosabelle felt as big as an elephant and was sure that she would never be slim and light on her feet again.

She was very overdue and beginning to wonder if the child inside her would ever come out. Was it going to stay hidden for ever?

Though it heaved around inside her, she could not think of it as another person, never speculated to herself whether she was carrying a boy or a girl, and deliberately avoided picking names for it, though Effie asked her about that often enough.

The door to Effie's kitchen was narrow and she sidled in sideways to find her mother-in-law lovingly cuddling Jessie's daughter, cooing to it and smiling down at its face. It had very blue eyes and stared back at her like a little doll.

'I saw Jessie running along the street just now,' said Rosabelle enviously as she slumped into a chair.

'She's taken on the job of washing Stanhope's shop aprons and left Henrietta with me. I think I'll be getting her every night if she makes a good job of the washing,' Effie told Rosabelle. It was obvious that the possibility of taking over the baby delighted her.

Rosabelle put a hand on the small of her back and groaned, at which Effie hopefully asked, 'Have you a pain? Are you all right?'

'No. I'm just tired of this. I hate being so big that I can't turn in bed at night. Will this baby never get born? It must be two weeks late now.'

Effie frowned. 'If it doesn't come soon, we'll have to do something.'

'Do what?' Rosabelle looked scared as she remembered Jessie's noisy labour.

'I might have to give you a draught to bring it on. But don't worry: they always come eventually, even the ones that aren't in a hurry. We'll wait a few days, though, and give it a chance to start on its own.'

Nothing happened, and Henrietta was asleep in her cradle three days later when Rosabelle arrived to be dosed in the hope of persuading her own child to get itself born.

First of all she was given a glass of liquid paraffin, and made to sit in a hipbath of hot water. When nothing happened, Effie went along to the Ship Inn for some gin, which she made Rosabelle sip while she topped up the bath with hot water from the kettle.

At last there was a twinge of pain. It started small and then suddenly hit Rosabelle in the back, almost doubling her up.

When her waters broke, Effie was jubilant. 'It's coming, it's coming! Oh I hope it's a boy. Let it be a boy!' she cried as she helped the moaning girl into bed.

The baby was in no hurry. For twelve hours Rosabelle writhed and groaned, trying not to scream like Jessie, but finding it hard. From time to time people, including her distracted mother, looked in on her, but the ones who stayed with her throughout were Effie and Euphen.

It was to Euphen that Effie confided her fear that Rosabelle was labouring too long. 'I wonder if the baby's lying the wrong way?' she whispered. Rosabelle heard this, and her eyes rolled in terror.

Calmly Euphen put her cold hands on the girl's bare belly and then said, 'I think it's all right. Try to push harder, Rosabelle.'

Downstairs she said to Effie in private, 'I'm afraid she doesn't want to have it. It's as if she's trying to hang on to it for ever.'

So they went back to the bedroom and gave the labouring girl more gin, which sent her into a wonder-world full of flowers and sweet smells. She thought she was in paradise.

Nature at last had its way and at three o'clock in the morning Rosabelle was delivered of Dan's son.

His mother was jubilant. When she held up the baby and

it gave a mewling cry, she cried out, 'Oh thank you, Rosabelle, you've given Dan back to me. This baby's his living image.'

The girl turned her face into the pillow and began to cry terrible raking sobs that had been building up in her for months. 'It can't be. It isn't Dan. I wish it was my Dan instead of just a baby.'

The next day, because Isa was alone and everyone was afraid of what she might do without supervision, Effie organized two men to carry Rosabelle and her baby back to her own home in an improvised litter. A bed was made up in the kitchen where the girl could lie and watch her mother, while Isa was told that it was her task to look after her daughter and the new baby.

She seemed very happy to do that and busied herself at the hearth stirring an enormous pot of soup. She still insisted on cooking enough to feed a hungry husband.

When Rosabelle was comfortably tucked up in the warm box bed, Effie patted her arm comfortingly and said, 'Don't worry about anything and don't get up. Euphen and I will keep coming in to see that you and Isa are all right. If you don't want soup, we'll bring you something else to eat. All you have to do is feed and cuddle your wee boy.'

The girl looked hollow-eyed and wan, but the child lay peacefully in the crook of her arm, his eyes closed, long dark eyelashes lying on his plump cheeks. He was a beautiful baby, with Dan's closely curled black hair and firm chin.

When she looked down at this stranger, the likeness to his father angered Rosabelle in a strange way. *But he's my baby and I must love him*, she thought guiltily; so she bent her head and kissed him. Effie saw this and the worries that had been plaguing her about Rosabelle's state of mind grew less.

'What are you going to call him?' she asked softly before she left.

'I don't know yet,' said Rosabelle.

'Daniel maybe?'

The girl visibly flinched. '*No*, not Dan. I couldn't call him Dan. There'll only ever be one Dan for me.'

Abashed, Effie stepped back from the bed. The new mother and baby were soon sleeping and before she left she tried to impress on Isa that Rosabelle needed rest and quiet.

'She had a very long labour. It wasn't easy for her,' she said.

'Oh poor lass. I had a bad time with her too, but it was easier with Clara. I'm glad you were able to help her, Effie, and I'll take good care of her now. Won't her father be pleased to have a wee grandson? He's aye wanted a boy and we only had the two girls. His boat'll be in soon and then he'll see the baby.'

Effie sighed and patted the other woman's shoulder. There wasn't any point reminding her again that her husband was dead.

For the next twelve hours Effie was rushed off her feet, dashing between her house and Rosabelle's. On her fourth visit, when darkness had fallen, she found Isa wringing her hands. Grabbing Effie's arm as she came into the kitchen, she cried out, 'The bairn never stops greetin'. I think something's wrong with it.'

The child was squawling the heart-piercing cry of the new born. Effie ran across to the bed and, in the light of the lamp, she saw Rosabelle staring up at her with a terrified expression on her face. 'He never stops, he never stops,' she sobbed.

Calmly Effie lifted the child. His face was scarlet and he looked furious. 'I think he's hungry,' she said.

With gentle fingers she pulled open the front of Rosabelle's nightgown and saw to her horror that the nipples were scarlet and inflamed.

'Does it hurt you to feed him?' she asked.

The answer was a sob. 'It's agony. I can hardly bear it.'

'But he must feed. Take him and let him suck. Then your breasts won't hurt so much.'

When the baby was laid against a breast, he turned his head and clamped his mouth on the nipple, sucking away so frantically that Effie was reassured nothing was wrong with him. The problem was with his mother. Rosabelle was in such distress that she was unable to stop herself from crying out.

'I can't bear the pain. It hurts me terribly,' she said. Tears were squeezing out from her closed eyelids and trickling down her cheeks. Effie leaned closer and saw that the nipples were engorged and bloody.

'Oh, that must be terrible sore for you. I'll go home and

make up a lotion to bathe them. I'll be back with it in half an hour.'

'Effie, you're so good to me. I don't know what I'd do without you,' sobbed Rosabelle, overcome, and Effie leaned over the bed to hug her.

'Just take care of my grandson. That's all the thanks I need,' she said.

While Effie was away, Jessie, smelling of soap suds and clean washing from a stint of laundry work, arrived to admire the baby, and exclaimed at the likeness to Dan; but when she saw the look on Rosabelle's face, knew better than expand on that subject.

'How are you?' she asked and Rosabelle sighed, 'Not very well. My breasts hurt terribly when he's sucking and I feel as if I've got the ague.'

'You're tired out. It'll be better tomorrow. Don't worry. Euphen's coming to give you and your mother something to eat.' Isa was pottering about in the cupboard off the kitchen, dragging out pots to make food for a man who would never come, and muttering to herself.

'Tell Euphen not to bother about me. I couldn't eat, but it would help if she could persuade my mother to go to bed. She's making such a noise.'

At ten o'clock, when Effie looked in again, she was horrified to hear the child howling the moment she opened the door. Isa was nowhere to be seen but the fretful baby lay in bed with its mother, its little face red with fury and its mouth wide open. Rosabelle lay beside it, sweating and fretful. When Effie put a hand on the girl's forehead, it was burning with fever.

Fear gripped her; she'd seen a new mother suffering like that before, and that girl died.

She ran for the door and headed for the doctor's house in St Ella's Square.

Dr Wilkie had finished evening surgery and was about to go to bed when she thudded on his door knocker. Her urgency told him that this was no false alarm and, throwing down his napkin, he stood up to go with her. Fisherwomen like Effie Young did not waste money on doctor's visits unless the case was serious.

Rosabelle was semi-conscious and delirious when he stepped into the room.

'She's running a high temperature. Her breasts are very sore and that could be causing the fever – or it might be something else. You're sure you got out all the placenta, are you?' he asked.

Effie, whom he respected as an efficient helper at childbirths, nodded. Like him, she knew that placental remains could cause the dreaded childbed fever that carried off young mothers.

'Has she been bleeding?' he asked.

'Not too much. It was a long labour but the birth was easy at the end. The baby came away without any trouble,' she said.

'Maybe she's only tired out, but we can't take any chances. You'll have to sponge her down till the temperature falls, and take away this little chap. She's not able to feed him at the moment anyway. He's probably starving,' said the doctor, lifting up the child.

He looked down at the little black head and said, 'What's his name, Mrs Young? He's your son's baby, isn't he?'

'Rosabelle hasn't decided on a name yet. She's still awful sad about losing Dan in the big storm,' she replied.

He nodded, thinking, *Poor little thing, another fatherless orphan for the relief fund.*

When they went back outside, the doctor put a reassuring hand on Effie's arm. 'I know what's worrying you, but I don't think it's childbed fever. The inflammation in her breasts has driven her temperature up. If you have any worries about her during the night, come and fetch me. That's a fine baby. It's good to see another generation of men being born in spite of the terrible thing that has happened to this town.'

She looked at him with swimming eyes and reached into her pocket. 'Thank you, doctor. I want to pay you for coming out.' In her hand she had one of Jimmy Dip's sovereigns.

He folded her fingers back over it. 'I make no charge for orphans of the storm, and don't hesitate to call me out to your daughter-in-law at any time,' he said.

Isa stood in the kitchen, wondering what to do with the furious baby that kicked and yelled in her arms. 'He's awful noisy,' she said.

'He has a temper and that's not a bad thing,' said Effie as she lovingly took the baby back. 'He's only hungry. It's a pity Rosabelle can't feed him. That makes a bond between a mother and her bairn. We'll have to get some good, creamy milk and we need another cradle. I gave my boys' one to Jessie.'

'I've a cradle,' said Isa, 'but I'm keeping it in case I fall wi' another bairn. You never know, do you? I'm not too old yet. My mother had me when she was forty-four. And Davy would like another one.'

Effie's patience snapped. 'Get your cradle out for this wee lad. He's your grandson and Davy's not coming back. *He is dead* – get that into your head. A sick lassie here needs your help, and you shouldn't be wandering around pretending you've forgotten the terrible thing that's happened to all of us.'

Isa's face went stiff. The eyes that stared back at Effie showed she understood every word. Without speaking, she went into the deep cupboard beside the hearth and dragged out a beautifully carved wooden cradle on rockers. In it were three neatly folded woollen blankets.

Effie knelt and laid the howling child in its little nest. 'Now fetch some milk and warm it on the fire. That should satisfy him, and when he's been fed I'll take him home with me. Euphen can come over and look after Rosabelle. She'll sponge her down to make that temperature fall,' she said.

'Thank you,' whispered Isa.

At six o'clock next morning Effie returned to Rosabelle's home and found the patient much cooler but no sign of Isa. When a hand was laid on Rosabelle's forehead, she opened her eyes to whisper, 'Where's my baby?'

'He's in my house with Jessie's Henrietta. He's fine. He's been drinking milk and now he's asleep.'

Rosabelle closed her eyes. 'Good,' she said and fell asleep again.

Noises came from upstairs and Effie thought that Isa was there, so she called, 'Come in and make a cup of tea for this lassie. She's much better, thank God.'

Euphen's face appeared at the foot of the stairs and she replied, 'I know, I went upstairs to look for Isa. I stayed here last night and Rosabelle's temperature fell at about three o'clock. I went home to look after Alex and my laddie. It's not childbed fever after all, thank God. I was afraid for her for a while.'

'So was I, but where's her mother?'

'I don't know. She was here when I left at five, but when I came back the door was unlocked and there was no sign of her.'

'I told her off last night and she knew what I was talking about. She'll come back when she's ready,' said Effie.

By nightfall Isa was still absent. Rosabelle slept for most of the day, waking only for short periods, and no one told her about her mother leaving home.

When the boats came back from fishing, a search party was organized. Men walked the beach and the fort on top of the cliff to see if they could find the missing woman – living or dead – but there was no sign of her.

One of the searchers went along the main road as far as the station at Burnmouth, where a porter told him that he had seen a woman of Isa's description boarding the train to Berwick early that morning.

'She spoke to me. She asked what time the train got in at Berwick and if I knew when high tide was today. I thought she was maybe going to gather mussels for bait or something,' he said.

Alex Burgon listened solemn-faced when his wife told him about Isa's disappearance. 'I'll go and look for her at Berwick,' he said, pulling his cap off the hook on the back of the door.

He went by train because it was faster and his first call was at the police office.

'I'm looking for a woman who wandered off from Eyemouth this morning,' he told the sergeant, who looked back at him with sharp eyes.

'What age of a woman?' he asked.

'In her forties. She's one of the disaster widows.'

'Poor soul,' said the sergeant and lifted the flap on the end of the counter as he said, 'Come on downstairs. I think she might be here.'

Lying on a slab in the police-station cellar was Isa, covered with a white sheet.

Alex looked at her and then at the sergeant. 'What happened?' he asked.

'Somebody saw her getting off the train this morning. Then she walked down to the pier, right along to its end. There was only one old man out there fishing, and before he could stop her she jumped off into the sea. It was running high . . .'

'She wouldn't have a chance,' said Alex sadly, pulling the edge of the sheet up and laying it over Isa's face.

'I don't think she wanted a chance. She knew what she was doing,' said the sergeant.

The tide had been running fast and the waves were high. Isa hadn't struggled, and when the tide turned, her corpse was washed up on Spittal sands. After Alex identified her, the black mortuary van, which had brought so many corpses to Eyemouth only a few weeks ago, was back again. Another victim of the terrible storm was coming home.

Raucous little boys yelling, 'Another yin, another yin,' ran alongside as the van trundled into the town.

Effie and Euphen conferred about how to break the news to Rosabelle.

Along with Jessie, Alex Burgon and Duncan, the coast-guard, they held a whispered council outside Isa's door, mindful of the girl lying inside.

'I canna tell her,' said Jessie, wiping her eyes.

'Nor can I. I'd start greetin' before the words were out of my mouth,' said Effie.

'Alex hasnae seen the baby yet. I'll take him in and he'll tell her,' said Euphen.

Rosabelle, ash-white and drawn, was lying back against her pillows with the baby beside her when the Burgons pushed open the door. Though she was surprised to see Alex, she smiled and asked, 'Have you come to look at my son?'

He bent over the baby and put out his enormous, gnarled hand to pat its tiny head. 'He's a handsome lad. What are you going to call him?' he asked.

She frowned. 'Everybody seems to think I should call him Daniel, but I don't want to – I want him to be different.' In her secret heart she didn't want him to follow his father's way of life either.

'I've been thinking I'd like him to have one of those old-fashioned names from the Bible – like Absalom or Jonathan.

I loved to listen to those stories when I was at the school,' she went on.

Alex's eyes lit up. The Old Testament was his own passion. 'Aaron's a good name. It means *mountain of strength*,' he said.

Euphen could see there was a danger of her husband being distracted from the real reason for being there. 'There's no hurry. You'll find a name,' she said as she shot him a look that made him straighten up and become more serious.

Rosabelle caught the look between them and asked, 'What's the matter?'

Alex cleared his throat. 'It's about your mother.'

The girl sighed. 'I know. She won't face up to the truth. She's in another world. Clara thought it would pass, but it hasn't.'

Euphen sat down on the bed and took her hand. 'She is in another world, my dear, in a better world. I'm sorry, but your poor mother's dead.'

Rosabelle surprised even herself by feeling very little sorrow when she heard this news. Her capacity for grief was all used up. Wary-eyed she looked from one face to the other. From their expressions she knew this was no normal sort of death.

'What happened?' she whispered.

'She went to Berwick and jumped into the sea off the long pier. I suppose she thought it was best to do it away from home. Perhaps she hoped they'd never find her.'

'So the sea took her too. I hate the sea. I hate it!' Rosabelle cried out angrily, while they looked on helpless, not knowing what to say.

Behind them the door opened again and Effie came in. Moving very quietly, she went to the side of the bed and lifted the baby. 'He'll need feeding. I'll take him down and do that,' she said.

Rosabelle looked up, dry-eyed. 'Yes, take him away. I'm going to call him Aaron. He'll need to be a mountain of strength to survive in this terrible place.'

Fourteen

At midnight on a cold night in March, a handful of mournful-looking men came out of the pubs and stared up at a sickle moon sailing across a dark-purple sky. Frost was silvering the pantile roofs of the houses and the decks of moored fishing boats.

Before they went off to their various homes they stood talking about a sad death that had taken place that afternoon.

'He'll be sorely missed,' they agreed.

'He will that. He's the only decent one on that committee. The big man'll have things all his own way now,' said a sorrowful voice.

Willie Wake, who'd been sleeping in an abandoned scull, heard them talking and sat up. *Who's died?* he wondered. Folk only talked in that tone of voice when someone passed on.

In an unwanted flash of returning memory he thought of men he'd known: Jimmy Dip, his own son, Robert Johnston and so many others – all swallowed up by the sea.

At least they'd been spared the curse of old age. He wished death would come and take him to join them. Sinking his head on to his knees in his characteristic crouch, he silently mourned for a moment; but his curiosity was strong and he clambered out of his perch to stumble after one of the Purves' sons who was making a slow and unsteady way along the pier.

'Whae's deid?' he asked when he caught up with the man.

'Dinna you bother, Willie. It's naebody ye know.'

'But whae is it?'

'It's Mr McIntyre at the bank. He died in his office this afternoon. Apoplexy, the doctor said. He was a good man.'

'Aye and one of our ain. Not like that galoot from Edinbury.' Willie was developing a loathing of Anderson.

Young Purves said, 'That's what I think too. You're not that daft sometimes, are you?'

The fishing community mourned McIntyre's death because he'd been a considerate, reasonable man who understood their ways. His death meant that only Duncan remained on the relief committee to speak up for their interests, but the coastguard was consistently patronized and outvoted when Anderson and the ministers imposed their strict prejudices on the women and children in their power.

Alan Cochrane still maintained a neutral stance, not wanting to antagonize his fellow clerics too much, but basically sympathetic to the ordinary people. He confided his feelings and growing disquiet to his journal but could do nothing to rein in Anderson, who was growing more overbearing every day.

Three days after McIntyre's death his funeral service was held in Cochrane's church before a crowded congregation. Steven Anderson, dressed in deepest mourning, arrived early and took a prominent seat but had difficulty in maintaining a suitably solemn expression because he was delighted that the troublesome banker was dead.

McIntyre had been too punctilious – carefully handing out the relief money from his bank every week and requiring meticulous accounting for every penny disbursed. It was only by subterfuge that he'd managed to sneak away small sums by withholding some payments, and he knew he was lucky not to be discovered.

The troublesome banker had also obstructed all Anderson's efforts to regulate the lives of the people of Eyemouth. This was becoming something of a crusade with the newcomer. Now, with the banker out of the way, he'd have a free hand and intended to make good use of it. He sank his head into his hands during the first prayer and allowed himself a secret smile of triumph.

Power went to his head. When he walked out of the church after the funeral service, he seemed to have gained in height. Seeing him striding along in front of her, Hester Stanhope was even more determined to marry him.

As far as he was concerned, it seemed as if his skin was not big enough to contain him. Anything was possible.

On the day after McIntyre's funeral, a woman who was

known to be cohabiting but still claiming her widow money, appeared in his office to claim her payment.

He sat at his desk with his hands on the tin money box and watched her approach his desk. She was a bold-looking woman of about thirty-five with large, prominent breasts.

'Yes?' he asked.

'I've come for my money. I'm Mrs Fairbairn and I'm due two weeks.'

He made a show of looking up his ledger. 'Sorry. There's nothing for you.'

She eyed him, starting at his head and working down. 'Why?' she asked.

'Because you're sleeping with Willie Purdom.'

'Is that a sin?'

'I don't know, but if you're sleeping with him every night and he's not got another wife, you should marry him. And if you marry him, you'll lose your relief money.'

She sighed and shrugged. 'I didn't sleep with him last week. You owe me five shillings.'

He shook his head. She leaned forward with her hands on his desk top and, he knew, deliberately letting him see the white cleavage between her breasts. 'How can I persuade you?' she asked.

He felt the breath catch in his throat. His only experience with women so far had been with Edinburgh streetwalkers and he knew they joked about the smallness of his penis . . . 'Wee prick,' they called after him in the High Street.

But he was a different man now. He had power and he had money. He wouldn't be surprised if the confidence that he felt had affected the size of his private parts as well.

The woman leaned nearer. He could smell the musty body odour coming from her.

'You could try,' he said.

She laughed and walked round the desk, leaned down and started expertly undoing the buttons of his fly. Before he knew what had happened he was on the floor with her on top of him. The whole thing was over in seconds.

When she stood up, she was still smiling and her hand was extended, with her eyes on the money box. Fumbling to hold up his pants, he opened the box and gave her two half crowns.

She looked at them quizzically and asked, 'That's all?'

'Don't be greedy,' he said and sent her on her way.

She talked, of course. Two days later another woman whose money had been docked came sidling in and said that Nelly Fairbairn had told her how kind and understanding he was. She was even more expert than the first, and easier to pay because she went away satisfied with half a crown. Both women began visiting him once a week and his self-satisfaction grew even more.

When he realized that knowing eyes followed him if he walked through the fishing town, he understood it was about time he took steps to safeguard his reputation. You could keep nothing secret in a town like Eyemouth.

The best way of securing his position in the town was to marry Hester Stanhope. There was not a doubt in his mind that she would accept him. It had only been a fancy for him to dream about the girl with the yellow hair – a passing passion.

He had not seen a glimpse of her for some time, but, he told himself, it didn't really matter. After all, she was a fisher-girl like the women who pleasured him on his office carpet whenever he wanted. Those people were debased, not respectable wife material. Perhaps one day he'd have a chance to have a fling with her, because she was beautiful; but all those women were immoral and, like the others, she'd have her price.

The courtship of Hester was almost too easy. She reacted like a girl when he invited her to go for a stroll on a fine spring evening, and they walked decorously up to the hilltop behind the town, with her hand resting lightly on his arm.

It's strange, he thought, *how I'm absolutely unmoved by her*. The easily excited member in his trousers never twitched when she smiled up at him or let him buss her gently on the cheek. That didn't matter. That sort of thing was better kept out of the marriage chamber.

It was almost two months before Rosabelle was sufficiently recovered in health and spirits to go out with her baby wrapped up in its shawl.

She had been the cause of a great deal of anxiety after her mother's death because she sank into a deep depression that even the sight of her son did nothing to lift.

Euphen and Effie whispered together about her in each other's kitchens. 'You don't think she's going like her mother, do you?' Effie asked.

Euphen shook her head. 'She's a sensitive lassie, very nervy. Everything that's happened has been almost too much for her; the death of her father, then seeing Dan drown like that was awful, then Clara going away, and then her mother drowning herself – all within a year. We'll just have to treat her gently and let her take her own time.'

'It must be the foreign blood,' said Effie darkly.

'When the spring flowers come out she'll cheer up,' said Euphen.

'Aye, maybe she'll want to carry that poor wee laddie of hers out into the sunshine. Sometimes I think it's an effort for her even to touch him,' said Effie sadly, because she'd watched the tentative way Rosabelle approached her baby and was not sure whether she was frightened to handle him for fear of hurting him or whether she disliked him.

Either way, it made Effie all the more affectionate towards the child and she spent hours dandling him, kissing him and singing him old songs. She loved Henrietta too, but the little girl had a very loving mother. Aaron had nobody else.

For many weeks either Effie or Jessie collected Rosabelle's relief money, but when she'd been ill she had not claimed anything for the baby and refused to allow either of the others to do it for her.

'I want to do it myself,' she said. Effie went along with that because she hoped it meant that a bond was growing between mother and child. At last, on a May morning when the banks of the fort were spangled with butter-yellow rosettes of primroses, Rosabelle picked the baby out of his cradle, pulled on her shawl and said, 'I'm going to the Town Hall to collect Aaron's money.'

Effie started up. 'Will I come with you?'

The answer was a shake of the head. 'No, I prefer to do it myself.'

Because of Rosabelle's previous experience with Anderson

she took care to have the necessary papers with her – her marriage lines and Aaron's birth certificate.

Anderson's voice sounded abrupt when he answered her knock with 'Come in'; but when he saw who it was, he half-rose from his chair and offered her a seat, an unusual courtesy for him.

She perched on the chair opposite him, with the child in her arms, and said, 'I've come about the money for my baby.'

As she spoke, she pulled some papers out of the shawl and pushed them across his desk.

'I believe that you and your baby are genuine applicants,' he said in a joking voice, but she did not smile.

'Your mother-in-law told me you were ill when she collected her relief, and I've not seen you around the town. Are you better?' he went on.

She frowned, dismayed by the thought that he looked for her in the street.

'I'm better,' she said shortly. For want of something to do, he opened her papers and studied them carefully. 'But the child's two months old. You've missed eight weeks. That's a lot of money,' he said.

She nodded. 'I know, but I haven't been able to go out till now. I wanted to claim my son's money from you myself.'

She wanted to see me! he thought, and his old fixation with her sprang back into life. If she'd come deliberately to see him, perhaps she was making some sort of an approach.

Putting on a grave face with an effort, he tut-tutted in sympathy. 'Don't worry about your back money. I'll pay it to you now. I'm sure you need it with this little fellow to care for.'

She looked down at the sleeping baby's face and made a sound that she hoped sounded like agreement. His cordiality surprised her, for his reputation as a penny-pinching tyrant was widespread; yet here he was unlocking his money box and producing two golden coins. He walked round to her chair and held them out, like someone offering a titbit to a dog. She stared at the money and then up at his face.

'That's two guineas,' she said.

'You're right. Forty-two shillings.' He gave a short laugh that exposed his big square teeth.

'But my baby is only due one pound – eight half a crowns.' Her voice was stony.

He was still holding out the money in his open palm. 'Take it as a present for him. It's customary to give newborn children a bit of money, isn't it?' he said.

'Do you give all new babies extra money?' she asked.

'Of course I do. It's fund policy,' he lied, and stepped so close to her that he could see the silky gold strands of her hair and the exquisite whiteness of her skin. He wanted to stroke it.

She sensed what he was thinking and shrank back, but that only increased his ardour. 'Take it for the baby, Mrs Maltman,' he said in a soft voice.

He could not bring himself to call these women by their single names. It was as if he felt that by persisting with what he considered to be the proper usage he would change the custom of the community.

Reluctantly she held out her hand and took one glittering coin. He reached down, put the second coin beside it and closed her fingers around them both. A smell of hair oil and tobacco wafted off him as he leaned over her.

She shivered, wishing she could refuse to take any money from him. Standing up, and hefting the baby on to one hip, she lifted her papers off the desk top and deliberately laid the extra guinea in their place.

'I can't take so much,' she protested again.

Seeing her discomfort, he stood aside so she could get to the door, but made the mistake of letting his tongue run away with him.

'You shouldn't be so proud. Take the money and pay me back one day.'

She stared at him, pale-coloured eyes wide. 'Pay you back?' she whispered.

'Yes, go for a walk with me now that the weather's getting better. It's spring. We could walk along the cliff top. That's where you people walk out together, isn't it?'

'The cliff top?' She almost staggered with surprise. She knew he was walking out with Hester Stanhope – everybody knew.

'Yes, we could walk to the fort. I've heard that's where

couples go when they want to be alone. You must have been there before. Wasn't that where you did your courting?'

'You and I aren't courting and never will be,' she said firmly, turned back to the desk and laid Aaron's guinea on it. Then she brushed past him and made her escape.

Outside she found she was shaking. A guinea would have been very welcome, but he'd made it very clear what he wanted in exchange. His effrontery horrified her. How could he ever imagine that she would consider him – with his broad, ugly face, and that horrible moustache – a substitute for handsome Dan?

Not that she was under any misapprehension about what he wanted from her. It wasn't marriage he was after; it was a dalliance.

'That's where you people walk out together,' he'd said. She remembered warm summer nights when she and Dan made love in grassy hollows on the cliff top. What did he think she was before he imagined that she would go back there with *him*!

But she needed money. Five shillings a week wasn't enough to keep her and Aaron. Clara had written to say that she and Tom were finding it hard in America, and now that Isa was dead she probably considered her duty to send money home at an end.

Effie, who seemed to have money secreted away some-where, always generously offered to help out, but Rosabelle wanted independence. She admired Jessie for finding a way of raising extra money and decided the time had come to do the same.

At the end of the street leading to the hotel stood Mrs Lyall's dress shop, and Rosabelle remembered the offer of future employment when she left to get married. Clutching her baby close, she hurried along the cobbles and pushed open the door. A bell rang in the workroom and Mrs Lyall herself hurried through. She looked surprised when she saw her visitor.

'Oh my dear, I heard about your poor mother and this is the first time I've seen you since. What a terrible accident. What was she doing in Berwick anyway?' she said.

'It wasn't an accident, Mrs Lyall. She drowned herself. She

lost her mind because of my father being drowned.' Rosabelle knew that Mrs Lyall was well aware of the details and only wanted to rehash it again.

'Poor soul; but other women have lost their men – you did, and so did your mother-in-law.'

'My mother was a very nervous person,' said Rosabelle stonily. She was not going to discuss Isa's mental state with this woman.

Mrs Lyall saw she was on dangerous ground and changed the subject. 'And this is your son!' she exclaimed, bending towards the bundle in Rosabelle's arms.

The girl pulled the edge of her shawl off the baby's head to show his fine curls. Aaron woke, opened his eyes and smiled like a cherub.

Mrs Lyall clasped her hands. 'What a lovely little boy. He's not blonde like you though, is he?'

'Dan had black hair,' said Rosabelle.

'Poor little soul,' said Mrs Lyall, putting a hand on Aaron's cheek before going behind her counter and, reaching into the money drawer, brought out a silver sixpence, which she pressed into the baby's fist. 'For luck,' she said.

'Thank you. That's very kind. I came in because I was wondering if you still needed some help with sewing,' Rosabelle said more warmly, won over by the kindness.

Shrewd eyes assessed her. Mrs Lyall could smell desperation, but she knew the girl was very skilled. 'I'm not very busy at the moment, but I can always do with occasional help. You're thinking of out-work, I take it.'

'Not necessarily. My mother-in-law will take the baby for me during the day. She likes having him, and she also keeps her other grandchild for Jessie, Henry's girl.'

Mrs Lyall knew all about Jessie. 'She's the one that does the washing for the Stanhopes, isn't she?'

'With her sisters, yes.'

'If you could come into the shop and sew here, I might find work for you, but you'll have to dress in something different. I can't have people seeing you in here dressed like that.' Mrs Lyall pointed at the fishwife's skirt and shawl.

'I've got the blue dress I wore when I worked for you before,' said Rosabelle.

'Does it still fit?'

'I'm even thinner than I was then,' said the girl bitterly.

'All right, come in for four days a week – Wednesday, Thursday, Friday and Saturday. I'm afraid the wages won't be as good as they were before. I can only pay ten shillings a week.' Before her marriage, as a skilled seamstress, Rosabelle had earned more than twice as much but, being in no position to argue, she accepted the offer.

When she was leaving the dressmaker's shop to head back home, Jessie came bursting out of Stanhope's shop front door, smiling all over her face. 'Byee,' she called, waving her hand at a figure behind the big glass door.

Rosabelle stared in astonishment. 'That wasn't old Mr Stanhope, was it?'

Jessie giggled. 'It was, and look what he gave me. Have you ever seen the like?'

From beneath her apron she produced an unpainted wooden box that looked like a miniature crate with fancy scrolled lettering on its lid.

'What is it? What does it say?' asked Rosabelle, looking at the pretty script and regretting her inability to read. Her education in school had concentrated on learning to sew.

'I can't read either, but it's what's called crystallized fruit – mandarins, whatever they are, pears, lemon and orange slices. He says they're delicious and very expensive,' said Jessie.

'Why did he give them to you?'

'Because he likes the way I wash his aprons, and because he likes the way I smile at him – and, most of all, because his daughter's not in the shop to stop him!' Jessie burst out laughing again, and Rosabelle joined her.

They walked home back into the fishing town, nibbling sugared orange peel and licking their fingers in delight.

'Yesterday he gave me three thick slices of cooked ham. It made a supper for everybody at home. I always try to go in for my money or collect the washing when his daughter's out of the way. She's all taken up with courting that relief-money man,' giggled Jessie.

'What's Stanhope after? They're always after something,' said Rosabelle, thinking of Anderson's guinea.

'He's after a kiss, or a feel of my titties. I might even let him one day,' said Jessie.

'Would you really? I couldn't do that,' Rosabelle replied, and the story of her experience in the Town Hall came bursting out.

Jessie listened with a suddenly solemn face. She'd heard of Anderson's dalliances with other widows. 'He's a scallywag, but I think you're taking it too hard. You should string him along. You need the money, don't you?'

'But go to the fort with him! Everybody knows you don't go to the fort just to walk.'

'You don't need to. All you do is string him along, promise to go one day, and keep him wondering if you ever will. The way you've handled it, he'll be angry and hold back your money if he can. You'd better make sure when you go to collect it you have somebody else with you. I'll see him off for you. He'll get my boot in his goolies if he doesn't watch out,' Jessie said.

Fifteen

It was a disappointment to Anderson that whenever Rosabelle came to collect her relief money she avoided looking directly at him and, worse, was always accompanied by her cheeky sister-in-law Jessie, whose eyes met his only too provocatively, as if she could read his mind and was enjoying his frustration.

He was in a state of confusion about the girl. Other women in the town treated him with deference; why not her? The idea that she disdained him was unthinkable. It had to be that she was leading him on.

Surreptitiously he began checking up on her movements and knew where to stand to see her hurrying home from work. The best place was in the corner of a twisting alley that led from St Ella's Square to the harbour. There was an empty shop there and he lurked in the shadows of its doorway to watch her running by.

One midday he stepped out in front of her. The alley was narrow – only wide enough for a wheelbarrow to pass through – and there was no way she could avoid him.

At first she did not recognize him, because he was blocking the light and loomed in front of her like a large, dark shadow. With a nervous smile she side-stepped to slip past. He took the smile to be an encouragement. He was right: she *was* leading him on after all!

He'd rehearsed what he intended to say, but it came out strangely garbled. 'It's a fine day, er – the weather's changing . . . yes, changing – it'll soon be summer – things are better in summer, aren't they?'

Now she recognized him and her face hardened. Lowering her head, she said curtly, 'I suppose so.' He was deliberately blocking the alley and she could not slip past him. Desperately she looked back over her shoulder to see if it was possible to retreat. To her relief a pair of women carrying baskets were coming along behind her and he was forced to stand aside to allow them to pass.

She knew the women and in an instant she joined them, grasping one by the arm as she asked after her children. Anderson stood staring after her with the characteristic puzzled expression that made him look dumbstruck.

Even the failure of that attempt did not discourage him. *She'd have spoken to me if those women hadn't interrupted us*, he thought angrily.

Day after day he brooded, sometimes as lovesick as a boy, at other times frustrated and angry, maddened by the idea that a fishergirl disdained him. She needed bringing to heel. She had to realize his importance and see how essential it was for her to be nice to him. He came up with an idea to take her down a peg or two.

At the weekly committee meeting he leaned forward and said, 'It's come to my attention that some of the women who are drawing money from the fund are also working and earning wages. Miss Stanhope tells me that a woman called Jessie Johnston washes the aprons for her father's shops, and another one, Rosabelle Scott, is employed by Mrs Lyall, the town dressmaker. I think their fund money should be cut if they have other sources of income . . .'

This was too much for Alan Cochrane, who sat up straight in his chair and protested violently, 'Surely that's unfair! Some other widows have been working as fish gutters ever since the disaster. They only earn pittances, and it doesn't make up for what the men used to bring in to their houses. It would be wrong for us to treat them harshly if they are prepared to work in an effort to better themselves. After all, five shillings a week is not a fortune.'

There was an outburst of discussion and, for once, the rest of the committee agreed with Cochrane. With bad grace Anderson backed down.

'It was only a suggestion. I don't like to see the fund being misused or wasted,' he said in a placatory voice.

Secretly burning with resentment, he began helping himself to more of the money from his cashbox, but only small coins at a time, and always soothing his conscience by intending to repay the money, though somehow that never happened.

It was almost too easy. Since McIntyre died a bank clerk handed out the fund money to him every week and, even if he did notice that there were small shortages, he was too scared of the overbearing Anderson to question him.

The failure of his attempt to waylay Rosabelle acted like a spur to him too. She no longer used the narrow alley, so he was forced to pretend to bump into her in the street, hoping to make her stop in her tracks and speak to him, even if it was only to protest at his clumsiness.

She never rose to the bait, however. All she did was stop, stare down at her feet and pretend that she had not seen him.

Of course this made his ardour and frustration grow, and it became a battle to force her to acknowledge him.

She'd have to if he held her in his arms.

She'd have to if his mouth was pressed against hers. Common sense left him completely, and he did not realize that he was in the grip of an obsession.

Though he always made it appear that he was extremely busy, in fact he had very little to do. Sitting at his desk in an empty office, he had plenty of time to stare out of the wide window that overlooked the main street and brood.

He knew only too well that he was on borrowed time, for he recognized that the fund committee must eventually realize that a clerk was all that was needed to disburse the pay-outs every week. It was necessary to devise some other way of ensuring a place for himself in Eyemouth.

If only he had a confidant, someone to listen to him and give him advice. The person who listened to him most was Hester, but he knew better than to consider entrusting her with the secrets of his heart. If she knew how he dreaded being forced to return to Edinburgh and insignificance, she would suspect that his intentions towards her were not entirely romantic. If she knew how he feared going back to live with his mother and sister in their two-roomed flat at the top of Leith Walk, she would suspect that his admiration for her family home was not entirely disinterested.

Just as he soothed his conscience about pilfering pennies

from the petty cash, he told himself that he was doing Hester a favour by courting her. After all, no one else was interested.

There were advantages in marriage for both of them: she gained a husband; he got status in the town, an imposing home and, best of all, money, because Hester's father was growing old. He would not be able to continue running his businesses for ever, and her brother was making his way as a lawyer in Edinburgh, so he wouldn't want them.

Anderson leaned his elbows on his desk, fished a cheroot out of a box in the drawer and indulged in a pipe dream of driving his own carriage and lording it over the big grocery emporium and the chandler's store that occupied a large area of the harbour side. As Hester's husband he'd be a man of substance in the town. The fishergirl would be impressed by him then.

Pulling on his jacket, he closed the office and went off to pay court to Hester, who was parading on the floor of the grocer's shop.

She brightened at the sight of him and became quite girlish when he said, 'It's a pleasant day, Miss Stanhope. I came to ask you to take a stroll with me along the harbour side.'

She fluttered, 'That's a good idea. I'd like to feel the wind in my face. Wait till I fetch my bonnet.'

They walked out, scrutinized by many knowing eyes, and she put her arm through his before they were out of the shop.

Racing thoughts were running through both their heads.

Why does he want to walk out in the middle of the day? He usually calls for me in the evening. Has he something special to say? she wondered.

Am I doing the right thing? was his main confusion, because he felt no thrill to have Hester in person hanging on to his arm.

They paraded along, self-consciously making pointless conversation, till, driven beyond endurance by his failure to come up with any reason for their promenade, she said, 'What a nice thought of yours this is.'

He peered down at her, eyebrows raised.

'I mean, to invite me out for a lunch-time stroll. The shop is very tiring sometimes,' she went on.

'That's what I thought,' he said.

She pouted: 'So you were doing me a favour? I thought you might have something to say to me.'

The moment had come. It was now or never.

'I'm growing very fond of you, Hester,' he said as they neared the end of the pier, '– very fond indeed, my dear,' he went on in a tender voice.

She paused and felt a surge of disappointment. This was not how she imagined her first proposal would be. Where were the fervent kisses? But he was staring out over the sea with a fixed expression on his face as if he was a doctor delivering a fatal diagnosis. *He's shy. I'll have to say it; I'll have to say it now*, she thought.

'Fond enough for us to marry, perhaps?' she asked tentatively.

He sighed. 'There is nothing I'd like more than that, but I can't aspire to you.'

She stared at him, eyes wide and disconcerted. 'Why not?' *Perhaps he's married already* was the thought that was running through her head.

He looked down at his feet and said slowly. 'I'm not a rich man. I have only a modest income, and small savings. People would say I was marrying you for your money . . .' In fact he had no savings at all, but he intended to change that.

She turned her face towards his and put out a hand. 'Oh Steven, how silly you are! Is money all that's coming between us?'

With an effort he managed to make tears spring into his eyes. 'That is all, Hester, but as far as I can see the barrier is insurmountable.'

'What nonsense! You are a man with a great future and fine potential,' she said sharply.

His tears dried up. 'Can I hope, then?' he asked.

'Of course you can. In fact, if you were to ask me to marry you, I'd say *yes*!'

His heart was singing and he did not have to act as he took both her hands in his and said, 'Miss Stanhope, will you marry me?'

It was only when she leaned against him and whispered, 'Of course,' that he remembered he ought to kiss her.

It was a marriage of convenience on both their parts. Hester was as calculating as her husband-to-be. In spite of her seeming trustfulness, she was not a fool and had heard the whispers about illicit goings-on in the Town Hall office.

When she first heard the innuendos, she thought the rumours were untrue, and only malicious gossip put about by the hotel maid, who made no secret of her dislike for Steven.

'Mr Anderson is not like that. Those fisherwomen are only trying to blacken his name because he is so proper about paying out the money,' she snapped to a friend who tried to raise the subject with her.

But after thinking hard and realistically she secretly accepted that the stories were probably true. He was young and lusty. Fisherwomen were notoriously easy in their ways. How could he resist if one threw herself at him?

Now, as she accepted his proposal of marriage, she did some quick thinking. If she confronted him with the rumours and accused him of philandering, what would he do?

Deny it, almost certainly.

And then what would she do?

Challenge him? Make secret enquiries? Change her mind?

Definitely not. She was twenty-five years old and there were no other suitors on the horizon except Cochrane, who was not a lusty man like Anderson. There would never be any problem about fishwives making approaches to the reverend gentleman. When the ring was safely on her finger, Steven Anderson would toe the line. She had already spotted his moral weakness and knew she could easily dominate him.

So, on the harbour side, on a pleasant afternoon, the matter was settled between them. The only embraces they shared were squeezes of the hand and discreet kisses on the cheek. Hester was playing safe and would allow no greater intimacies until they were married.

That suited him very well. He was not lusting after her as he lusted after Rosabelle. If Hester was a virginal bride, he'd be the first and only man that ever slept with her and there was no urgency in him for that.

They strolled back into town, arm in arm, and when they parted at the door of the shop, she told him, 'I'll tell Father tonight, and then we'll make an official announcement. I think we should set the wedding date for October. We don't want it to look *hasty*, do we?'

'That will be perfect,' he said, kissing her cheek.

As she walked up through the garden, she ruefully wished

he'd said October was too far off, because he wanted to marry her tomorrow.

A week later, Alan Cochrane sat in the book-lined study of his manse and stared out of the window as he pondered the problem of writing next Sunday's sermon.

His congregation was always small and growing smaller; the people who regularly filled the pews were self-satisfied and sure of their godliness. There was no question of trying to win converts for God. Sometimes he felt that the only doubter in his church was himself.

He wished he still had the certainty that filled him when he'd first arrived in the town and looked back on the young man he'd been with something like disbelief. Was he really so green? Had he ever considered marrying Hester Stanhope?

She and her father were among the most prominent members of his congregation, and for the last few weeks, since she'd begun walking out with Anderson, she'd adopted an annoying, sisterly attitude towards him as if he was not capable of looking after himself or thinking independently.

He was not looking forward to the evening, because Hester had sent an invitation for him to dine at Beechwood that night. His first impulse was to refuse, but knew he must not. The Stanhopes wielded such power that they could drive him out of his living and, though he was beginning to question his own belief, he must stay, because he was the sole support of a widowed mother and a brace of querulous aunts.

One of his uncles had paid for him to become a minister, and he was expected to be suitably grateful. There was nothing else he could do than join the Church, for his lanky frame was not robust, and his only interest was reading books. At least that had been his only interest until he came to Eyemouth.

After the terrible storm, things changed. It was as if blinkers were snatched from his eyes. Where once he considered the way of life of the fishing community as incomprehensible and immoral, he was more won over to them every day.

Their morals were not his morals, their beliefs not his beliefs, their aims not his aims; but he respected their independence, their hardihood and stoicism as much as he overlooked their shortcomings.

The fact that he was on the relief committee was a blessing and a curse. When Anderson and his cohorts dispersed their niggardly handouts, or tried to impose their narrow values on people in receipt of the money, Cochrane stood up for the recipients, though he knew he would be voted down. *At least*, he thought, *I have to show them there may be another point of view.*

When George Aitken's widow was refused relief money, he took to removing a few coins every week from his collection plate and putting them aside for her. Every little helped.

What was so bad about giving suffering people a little comfort or even occasional luxury? Why make sure they were kept on the verge of starvation? What was so bad about men drinking to forget the horrors of battling high seas? What was so terrible about a grieving, heart-broken widow trying to find solace in another man's arms, even if it was only for one night? He couldn't condemn that.

Like Anderson, he longed for a confidant and his substitute was his journal, which had grown into a thick wad of closely written notes.

He'd started off by making a list of the men who died in the storm, noting their relationships to each other, their ages and their local reputations. He also listed their wives and children, amending the list as more were born – or died.

It was easier, he discovered, to find things out if he went about the town in plain clothes. When he dressed like everybody else, the fishing people were prepared to forget his calling and answered honestly when he asked about the fishing, enquired about boats, and tried to find out how much they cost. He also wanted to know how hard it was to make good catches, where the fish were sold and who bought them.

The biggest hurdle he had to overcome was when he asked about the local superstitions; but little by little people became less suspicious of him and told him their secrets. In his leisure time he walked the churchyard, reading the memorials. On fine days he roamed the abandoned fort and asked Coastguard Duncan to show him the honeycomb of cellars below the Customs House. He borrowed history books from the town lawyer and persuaded him to give him access to old records in an effort to draft the story of the town from its origins till the present day.

This interest soon became an obsession and, instead of writing sermons, he spent hours pouring the results of his researches, anguished thoughts and suspicions about the distribution of the relief money on to the pages of his journal.

When he put down his pen on the day of Hester's dinner party, he realized that he was writing a book about a town and its suffering. He wanted to show the truth about the self-contained little community and what happened when a hurricane ripped its life apart.

From sitting on the committee he was aware that part of Anderson's duties was to send regular reports on Eyemouth to the charity commissioners. That official account would be read by people in authority, but it would be biased. If he, Cochrane, had the courage to give a different version, it might in time appear between hard covers and tell a different tale.

In the meantime his notes had to be kept secret. None of the servants must see them. He did not know if his maids could read, but they certainly loved to gossip. Rising from his chair, he unlocked a drawer in his desk and put the papers in, feeling as if he was hiding a bomb.

When he looked at his clock, he realized time had passed without him noticing. Now he must prepare himself for the dinner party at Beechwood.

While he was changing into his clerical black, the kitchen of the big house where he was to dine was full of steam, and the cook was raging at the scullery maid because she'd let the carrots boil over.

The scullery maid was sobbing because the cook slapped her about the head and made her ears ring.

The two table maids were quarrelling between themselves about who should serve the wine – for the Stanhopes kept no butler and neither of the maids wanted the job.

Jessie, on her way to the washhouse bearing another bundle of dirty white aprons from the shop, heard the din and stuck her head through the kitchen door to ask the boot boy, 'What's going on? It sounds as if you're a pack of wild animals having a fight.'

'They're holding a dinner party tonight. Ten people will sit down and there's enough food to feed a regiment. Dinna let Miss Hester see you in here. She's ready to fight with her shadow,' he told her.

'I don't want to see her either. She's a sour bitch.' Jessie didn't mince words.

The boot boy laughed. 'Maybe she'll be a bit better after tonight. She's got that Inspector of the Poor to propose to her.'

'Do you mean the relief-money man?'

'Aye, that galoot Anderson. She's been after him ever since he arrived. She tried the big tall minister first, but he's too fly for her.'

Jessie laughed. 'If she gets her hands on Anderson, maybe it'll stop him making advances to the fisherwomen.' *Rosabelle will be relieved*, she thought.

At first, the conversation around the Stanhope dinner table concentrated on local gossip, particularly the vicissitudes of various women in receipt of relief – who was drinking too much, who was sleeping with whom and who was pregnant again were the themes mulled over with disapproval, especially by Hester.

'When I have to tell them that their money is being held back because of their way of life, they give me stories about sick children, no coal for their fires, no food on their tables, and I have to harden my heart, though it's not easy at times,' said Anderson sanctimoniously.

He was facing Hester across the table and she smiled at him with unhidden admiration. 'It must be very trying for you,' she said.

'It is, but I always keep in mind that it's not my money I'm giving out. It's been donated by kind people who wanted to help, and I must make sure it's not frittered away or wasted. We've been given a chance to make those people see the light and live lives of godliness. In a way, the storm might be a blessing in disguise in the end,' he said.

Cochrane visibly flinched, but managed to say, 'There's not much chance of all the relief money being frittered. It was a considerable sum. Properly invested it should bring in enough to provide weekly incomes for the pensioners for years. Who is doing the investing now that Mr McIntyre's dead?'

'Friends in the business community in Edinburgh are advising me,' said Anderson, and an idea that had been lying at the back of his mind suddenly flowered in his head like an exotic orchid.

'Good, Edinburgh's a well-known centre for handling money,' said the minister of the local Methodist church.

'Shouldn't the committee have a say too?' Cochrane asked blandly.

'My dear man, I haven't a clue about how to invest money without expert advice. Have you?' laughed another of the men at the table.

'Not really,' Cochrane admitted, aware from her hardened eye that Hester was annoyed with him for questioning Anderson.

She was looking elegant in a striped taffeta gown of pale lilac and pink that gave her the illusion of a full bust and generous hips. Candlelight from silver candlesticks placed along the middle of the table gave her skin an attractive ivory glow. She'd stage-managed the setting very well and Cochrane wondered if she hoped to make him regret his failure to respond to the overtures she once made towards him.

When the soup plates were removed, wine was poured by a nervous table maid, and it glowed a deep, glorious red in crystal goblets.

Mr Stanhope lifted his glass to his lips and sniffed appreciatively. 'Drink up, it's France's best,' he said.

They all sipped and Anderson smacked his lips, sighing as if he'd tasted the wine of the gods. 'Unsurpassed!' he said.

Stanhope smiled and told the gathering, 'It's my last bottle of that consignment. The man who used to bring this particular Merlot over from France for me was drowned in the storm, unfortunately. I'm serving it tonight because this is a special occasion. I've received a piece of news that I want to share with you. Ladies and gentlemen, please join me in a toast to my daughter Hester and her husband-to-be – Mr Steven Anderson, who asked me for her hand this evening.'

Alan Cochrane put down his glass and clapped his hands. 'I'm very pleased!' he said with absolute sincerity.

Sixteen

With a baby in each arm, Effie sat on a wooden chair at her kitchen door and smelt summer in the air. To her surprise, she felt her heart give an unexpected thrill of hope and promise of future consolation. Perhaps the ever-present pain was lessening.

When Jimmy Dip and the boys drowned, she truly thought she would never feel anything other than black misery again; but these two little children in her arms were giving her new solace.

She looked after them every day except Sunday and, when she handed them over to their mothers, she fretted till they came back again. Sometimes Jessie left Henrietta with her overnight, and she loved to lie in bed with the baby, cuddling it like a little doll. She never asked where Jessie went on those nights. The girl was too young and vigorous to live like a nun.

Effie thought that a little flightiness would be a good thing for Rosabelle as well, but there was no sign of it. The poor girl's eyes still filled with tears whenever anything was said about the disaster – and nobody dared even mention Dan.

For several months Jessie fed her daughter herself, rushing back from the laundry at feeding times to whip out her generous, milk-dripping breasts, but after her first agonizing attempt to feed Aaron, Rosabelle never tried again. Fortunately the baby thrived on cows' milk and sucked on a rubber teat in a glass bottle, his lips curving round it in a placid smile. In spite of what his mother went through when she was carrying him, he was an exceptionally placid baby.

He looked so like Dan that sometimes Effie went back in time and thought she was cuddling his father. Eventually the resemblance ceased to pain her, but she knew it still harrowed

Aaron's mother and feared that Rosabelle was not able to give unlimited affection to her baby. In time, she hoped, the girl's pain would ease, but now she made up for his mother's reticence by cuddling and kissing the baby at every opportunity. He thrived on it.

Sitting in the pale sunshine, eyes closed and babies asleep, she heard a footfall on the paving and looked up to see Euphen staring down at her.

'What a bonny picture,' said Euphen.

'Get yourself a chair and sit with us. The sun's warm. It makes you feel good,' said Effie.

Euphen pulled a stool out of the kitchen and perched on it. 'The bairns are coming on well,' she said.

'Yes. They're both strong and handsome. This wee lad's as good as gold. One day I want him to have his own boat,' said Effie, planting a kiss on Aaron's head.

Euphen looked sad. 'Don't you think your family's given enough to the sea?' she asked.

Effie was shocked. 'How can you ask that? We're a fishing family on both sides. We've aye been fishing people. What else would he do but go to sea?'

'I sometimes wish there was an alternative,' said Euphen sadly.

Effie sat up straighter. Her friend's face was white and she looked tired. 'Are you all right?' she asked.

'I get weary. It's hard getting up at five in the morning and baiting the lines for Alex and our laddie. I wish he'd get married, then I'd only have Alex's to do.' Euphen always referred to her only child as 'our laddie' and Effie flinched when she said it.

'William's nearly twenty, isn't he? And he's a big handsome lad. The girls will all be after him soon,' she said.

'Some of their people wouldn't want him because of Alex bringing the boat back out of the storm. There's folk who resent that. Women still shout things after me in the street.' Euphen's voice was dejected.

'They're stupid. Ignore them,' said Effie briskly.

'I try to, but it's hard if old friends drop you. When Bella's in drink, even she says nasty things about Alex to me. My own sister!'

'You tell her that if it wasn't for Alex a lot of people round here wouldn't have bread on their tables. He gives money to Aitken's widow, and to other families as well,' said Effie indignantly.

'I know, but he doesn't want me to tell folk about that. He thinks if Anderson got to know he was helping some people, he might cut their money.'

'But Aitken's widow doesn't get any money.'

'I know, but others do.' Euphen sounded exhausted.

'I'm going to speak to the laddie of yours next time I see him and tell him to get himself married soon,' said Effie.

Euphen's eyes searched her friend's face. 'Dinna do that, Effie. You see he's taken a terrible fancy to your Henry's Jessie. I think they've been going up to the fort together.'

Effie frowned and thought about this. Jessie was burning for a man, she knew, and William was a good-looking young fellow though nervous and shy. 'But they're first cousins,' she blurted out.

'I know. And there's been a few funny bairns born in our family already. My grandparents were first cousins too, and my parents second cousins. We canna risk it.'

Both women were silent for a few moments, thinking about instances of first cousins marrying and the sort of children they produced.

Willie Wake is the child of first cousins and he began going funny in his thirties. His son was funny too, thought Effie.

'William's our only son. Alex and I want grandchildren. We want him to marry someone who isn't related, maybe a girl from another place,' said Euphen quietly.

'I'll speak to Jessie,' Effie promised.

That night, when she handed over Henrietta, she said, 'Have you found another man, Jessie? Don't think I'd object, I wouldn't. It's the best thing you can do. Just be careful who you pick.'

Jessie held the baby and looked defiantly at Effie over the child's head. 'I've no plan to marry anybody,' she said slowly.

'Don't hurt anyone while you're looking around,' Effie said.

'It's a new season. Things are growing. Life goes on. I like men and they like me. If I go up to the fort with a fellow, it

154

doesn't mean I'm going to settle down with him. I've got plans. I'm waiting to see what turns up and something will. Who's been speaking to you, Effie?' Jessie was not apologetic, only concerned.

'Euphen. She's worried about William. She says he's daft about you. But you're first cousins and you know what that means . . .' Effie's voice trailed off.

Jessie nodded. 'I know well enough. Poor Will. He's a handsome lad and a kind one, but he's not Henry and I've no plans to marry him. All right, so I've lain in the fort with him. It's good for me and for him too. I've never told him any lies. We're just enjoying ourselves. Tell his mother not to worry. He'll get over me and marry a nice lassie. Like I said, I'm taking care – I know how.'

She looked down at her baby and ran a loving finger round its lips before she went on, 'Anyway I don't want to go back to line-baiting and waiting for boats to come in. It's better to go on alone like I'm doing now, having a man when I need one, getting my relief money every week and washing Stanhope's laundry.' Jessie was more serious than Effie had seen her for a long time.

'I'll tell Euphen,' she replied.

Jessie was not the only woman made unsettled by the balmy weather. Rosabelle lay wakeful through long nights, her body aching as she remembered Dan's love-making. She knew how Jessie was working off her frustration, but she'd never been as free and easy with her body as her friend, and that release was not open for her.

Dan was the only man she'd ever slept with. No one would ever measure up to him. The thought of sleeping with anyone else not only felt like a breach of faith, but it frightened her. She fell asleep with the tears wet on her cheeks as dawn was breaking.

After she dropped Aaron off at Effie's and made her way through the alleys to Mrs Lyall's shop, she was still being spied on by Anderson. In her straw bonnet and blue working dress with a spotless white fichu, she cut a dignified, even elegant, figure.

She caught sight of him sometimes and realized he knew

her route and times. What she did not know was that he sought out every secret, hidden place to stand to watch her go by, and surreptitiously did that daily. Every time he saw her he was filled with a strange mixture of feelings that confused him: longing, admiration and a kind of hatred. He was furious not only because she rejected him, but also because she could inspire such emotions in him. His passion was growing so strong that sometimes he felt frustration would choke him. He was more determined than ever to make her yield to him.

Though he had promised to marry Hester, and was still being pleasured by two friendly widows every week, he did not stop lusting after the yellow-haired girl. He had to have her. She was an ever-present challenge to his manhood.

One evening, as he was escorting his fiancée from the grocery store up the hill to Beechwood, he saw the yellow-haired girl heading out of the square in the direction of the fisherfolk's houses.

It was not her usual finishing time and he wondered why she was leaving Mrs Lyall's so early. Was she meeting another man? He felt himself go cold at the very idea.

Suddenly he stopped in his tracks and said to Hester, 'I've just remembered that I've left the cashbox unlocked in my office and I have a few letters to write. You go home on your own, my dear, and I'll be up later.'

She did not object, and walked with him to the Town Hall, where they parted. He watched from his office window till she was out of sight and then rushed back out, almost running to the harbour side.

Because the work she was doing was completed early, Mrs Lyall had allowed Rosabelle to go home, and she was on her way to Effie's to collect her son. It was a fine evening and she intended to carry Aaron along to the pier end so that he could have a breath of sea air.

The baby seemed to get heavier every day and she hoisted him on to her shoulder as she walked back from the pier end to her mother's house, which, she supposed, was hers now, though she still thought of it as Isa's. Aaron was gurgling happily as he looked down at the paving stones beneath his mother's feet and she patted him softly on the bottom with her left hand as she walked along.

You are a sweet little thing after all. I just wish you didn't look so like your father, she thought. The resemblance pained her all the time.

At her front door, she bent slightly to turn the handle, but an arm came between the baby and the door and a voice said, 'Let me do that.'

It was Anderson. She knew him by his tobacco and pomade smell. Stiffening, and without turning her head to look at him, she knocked his hand off the handle and said, 'Go away.'

'I'll help you with the baby. Let me in,' he said, trying to open the door and push her through it. She pressed herself against the handle and looked frantically around for help, but in this quiet part of the afternoon there was no one about.

The boats were out and would probably stay out till tomorrow. Women who still had men were down on the shingle gathering bait. Others were shut up in their houses. Her own home was empty.

He tried to pull her away from the door, but she went rigid as she lowered the baby from her shoulder, clutched him to her breast, and, for the first time, looked directly into Anderson's face. The fixity of his features horrified her. He looked like a man possessed.

'Please! *Go away!*' she snapped, panicked now.

The note of entreaty in her voice encouraged him and he said, 'I won't go till you talk to me. You've been taunting me, teasing me, leading me on. Why won't you speak to me?' he rasped.

'I don't like you,' she said slowly and flatly.

He put a hand under her chin, not caring that she flinched when he touched her. 'You don't have to like me. You just have to be kind to me. I'll make it worth your while.'

She recoiled from him and cried out, 'No! Go away.'

The baby started to cry as if he sensed her fear. She stood with her back against the still closed door, and, emboldened by her obvious panic, Anderson put his hand on her lips to stop her calling out.

Suddenly her eyes flashed fire and, like a dog, she snapped at him, catching his forefinger between her teeth and biting hard into it.

'Never, *never* touch me!' she shouted.

157

With an anguished yell, he withdrew his hand. The finger was bleeding profusely and for a moment he considered hitting her, but she turned, dashed in through the door, and slammed it behind her. Standing outside, holding out his bleeding finger, he heard the bolt being driven home with tremendous force.

With a curse, he turned and ran, disappearing down the alley as if all the devils of hell were after him.

Rosabelle stood in the middle of her kitchen floor, staring at the bolted door. She laid the baby in its cradle and grabbed a long poker. If he tried to break in, she'd kill him.

It took a long time, and night had fallen, before she felt safe enough to wrap the baby in his shawl and run to her mother-in-law.

'My word, you're in a state. What's happened?' asked Effie when the girl came rushing into her kitchen.

'Lock the door, lock your door,' gabbled Rosabelle, and threw herself down in Jimmy Dip's chair. Only then did she burst into tears.

As always in a crisis, Effie was superb. She found her big door key and turned it in the lock. Then she went to her corner cupboard, brought out a half-bottle of whisky and poured out a small measure, which she gave to the weeping girl. 'Drink that and then tell me what this is all about,' she said.

'It's that relief man. He's been following me for weeks and tonight he tried to get into my house. I think he's mad . . . and he scares me. I bit his hand, Effie. I made it bleed.'

'Good, serves him right,' said Effie.

'Can I move in here with you? I'm frightened to go on living alone,' said the girl.

'Of course, but what are we going to do about him? Do you want me to go to see him? Do you think we should tell one of the men? Somebody like young William Burgon could put the fear of God into him.'

Rosabelle shook her head in panic. 'Oh no, that would only make him worse. And who would believe me anyway? They'd think I was leading him on – he said to me tonight that I *have* been. They'd believe him before they believed me.'

Effie nodded. It was a man's world, she knew.

When Jessie arrived to leave Henrietta with Effie while she did her laundry work, she was told the story and stood with her hands on her hips, looking gleeful. 'Don't you worry,' she told her friend; 'I'll fix him. I'll go to fetch your weekly money and I'll make sure he understands that he's got to leave you alone. I'll enjoy it.'

Next morning she hung around outside Anderson's office until he was on his own and then went in to tell him, 'I've come to collect the money for Rosabelle Scott, and I'll be the one collecting it from now on.'

He glared at her. 'That's very irregular. I can't allow it.'

Jessie glared back. 'You'd better, or I'll be going up to Miss Stanhope's and telling her *and her father* about the way you've been chasing Rosabelle and about the women who come in here and roll about with you on the carpet. I ken them all; I've heard their jokes about your wee pecker.'

It was the last crack that really threw him. He grappled for his cashbox, much hampered by a bandaged finger that looked like a big white sausage. Jessie watched as he scrabbled for the money and counted it out. Then she gathered it up and asked, 'What happened to your finger, Mr Anderson? Have you been sticking it someplace where it shouldn't be?'

'I was bitten by a dog,' he snapped as she made her smiling departure.

Jessie was gleeful when she reported to Rosabelle: 'You must have grand strong teeth. He has a big bandage on the first finger of his right hand and he cannae write in those books of his or get the money out of his tin box. You really bit him, didn't you? I asked what happened and he said he'd been bitten by a dog.'

The finger mended quite quickly, but the fact that the girl had bitten him so badly preyed on his mind long after her teeth marks disappeared. He took to cradling that hand in his other one, and stroking the scar, till an exasperated Hester asked him if it was giving him much pain. 'Maybe you should let the doctor have a look at it,' she suggested.

He dropped both hands like a small boy who'd been caught stealing from the biscuit barrel.

Because of Jessie's threat to talk to Mr Stanhope about him, he decided that his safest course was to keep out of Rosabelle's way till he was safely married. Once he and Hester were man and wife, there would be little her father could do.

He stopped lurking in the street looking for Rosabelle but spent hours in his office window staring out in the hope she would pass by; but she never did.

During this time his passion for her grew, but now it was fiercer and more dangerous. How dare she, a fishwife, treat him with scorn! How dare she injure him when all he wanted to do was talk to her. He wondered if she and Jessie joked about his 'wee pecker', as Jessie had called it. Women like that deserved to be taught a lesson, and one day his opportunity would come.

On a brilliant Saturday afternoon in the beginning of October, Hester Stanhope and Steven Anderson were married in Alan Cochrane's church.

There were many people who thought their choice of date was inappropriate – disaster day had been in October – but they never gave it a thought.

On the morning of the wedding Jessie tried to entice Rosabelle and Effie to go with her to watch the newly wed couple emerging from the church, but they rejected the idea with horror. Rosabelle did not want the man who so terrified her to catch a glimpse of her in the crowd.

'But don't you want to see her dress?' Jessie asked.

'I've seen it already because I helped to make it,' said Rosabelle. It had been Mrs Lyall's most expensive order of the year.

Jessie was determined not to miss the fun, however, and promised to come back and tell them every detail.

She returned at half past twelve and began talking the moment she came through the door. 'You've no idea how grand it was. You did a good job, Rosabelle; Hester's dress was lovely – grey lace with long flouncy sleeves. It made her look almost bonny. Her father ordered her bouquet of white roses from Covent Garden in London and they were sent up by the early-morning train. There were dozens of them, all falling down in a cascade, lovely . . .'

'Was there a lot of folk in the church?' asked Effie.

'Plenty. All the well-off folk from the town and all the gentry. That brother of Hester's – the one with the funny name – was best man. There was a line of carriages lining the road to away past the corn mill. Anderson was got up like the Prince of Wales in strippit trousers and a black jacket with a high cravat holding up that bull's head of his. He was grinning like somebody who'd found a gold mine.'

'If you're asking me, he has,' said Effie bleakly. She thought it was about time for her own family to have a little bit of good luck. It was so long since they'd celebrated anything or been unashamedly happy.

She was still worried about Rosabelle, who had been very set back by her experience with Anderson. When she looked downcast, Effie often asked if she was troubled, but she always shook her head and said, 'Of course not. No worse than usual.'

Yet she still burst into violent tears without any obvious reason, and, because she was a believer in the virtue of exercise and the open air, Effie persuaded her to walk to the pier end with her baby on fine evenings, but only when there were other people about. Discreetly, Effie followed at a distance, keeping an eye on her, because she remembered how Isa threw herself off Berwick's pier end, and she suspected that, though not so obvious, Rosabelle's depression was as devastating as her mother's.

The habit of bursting into tears exasperated Jessie who tried to rally her friend by saying, 'Pull yourself together. You've got to start living again. What you need is a new man.'

The reaction was horror. 'Another man! Never, never, never.'

Jessie screwed her mouth up. 'Oh dear me! But take my word for it, it's a grand cure for greetin'. There must be something wrong with you. Are you feeling all right?'

'I'm tired all the time, so tired that sometimes I can hardly put one foot past the other. Mrs Lyall works me hard. I designed and made Hester Stanhope's wedding gown and she charged ten guineas for it – but I got nothing extra. She says that if I earn too much, the relief man will take my payment off me. I don't want to have to go near him, but I need the fund money. Everything worries me, everything . . .'

Jessie made an exasperated noise with her tongue. 'You're being daft. Lyall's only making the relief money an excuse for not paying you enough.'

Neither of them knew that Anderson had already made a move to have their money cut but was thwarted.

'I wish I could be strong like you, Jessie, but I'm not brave,' Rosabelle said.

'You're brave enough but you're too arty. You're not down to earth like me. I dinna mind dirty work; I dinna mind going up to the fort when the urge is on me and I've a nice lad to meet; I dinna mind washing the dirty linen from Stanhope's shop. I'm happy to go on like that and stay here for the rest of my life, but you want something else. You need to get away from here, I think. It must be your mother's fault for having a bairn by that foreign captain. She should have stuck to the locals.'

Rosabelle looked at her friend with admiration. They'd grown closer over the months and now Jessie seemed more of a sister than the distant Clara.

Jessie's tears had stopped flowing, but that didn't mean that she no longer mourned Henry, just that she was a realist who valued life. Once more she was blooming, in the peak of her prettiness, plump, black-haired and more roguish than ever. She'd been gentle about letting William Burgon down, and he'd gone off to marry a girl from a fishing family in Cockburnspath. Euphen and Alex were delighted.

Once more Effie watched and compared the two girls as she had done that terrible day on the shore when they were gathering bait. 'My boys have left me a fine legacy and I love them both,' she realized.

Jessie, whom she first thought frivolous and giddy, had grown in her regard. In time, she knew, she would rely on this girl.

Poor Rosabelle was a different proposition. The girl was desperate. Her grief was growing worse instead of softening. Jessie was right to say that Rosabelle ought to get out of Eyemouth, even if only for a little while; but how could that be arranged? The thought of her taking Aaron away terrified Effie.

The baby was growing fat and chuckling, grabbing for his grandmother's hair whenever she bent over him. She wanted him to have good, warm clothes and toys like better-off children, and knew Rosabelle wanted that too; but luxuries were not bought on half a crown a week. Money had to be found from somewhere.

It was like a message of hope when she found an interesting advertisement in the *Berwickshire News*, a local news-paper that was passed from house to house by those of the fisher people who could read. Thanks to an ambitious mother, Effie was one of the few women of her community who had that skill.

When Rosabelle came home that night she was sitting with the paper spread out on the kitchen table in front of her.

'That Mrs Lyall isn't playing fair with you. You should look for another place,' she said, looking up.

'Where? Lyall's the best dressmaker in the town.'

Effie ran her finger halfway down a column on the front page and stopped at a neatly boxed announcement.

'Listen to this,' she said, and read out an advertisement put in by Mrs and Miss Gibson, milliners and dressmakers of Hide Hill, Berwick-upon-Tweed. Their advert said they sold hats, mob caps, feathers, velvets, plushes, silks and ribbons, hosiery and yarns to the fashionable ladies of the town. But what was most interesting was the last line of their advert, which said: 'An Apprentice Dressmaker Wanted.'

'There's a good place for you. I've seen their shop when I've been in Berwick. It's very grand,' said Effie.

Rosabelle protested, 'But I'm not a proper dressmaker. I've never really learned my trade, just picked it up.'

'You made Hester Stanhope's wedding dress, didn't you? Everybody says it was beautiful and that you're better with your needle than Mrs Lyall.'

'Do they?' Rosabelle was surprised.

'Yes, they do. You're a clever lassie and it's time you started believing it. Go to Berwick and see these women. Ride in with the carter tomorrow morning. If you get the position, I'll look after Aaron. Jessie's right. You need a wider horizon than this town. It's wearing you away.'

Rosabelle sighed. 'At least in Berwick I wouldn't always be afraid of meeting Anderson in the street.'

They were not the sort of people who received letters, but next morning one came for Rosabelle – only the second she'd ever had in her life. It too was from Clara, and when Effie pored over the words before reading them out, Rosabelle stood wringing her hands, worried in case it was bad news.

163

In fact it was anything but bad, and Effie was beaming when she looked up. In her hand she held a banknote. 'Look what she sent you,' she said.

'What is it?'

'An American ten-dollar bill.'

'What's that in our money?'

'Goodness knows, but it must be worth something or she wouldn't have sent it.'

Clara's letter said how she grieved over their mother's death, but she was happy in Boston now because Tom was working, they'd made friends and found a house with a garden, something they'd never had before. The ten-dollar bill was to buy a present for her sister's baby.

Exclaiming in pleasure and gratitude, they passed the crisp note between them, admiring its colour and fine calligraphy. 'There's nowhere in this town where you can change it. Now that Mr McIntyre's gone, we canna be sure that the bank people won't gossip. It doesnae do for folk to know your business, especially if you're afraid of getting your money cut. This is all the more reason for you to go to Berwick. There's two or three big banks there that'll change your money and you can find out about that dressmaker job at the same time. It's a sign,' said Effie.

By half past nine Rosabelle was on her way. She'd asked Mrs Lyall for a day off, and, when that was refused, in a rush of anger, she resigned. As she sat on the cart, rumbling along the high road, she chastised herself for impetuosity. How stupid to throw away good work because of a ten-dollar bill! She must find a position in Berwick, no matter what it was.

When a bank converted the ten-dollar bill into five golden sovereigns, Rosabelle stepped back out into the street feeling like a woman of property.

Smiling faintly, she looked around and felt her heart lift. The money in her purse gave her confidence. The next thing to do was find the Gibsons' shop.

Hide Hill was in the smart area of the town and the dressmaking business was established on the ground floor of an elegant Georgian building with long windows and a short flight of steps leading to the front door.

The elder Mrs Gibson was alone in the room she called her 'salon'. A sweetly spoken woman in her sixties, smartly dressed in a mauve foulard gown and a crisp, lace-trimmed cap covering her grey hair, she had two corkscrew curls hanging down the sides of her cheeks. They made her look like a lady of fashion from fifty years ago.

She examined the examples of work that Rosabelle brought with her and exclaimed, 'But you're no apprentice, my dear. If this is your work, you're highly skilled.'

'Please take me. I need work,' said Rosabelle simply, and without thinking poured out the story of how Dan died in the big storm. She was not trying to awaken Mrs Gibson's sympathy; it was because there was something warm and understanding about the woman that made her want to talk.

Mrs Gibson nodded encouragement as she listened in sympathetic silence, and then said, 'You poor girl, what a very sad story. I'm going to take you on, but as more than an apprentice. Have you any experience as a dressmaker?'

'Yes; I don't know if you've heard of Hester Stanhope, but I made her wedding dress. I enjoy making gowns for people. It's like painting pictures, I think,' said Rosabelle.

Mrs Gibson had heard about the chandler's daughter's pretty wedding dress and smiled as she replied, 'You're right. Dressmaking is a form of art. Come back tomorrow to start work. My daughter and I will be pleased to have you.'

Rosabelle carefully gathered together her scraps of sewing, before she summoned up the courage to ask, 'What will you pay me, please?'

'I wondered when you'd ask that,' said Mrs Gibson. 'Your starting wage will be two pounds five shillings a week, and if we're extra-busy, we'll pay you a bonus. We're busy now, actually, because the ball season is starting and the ladies of the garrison are all having dresses made. Is that money acceptable to you?'

It sounded princely to Rosabelle, so she smiled and said, 'Oh yes.'

Just then the front door opened, and there was a swishing sound of taffeta along the marble floor of the hall. Mrs Gibson looked over Rosabelle's shoulder and smiled at the newcomer as she said, 'Ah, Madame Rachelle, have you come for your fitting? My daughter is out on an errand but she'll be back directly. Please sit down.'

Rosabelle stood to the side and looked at the woman who entered the salon. In a flash she recognized Nisbet's mistress. Though only glimpsed twice before, the woman had made an indelible impression.

As tall as Rosabelle, and as dark-haired as the girl was blonde, very slim, erect and tightly corseted, she looked as elegant as a fashion plate in a sea-green gown with long tight sleeves and a lace inlay round the neck. Her hat was pale-yellow straw trimmed with matching green ribbons in luxuriant loops.

It was difficult to guess her age, because her face was so heavily made up and rouged that she looked like a china doll. The air of self-possession that she exuded awed the girl watching her.

For her part, Rachelle too immediately recognized Rosabelle. Her practised eye took in the shabby clothes, the black shawl covering the elegant shoulders . . . *Probably five foot seven, thin but full-busted, magnificent pale skin and that spectacular hair, curling like flower tendrils around a proud face . . . a beauty*, she thought without any jealousy, because her interest in Rosabelle was not as a rival but as a tool. She had a plan in mind that every day was becoming more possible as her nest egg from various 'protectors' grew. Soon she would have enough to launch herself in London, and she needed an assistant, an accomplice. This girl would be perfect.

She smiled and extended a hand to Rosabelle. 'I've seen you before, haven't I?' she asked.

'Have you?' Rosabelle found it hard to believe that this fashion-plate woman would ever notice her.

'Yes, in Eyemouth, at the funeral of an *ami* – a *friend* – of mine . . .' Her speech was stressed as if she was not quite sure of the meaning of friend, and her accent was strange, soft and sibilant with a rolling of the 'r's that made the words like whispered secrets.

Rosabelle nodded. An *ami*? What a lovely word. In Eyemouth, Nisbet would have been called this woman's 'fancy man'.

Rachelle was looking into her face with a strange dancing

light in her eye, as if she was secretly amused and totally uncaring whether any of them knew that she'd been Nisbet's mistress.

'You were at Mr Nisbet's funeral,' Rosabelle agreed.

'And you were watching? Did you know him?'

'He was my mother's cousin . . .' Almost every fishing family in Eyemouth had links with the others.

Rachelle clasped her hands in delight. 'You have style like he did!' she exclaimed.

Style. Another lovely word, especially when spoken in that strange accent. Rosabelle stood up taller and felt her shoulders drop as the tension in them relaxed. Watching her beginning to glow beneath Madame Rachelle's complimentary regard, Mrs Gibson was even more pleased about her decision to employ the girl. She could only be good for business.

Seventeen

This is the first anniversary of the disaster, and ironically it is a fine, bright autumn morning with a beautiful display from beech leaves and rowan berries, which are turning to scarlet and orange. It is cruel that the weather is so fine on such a terrible day, especially when I remember last 14 October, with its howling winds and raging seas.

I have been walking through the fishing town and the alleys and wynds are deserted. No boats have gone out and curtains are drawn over most of the windows. The school is closed in respect for the dead and some little bunches of flowers have appeared on the end of the pier and on top of graves in the burying ground, but no one has asked me to hold a church service.

It is hard to show the bereaved how much I sympathize with them. They still view me – and most clergymen – with suspicion. Yet as the weeks pass and one season follows another, I find myself more and more admiring of the people of this town. They are staunch and proud almost to a fault. They turned down Quarrier's offer, and have made sure that their children are suffering as little as possible from the tragedy. Not one single child has been sent out of the town, and there are no miserable, downtrodden beggar children like the ones you see in Edinburgh or Glasgow. There is no general starvation and malnutrition. The local diet, consisting mainly of fish, seems to sustain them very well. If a child's own mother is unable to look after him or her, a relative or someone else in the community does. I know they support each other financially too.

It is in the children that I see the hope of the future. They are as wild as ever, and though they are quiet today, they will be running shrieking through the streets again tomorrow.

Alan Cochrane put down his pen and looked through the manse window at an expanse of pale-blue sky. It was hard to believe that such weather could suddenly turn into a raging fury – but by now he knew only too well that it could. He remembered the storm vividly, and still superstitiously feared that he was in some way responsible for bringing disaster on the town.

'Cauld iron, cauld iron!' cried a voice in his head.

To banish these thoughts, he pulled his coat off the hook on the back of his study door and set out to walk off his sadness along the shore.

There was no one about. Even in the upper town, all the shops were closed in respect. His walk took him past Stanhope's shuttered grocery store, and along the shingle beach. When he turned at the base of the cliff to head back towards the harbour wall, he saw Willie Wake squatting against the wall on which the barometer stood.

As he approached the old man, he saw that he had his hands over his face. 'Are you all right?' he asked gently.

The head in its black woollen cap was raised. 'No, I wish I was deid. I'm trying to dee but it doesnae happen. God doesnae seem to want me.'

The conventional ministerial response would have been to try cheering the man up, but Cochrane knew this was not what was needed. 'I'm sorry,' he said.

'They're a' deid. A' the good men. What sort of God wants them all at once?'

'I don't know.' Nice phrases about being in a better place, and with their maker, were certainly not called for either.

The old man stood up and said dismissively, 'If you don't, then naebody does.'

Helplessly Cochrane watched him staggering off along the pier, his arthritic legs almost buckling with the effort.

He went up to the barometer, tapping on its long tube of silver mercury. It was high and did not move. He shivered and turned away to find a girl standing on the lower part of the stonework, staring up at him.

'It's set fair,' the clergyman said, for the sake of breaking the silence. The girl was not dressed in fisherwoman clothes but in a blue serge dress with a thin shawl over her shoul-

169

ders. Her curly yellow hair was drawn back in a thick bun and she wore no bonnet.

She nodded. 'They say there might never be another storm like that again,' she said, and he knew she was referring to the disaster.

He climbed down and stood beside her. She was one of the fishing widows, he knew. 'How are you managing?' he asked.

'I get relief money and I'm working in Berwick as a dressmaker. My son's with my mother-in-law.'

'I mean how are you in yourself?'

Her eyes were full of misery and sorrow. 'My heart is broken. I don't think it will ever mend,' she said simply.

His own heart ached at the words, so simple and, he knew, so true. Again the old truisms about time healing all pain were not appropriate.

'I'm sorry,' he said.

She turned her face to his and said fiercely, 'Today it's worse than usual. I had to get out of the house, but here I can't help seeing those rocks where my man died.'

She pointed at the Hurkars, which even on fine days looked sinister and black, and he realized that she was the wife of the man who had perished in sight of the people on the harbour wall. How terrible today must be for her!

She saw anguished pity on his face and said bitterly, 'You have no idea how much I hate this place.'

'Perhaps you should leave,' he suggested. Several families had done that already.

She shrugged. 'My sister's gone to America. I could go there, I suppose, but I have responsibilities here – my husband's mother especially. She lost all her men in the storm and she loves my son. I can't take him away from her.'

'Won't she go with you?'

The girl shook her head. 'She'll never leave here. In spite of everything that's happened, this is the place where she wants to be. I think she'll feel closer to the men she lost if she stays here.'

He was powerless to help her and there was nothing he could say. 'It's good that you have found work outside the town then,' he said.

She nodded. 'It's the only thing that makes my life sufferable.'

When they parted, both of them felt that they'd had a conversation of deep significance.

What it did for Rosabelle was to bring to the surface of her mind an idea that had been floating around for a while. How wonderful it was to get out of Eyemouth, and it would be even better to go further than Berwick. On bad days like today her mind was obsessed with the fear that the Hurkars would get her too.

When she eventually walked home, she found Jessie with Effie. The news she brought provided a small diversion in the grief-filled house.

'I came round to tell you both that my sister Fanny's getting married next month,' said Jessie.

Rosabelle draped her shawl over the chair back and said, 'That's good. Are you pleased?'

Jessie didn't look pleased, but today was not a day for smiling or showing pleasure. 'I don't mind her getting married, but it means she won't be at home to keep our mother in control, or help me with the washing for the shop.'

Effie turned round from the cradle where she was rocking Aaron and said, 'You don't do so much laundering yourself any more, do you? I've seen you serving in Stanhope's shop some days.'

'That's true. I like working in the shop and the old man sometimes lets me when his daughter's off putting her feet up in the afternoons.'

Rosabelle had not known that Jessie had been promoted to counter assistant and asked in surprise, 'What do you do?'

Jessie looked slightly shifty. 'Nothing much. I serve cheese, pack orders, and put stuff on shelves – this and that.'

'Did Miss Hester hire you?'

'Not her! He only lets me work there when she's out of the way. It's quite often, though, because she's taken up looking after that man of hers. The minute she takes her eye off him, he's off chasing some lassie or other – and some of them let him catch them. He's handing out relief money for more than charity.'

Remembering the box of crystallized fruit, and the slices of cooked ham, Rosabelle exclaimed in alarm: 'Oh Jessie, don't do anything rash. If she catches you helping yourself, she'll have the policeman after you. They'd send you to prison for that.'

'I'll not be helping myself to anything that I'm not entitled to,' said Jessie sharply.

It was obvious that she resented her honesty being questioned, so Rosabelle changed the subject back to something safer.

'Who is Fanny marrying?' she asked.

'A Harkins from Cove. His brother was one of the men who drowned.'

'What's he like?'

'He drinks, and folk say that when he drinks he fights.'

'That doesn't sound too good,' said her friend.

'Well Fanny can fight too even when she's sober. My chief worry is the laundry. Wee Mary's not big enough yet, so I'm thinking of talking one of the boys into helping,' said Jessie.

'It sounds as if you're setting up a family business,' was Effie's comment, but there was a hint of a smile round her mouth, even on this terrible day.

Jessie almost smiled too, but, seeing Rosabelle's stricken eyes, stayed solemn-faced. 'I came round to ask you a favour,' she said, turning to her friend.

'What is it?' asked Rosabelle.

'I want you to make me a new outfit and I want it to be purple,' Jessie said.

'Purple? Are you going to wear it to something special?' Rosabelle was surprised.

'To Fanny's wedding, of course. I'll wear it to show I'm glad to get her off my hands. She's a crabbit bitch. The Cove lad's welcome to her.'

'Of course I'll make you a dress, and I won't charge for my time. Mrs Gibson will let me buy the material and trimmings at cost price and I'll make it really pretty.'

'And I want a hat too, but I don't want it to be pretty: I want it to be *grand* – and big, with lots of ribbons and a stuffed bird on it. I've aye dreamed of a hat like that.'

Rosabelle reeled. The vision of wee Jessie at her sister's wedding with a stuffed bird on her head was almost comical.

Mrs Gibson, who had grown truly fond of Rosabelle, was also amused by the commission, and helped with it, so the outfit

172

was finished well in time and Jessie came to Berwick for her final fitting on a miserable November afternoon.

In her drab fishwife clothes she pushed the salon door open and entered, to find Madame Rachelle, bandbox-smart as usual, already there.

She called in often with orders and never forgot to congratulate Rosabelle on her artistry. Today she was making Gallic complaints about the weather – 'Thees terrible fog. It is here all the time. I have a terreeble cough. It is not weather for fine gowns,' she was saying as Jessie stepped into the room.

There was an immediate silence while Rachelle took in the newcomer's clothes, and the atmosphere chilled as the two women eyed each other like combative terriers sizing up the opposition.

Watching them, Rosabelle was astonished by their instant animosity, and then by how much Jessie had changed and grown in assurance over the last year. Almost unnoticed she had cast off much of her frivolity and grown up. Today, in spite of her old shawl and dark fustian skirt, she had the air of a woman of the world, someone to be reckoned with.

It was obvious that Jessie and Rachelle disliked what they saw when they looked at each other, as if they could spot each other's secrets and pretensions, perhaps because they shared them. People always resent their own faults in others, and Rosabelle suddenly realized that Jessie and Rachelle were both daring adventuresses with their own rules of morality.

Madame Rachelle seemed to be in no hurry to leave, although her latest purchase, a lace-trimmed peignoir, was already wrapped up for her. She obviously wanted to know what brought a fishergirl to the Gibsons' establishment, so she lingered on, congratulating Rosabelle again on her fine work and talking about new ball gowns.

Jessie stood back saying nothing, so Rachelle was forced to acknowledge her existence and ask, 'Is this clever girl making something nice for you too?'

'She's making me a dress and trimming my hat,' said Jessie grandly.

'You are getting married?' was Rachelle's next question as she ran her eye over Jessie's trim little figure.

The answer was a shake of the head. 'Not me, but my sister will soon be a bride.'

'Oh what a shame! You are so pretty, I thought it would be you. Have you no beau?'

Jessie looked her in the eye. 'I've lots of them. I take my pick.' She used the present tense, not the future, and Rachelle recognized the inference. Her look became even more appraising.

'You plan to travel somewhere in your new dress? London perhaps?'

Jessie laughed. 'London? Not me. I don't want to go any further than I've come today. From Eyemouth. I like my home.'

'You are fortunate. So you want to look smart at your sister's wedding? Will it be a grand affair?' Rachelle seemed even more like a dog as she worried away with her questions.

Jessie shook her head. 'No, quite small. We've had a family bereavement recently and our mother is not in the best of health.' Bella was a full-blown alcoholic by this time and 'not in the best of health' was a moderate way of putting it.

'Let me see your new outfit,' said Madame Rachelle, settling herself back into the waiting-room chair.

Rosabelle took Jessie into the curtained-off cubicle and they could be heard rustling about, trying on the new clothes. When she emerged, Jessie was a vision, so eye-catching that she took everyone's breath away – even Rosabelle's.

The dress was made of deep purple, stiff material and simply cut with a high neck, long tight sleeves and a generous skirt but no bustle or hoop. The hat made up for its simplicity, however, for it did have a bird on top, a gleaming-breasted bird of paradise with wings outspread and its beak slightly open. Mrs Gibson had kept it in her store cupboard for years after she bought a job lot of trimmings from a travelling theatrical company that ran out of money in the town. Jessie was delighted with it.

The women looking at her balancing it on her head were stunned into silence for a few moments.

Madame Rachelle was the first to recover. Eyeing the hat, she said in her heaviest accent, 'Oh such a bird! Was it shot, do you theenk?' then quickly added, 'My dear, you are wasting that outfit on a small wedding. That outfit could take you to the Palace.'

Mrs Gibson was the only one who realized that the Palace

sarcastically referred to was not the residence of Queen Victoria but a theatre. Jessie beamed, however. Slowly turning round on her heel like an actress on stage, she asked, 'Do you really think so!'

'Of course!' said Rachelle with unconcealed malice.

Rosabelle travelled home in the train with Jessie, who was clutching her precious striped hatbox. 'I'm so pleased with my outfit. You're so clever. It's exactly what I wanted,' she kept saying.

'You'll certainly outshine the bride,' Rosabelle told her, and Jessie giggled, 'That's what I want. But who's that woman who said I could go to the Palace?'

'She's Mrs Gibson's best customer. They say the colonel up at the barracks is keeping her now, but she used to be Tommy Nisbet's mistress. I think she loved him, because I saw her at his funeral and she goes all gentle when she speaks about him. I'm sure she was fonder of him than she is of her new man.'

'I've heard about her. Folk said she was part of Nisbet's smuggling business. I don't know what she did exactly – passed stuff on or stored it for him, perhaps. There's something funny about her, though, don't you think?' Jessie said slowly.

Rosabelle was entranced by Madame Rachelle's glamour, and Jessie's comment surprised her. 'How do you mean, funny?' she asked.

'I mean artificial. Not real. She's acting a part.'

'She's French,' said Rosabelle, as if that was sufficient explanation.

'It's not just that. It's something else. I don't trust her.'

'Oh, you're too suspicious. She's very kind to me, always saying how good my work is . . .'

'Watch out. If you ask me, she's wanting something off you.' Jessie was not going to change her mind, but Rosabelle only shook her head in disbelief. 'Off me? What could she want that I've got?'

When the girls got off the train at Burnmouth, it was dark, and Jessie, knowing how scared Rosabelle was of Anderson, patted her arm and said brightly, 'Let's run all the way home. I'll race you.'

Both were young and fit and, as they went pelting down the hill into the town, watching the lights drawing nearer all the time, they were filled with a wild exhilaration that rapidly disappeared when a figure stepped out from under a beech tree that stood on the last sharp bend in the road.

He held out a hand to stop them. 'What's the hurry? You'll fall if you run so fast,' he said, smiling in an oily way.

Rosabelle, who was winning the race, skidded to a halt and turned back towards her friend, who came panting up, hatbox swinging from her hand. He had not known Rosabelle was with a companion and disappointed surprise showed on his face at the sight of Jessie.

She wasted no time but swung at his head with the striped box, catching him on the temple.

'Fuck off!' she yelled, grabbing Rosabelle's arm, and pulling her along in a headlong dash for home.

The knowledge that Anderson had not given up stalking her unnerved Rosabelle, and next day she stayed in bed, weeping constantly and refusing to eat. It was as if her first terrible grief after Dan's death had returned and was sweeping her away again.

Effie and Jessie were both dismayed because they had begun to hope that working in Berwick would cheer the girl up and give her a new interest in life.

'I'm always feared that she'll go like her mother,' Effie whispered as they stood shaking their heads in the kitchen.

Jessie bent down and lifted Aaron out of his cradle. 'I'll take the bairn up to see if he can brighten her up,' she said, and headed for the stairs.

In a few moments she was back, Aaron beaming happily in her arms. Effie raised her eyebrows in a silent question and Jessie shook her head. 'She cried all the worse when she saw him. She told me to take him away,' she said.

Effie took the baby, kissed the top of his head and laid him back in his cosy nest. 'It's being scared by Anderson again that's put her back,' she said sadly.

'I could kill that bastard,' Jessie replied in a belligerent tone.

Next day Jessie went back to Berwick and told the Gibsons about Rosabelle's illness, but not about her fear of Anderson. The good ladies were upset because they had both come to love their gentle seamstress, and told Jessie that she was to stay at home till she recovered fully.

176

'Things are quiet at the moment and we can manage. The position will be kept open for her and she is not to worry,' said Miss Marie.

Through her wakeful nights it seemed to Rosabelle that she was hanging over the edge of a high cliff and below her was only blackness. She was afraid to go to sleep in case she fell into the abyss and never stopped falling, so she napped intermittently, and when she woke she began crying again.

Effie padded up and down the stairs, bringing food that was always refused, or carrying cups of beef tea laced with teaspoons of whisky, which were accepted.

On her way out to buy food on the fourth morning Effie met the doctor and stopped to say, 'I'm worried about Dan's wife, doctor. Remember her? She's the lassie that had the wee boy and we were afraid she had childbed fever . . .'

He stopped and nodded. 'I remember her well, poor lass. What's the trouble?'

'It's not that she's ill really. It's just that she seems to have given up on life. She lies in bed and weeps, and doesn't care about anything, even the baby. It was her mother that drowned herself and I'm scared in case she tries something like that too.'

He frowned. 'Is she eating?' he asked.

'Beef tea, that's all,' said Effie bleakly.

'Do you want me to come to see her?' he asked, and she nodded.

Rosabelle looked scared when she opened her eyes and saw a man standing by her bedside. Effie, on the other side of the bed, said reassuringly, 'The doctor just wants a wee talk with you,' and went out of the room, leaving them together.

When he asked her what the trouble was, she burst into tears again, 'I don't know, doctor, I just don't know. I keep seeing Dan trying to climb that rock and falling into the water. I can't get it out of my mind. And I feel so tired all the time. All I want to do is sleep but I'm afraid to . . .'

'It was a terrible thing for you to witness,' he said, sitting down by the bed, as she talked and talked in a distraught stream of words, taking him through the death of her beloved husband and her terror of the darkness, though she said nothing about Anderson. In a strange way she was ashamed of arousing such violent feelings in a man.

177

Being listened to by an outsider helped. The sobbing became less anguished and eventually she said, 'Don't tell me I have to go on living, doctor. I know that already. I'm ashamed of myself for being so weak. Jessie lost her Henry and she's not carrying on like this.'

'Take your time. Different people act in different ways. One day soon you will begin to feel better,' he said sympathetically; but, as he walked down the stairs, he wondered how long that would take.

When he heard Effie clinking money in the kitchen, he told her, 'If you try to give me money for talking to that poor girl, I'll be insulted. It's going to take time, but she'll recover. She's lucky to have you to help her.'

Rosabelle got out of bed on the morning of Fanny's wedding, so that she could watch an excited Jessie in her finery going off with the bride and groom to Lamberton Toll.

They walked to the carrier's cart, with Rosabelle carrying Aaron and Effie hugging Henrietta, who was not included in the wedding party and had been specially weaned for the occasion. All stood waving as the wedding party climbed aboard.

Poor plain Fanny, dressed in grey with a black straw bonnet, looked as if she could murder her overdressed sister, but Jessie did not care.

In pale, sparkling sunlight, she sat up high on the carter's box, giggling and ebullient in purple. The outrageous hat looked as if it was about to soar off into the heavens on its own.

'I hope naebody tries to shoot her when she crosses the moor,' Effie muttered, and was delighted when her joke brought a smile to Rosabelle's lips.

Bella, Mary and the boys sat on the back of the cart, sharing a box of caramel sweets that Jessie had given them. Effie hoped they had the sense to keep the box hidden till they were out of town. If Hester Stanhope saw it they would be in trouble.

Jessie turned in her seat as she rode off and waved. She wished she could tell Rosabelle that the reason she was so dressed up was not only because she wanted to annoy Fanny.

She had an assignation after the wedding and was very much looking forward to it.

Eighteen

Marriage brought unforeseen problems for Steven Anderson. The first was his family, and the second was expense.

Because he was ashamed of his mother and sister, he did not invite them to the wedding, or even tell them that he was getting married. Hester was told that both were too unwell to attend.

She accepted that, but continually pressed him to take her to Edinburgh to visit her new in-laws.

'It seems so terrible that we are strangers to each other,' she said.

He made excuses, pleading pressure of work and secretly hoping that his female relations would die before she wore him down. Eventually she dropped the subject, thinking that his mother must be so possessive and jealous of her son that she could not bear the idea of him taking a wife.

In fact, when he imagined leading Hester up the worn stone steps to his family flat, he quailed. The contrast with Beechwood was too glaring to contemplate, because the tenement where his mother lived was truly squalid. The stairs smelt of urine and various vagrants could always be found sleeping on the steps of the lower flight after running the gas from the lamps in the narrow hall into mugs of cheap wine or, occasionally, methylated spirits.

One day, he promised himself, he'd find his family a more salubrious place to live – but that would have to wait, because at the moment he had debts. The elegant suit he bought for his wedding cost more than he'd ever paid for a whole year's clothes before and, moreover, he needed money to jingle in his pocket when he walked round the town with Hester's father.

The tin money box on his desk was a constant reminder of the huge sum of money that he had under his control – money that would probably never be spent. Nobody would ever know if he helped himself to a little of it.

He and his committee had become even more stringent about punishing wrongdoers by withholding their money, and much of the unused surplus went straight into the relief man's pocket; but even that was not enough. Hester was proving to be extremely parsimonious about handing out pocket money to him, and though he now lived in Beechwood with no expenses for food or rent, he still needed funds, because his wage was too low for his newly adopted lifestyle.

Sitting at his desk on a hot summer day, he painstakingly worked out exactly how much of the fund had been disbursed, and what was left.

The pay-out was minuscule, which made him feel virtuous. He'd certainly not thrown money around. There was still £49,000 left. Some of the capital was invested, but the majority of it was lying on deposit. Something ought to be done with it.

He mopped his brow, put on his jacket and walked to the bank. 'I think we ought to do something about investing more of the fund money,' he told the young manager who had replaced McIntyre.

'Were you thinking of government stock?'

'No; a friend of mine is starting a friendly society and it will be very secure and profitable. I think we should put five hundred pounds into it.'

The bank manager furrowed his brow. 'Can we legally do that?'

'Of course the other committee members will have to agree. I'll ask them and let you know.'

It was easy to win round his colleagues to his plan. He deliberately did not ask Alan Cochrane, who seemed to go out of his way to question everything these days.

On the following day he told Hester that he was going to Edinburgh on fund business. Her face brightened. 'I'll come with you. We can go to see your mother.'

He shook his head. 'It's money business, my dear. I'll go up on one train and return on the next. There'll be no time for visiting.'

With the money in his pocket, he opened a bank account in his own name at a palatial bank in George Street. It was difficult to conceal his awe and admiration as he stared round the magnificent central hall with its stained-glass windows, highly polished wooden counters and marble pillars rearing up to a domed glass roof. Because he had a considerable sum to deposit, he was received with a politeness that made him feel godlike.

After the transaction was completed, he said to the clerk, 'I think I'll take out some money to tide me over for the meantime.'

'Certainly, sir; how much would you like?'

He frowned. 'A hundred will do for now, I think.'

Before he returned to Eyemouth he paid a call on his mother and sister and gave them five pounds each. Even then he did not tell them that he was now a married man.

There's no point confusing them with too much information, he told himself.

Having money in his pocket was heady. He bestowed a few coins on the complaisant widows, and next day slipped sixpence to Jean, the little scullery maid at Beechwood, who could not fight him off when he slipped his hand inside her blouse and threw her on to the floor of the back pantry where she was meant to be cleaning the knives. Like all his encounters, it was over in seconds, and she was too scared of him to scream.

The other maids found her weeping and she told them her story. When they saw him after that, they fled at his approach. Once again, the thought that women were rejecting him acted like a spur, and he began stealthily prowling the corridors at night, trying to get into the maids' bedrooms. Fortunately for him, Hester was a heavy sleeper and the girls were careful to shove chairs under their door handles to keep him out.

But they talked about him to the girls in the washhouse.

'Imagine, he took poor wee Jean against her will and him only newly married!' they exclaimed.

'He's a bad lot,' said Jessie. 'Why didn't Jean tell Miss Hester what he'd done?'

The oldest maid stared hard at her in disbelief and asked, 'And what do you think would happen then? Jean would be sent off without a reference. Miss Hester wouldn't believe a word of it. She'd say it was all lies.'

Two months after he first took money from the fund, Anderson was back at the Eyemouth bank. All smiles, he laid fifty pounds

181

left from his original hundred on the manager's desk and said, 'Pay that into the fund, sir; it's interest on the five hundred I invested with my friend. Ten per cent is a good return in such a short time, isn't it?'

The manager was suitably impressed, and when Anderson returned a month later – *You mustn't rush these things*, he thought – to ask for another five hundred to invest, he was given it with alacrity. It was almost too easy, and he wished his father and sister knew how clever he was. That would make them eat all those cruel words about him being a dunce.

During all those machinations he could only spare an occasional thought for the girl with the yellow hair. He knew she was no longer working with Mrs Lyall because he kept his eye on the dress shop. When Jessie collected her weekly money, he dared not ask where Rosabelle had gone, because he remembered her violent reaction to his attempt to waylay them on the way from Burnmouth.

His wife was the one who told him the girl had gone to the Gibsons in Berwick. When she was planning her winter wardrobe, she paid a call on Mrs Lyall and asked if Rosabelle would make her a dinner gown.

'I'm afraid she no longer works with me. I had to get rid of her. But I'll be happy to make you a dinner gown, Mrs Anderson,' said Mrs Lyall.

Hester's face fell. She'd been happy enough with Mrs Lyall's creations for years, but the wedding dress had raised her standards.

'I suppose that girl's gone back to fish-gutting,' she said.

The dressmaker shook her head. 'Not yet. She's found a position with the Gibsons in Hide Hill at Berwick. They make a lot of clothes for the garrison wives, but I don't think Rosabelle is up to that. Those women are very demanding.'

Hester shook her head and ordered a dinner gown. But she could afford more than one, and was determined to make a trip to Berwick to try out the Gibson establishment.

That night at dinner she said to her husband, 'What about going to Berwick soon? We can borrow Father's barouche for the trip.'

Feeling expansive because of the money in his pocket, he

beamed. 'Anything you want, my dear. When would you like to go?'

'Tomorrow, perhaps. There's a dressmaker there I'd like to see. Do you remember my wedding dress?'

He nodded. 'Indeed I do. You looked like a queen in it.'

'Well, the girl who made it used to be employed by Mrs Lyall in the town, but she's gone to Berwick and works there for another dressmaker. I want a new winter wardrobe, because I seem to be growing a little larger round the waist. I think I might have something nice to tell you soon.' Her voice became coy.

Her father, who was glumly and silently eating his dinner without apparently listening to what they were saying, looked up with new animation and asked, 'Are you expecting a child, Hester?'

She blushed scarlet. 'Oh Father, don't be so direct. It's just a suspicion . . .'

'Then let's hope it's well grounded. I want a grandchild. I miss having children around the house,' said the old man.

Then he looked at his son-in-law and thought, *Maybe he's good for something after all*, because as far as he was concerned Anderson had not improved with greater acquaintance. In fact, he would even have preferred her to marry the minister, because there was something about the relief man that disturbed him.

Anderson felt as if he'd received a jab in the chest when he heard Hester talking about the girl in the dress shop. As casually as he could manage, he asked, 'Do you mean that tall girl with the yellow hair, one of the disaster widows?'

'Yes, that's her. She's some relation to that pert little piece who washes our aprons, but she's a clever dressmaker. I want to give her a try.'

'I'm rather busy, but I'll come with you to Berwick,' he said benignly, cutting a chunk off a slab of Cheddar cheese. He was looking forward to the trip and thought it would be amusing to confront Rosabelle at her new place of work.

They rode to Berwick in style on a fine autumn afternoon and alighted at the door of the Gibson establishment. When old Mrs Gibson saw a man with her new client, she was discomfited: to be fitted, women had to take off their dresses and stand in their petticoats. It was not appropriate for men to be present.

'Would you mind waiting in the parlour, sir?' she asked, and he was forced into a little, over-furnished room on the other side of the hall. This did not please him at all.

'Will it take long?' he asked, pouting.

'Oh no, sir. I will just discuss your wife's requirements and call in my dressmaker to measure her. It won't take any time at all.'

The information about calling in the dressmaker was what he wanted. 'I'll wait,' he said, and took care to leave the parlour door slightly ajar.

After about ten minutes, he heard a bell ringing in the salon. From upstairs a door opened and feet sounded on the stairs. Jumping up, he ran across to the door and peered into the hall. Rosabelle was coming down the stairs and she looked even more beautiful than before. His heart leaped at the sight of her.

When her foot landed on the tiled floor of the hall, he stepped through the door and smiled at her. Caught unawares, she looked straight into his face and staggered, putting out a hand to the newel post.

'Good afternoon Mrs Scott,' he said, bowing in what he hoped was a sarcastic way.

She said nothing, only stared wide-eyed at him. *I'll never be rid of him*, she thought. Her eyes were blue-green like the sea, he noticed.

There was another ring from the bell, and Mrs Gibson's voice called out, 'Rosabelle!' so she brushed past him and ran into the salon.

Satisfied at having upset her, he went back into the parlour and settled down to wait for Hester. The girl he'd waylaid was shaking and her heart racing when she went into the salon. It was only with a great effort of will that she calmed down and was able to concentrate on the task in hand.

To her relief, Anderson and his wife rode off in their carriage before she emerged into the hall again. *It doesn't matter if he knows where I work now. He can't do anything to me*, she told herself.

Seeing Rosabelle again, however, re-awakened Anderson's passion. He did not accept that she was too startled to compose herself when he appeared, and went over and over the way her blue-green eyes fixed themselves on his face. Her look had been open, direct, even challenging – not disdainful any longer. She'd learned her lesson.

Now that he had money in his pocket and was wearing smart clothes, he was sure that she wouldn't withstand him. She was just a seamstress. He could buy her.

He knew that she had two possible ways of getting to Berwick: by the carter, or on the train. Next evening he lurked in the dark passages of the fishing town till he saw her hurrying home.

After that he waited on the outskirts of the town at the same time and saw her walking down the hill from Burnmouth, so worked out that she used the train.

Though he watched her, he hurried away and did not accost her. He was laying his plans carefully.

By the time of Mrs Anderson's visit – and substantial order – Rosabelle was well established in Mrs Gibson's esteem.

The main business of the shop on Hide Hill had always been selling frills and furbelows; a small but select group of women, however, also went there to have gowns made, and as the new girl's fame spread, that clientele was growing.

As she felt easier in her new job, Rosabelle's confidence and peace of mind grew too. The kind Mrs Gibson and her daughter Marie were pleased to notice that, a couple of weeks after her return from the bout of illness, her tense expression began to soften and she even smiled sometimes.

For her own part, Rosabelle was feeling a little happier, especially because during her working hours she was out of sight of the sea. She had not realized how much she hated it, and how much it dominated her life at Eyemouth. Even on fine days, she was aware of it murmuring away in the background, and on wild days its roaring terrified her. Whenever she raised her head and stared at the horizon, she saw the Hurkars and remembered Dan's terrible death.

In Berwick, her view was of busy streets, shops and Mrs Gibson's pretty garden. The sea was well hidden beyond the ancient town walls.

When her employers found out that she rose at five o'clock in the morning to ride in the carter's dray to work, they were horrified and asked, 'Why don't you come by train?'

'There's no station in Eyemouth – only at Burnmouth, two miles away.'

'But wouldn't that still be quicker for you?'

'Probably, but the carter brings me in for nothing because he knows my mother-in-law. I'd have to buy a ticket for the train.'

'My dear, we were going to give you a rise because your work is so good, but let us pay for your train ticket instead,' said Miss Marie.

So Rosabelle could now stay in bed till half past six and arrive fresh, dry and not wind-blown even in the worst weather.

She liked the Gibsons and her confidence grew as she realized that they liked her too. Because she'd never really been out of Eyemouth, she was shy and unsure of herself anywhere else. What also boosted her was the praise her work received from the Gibsons' clientele – especially from Madame Rachelle.

Some customers specified precisely what they wanted, or brought illustrations cut out of magazines for her to copy; but others, like Rachelle, came in with swathes of materials and asked the Gibsons to devise eye-catching creations out of them.

She was the most demanding client of all and preened and pirouetted in front of the pier glass, holding lengths of cloth up against herself. 'Give me some ideas! What do I do with this?' she imperiously demanded in her strange foreign accent. She gave them to understand that English was not her native language, though she never seemed to be at loss for words.

To please her, dresses had to be extravagant and daring, more London or Paris in style than Berwick, and heads turned in the streets of the town when she swished by, which, of course, was the effect she wanted to create.

At first Rosabelle was too much in awe of her to speak during fittings, but stood silent beside Miss Marie, carrying tailor's chalk or papers of pins while the worried little woman ran round Madame Rachelle pinning up here or draping there. It was on the day that the customer brought in a luscious length of figured crimson satin that the girl found her tongue.

'I want a ball gown. I see it with a huge skirt – over a hoop at the back, perhaps – and a train that I'll carry over my arm,' said Madame Rachelle.

Unable to stop herself, Rosabelle fingered the material. It

186

was so soft and luscious, she wanted to rub it against her cheek but didn't dare. The colour was like rubies, which would set off Rachelle's milk-white skin and jet-black hair.

'Don't have a big skirt and certainly don't have a hoop. This dress should be fitted, long and flowing, like a statue . . .' she blurted out, making a long, elegant shape with her hands.

Rachelle stared at her, eyes sharp. 'Could you make a dress like that?' she asked.

'I could try.'

'It's not a question of trying. This material is French and cost a fortune. Could you make the dress?'

'Yes, I could.'

Rachelle bundled up the valuable cloth and thrust it at the girl. 'All right. Do it. I want to wear it in three days' time at the garrison ball.'

As she held the lovely stuff in her arms, Rosabelle wondered how she was going to carry out the commission in such a short time; but she'd said she could, and she was not going to let the Gibsons down by changing her mind.

The first thing to do was make a template pattern. Mrs Gibson helped because she had Madame Rachelle's measurements. The two of them ran to and fro round the cutting table with enormous scissors in their hands, almost afraid to be the first one to cut into the lovely material.

Rosabelle eventually took the plunge and daringly clipped out a panel for the front of the skirt.

On the third day the scarlet gown was almost finished, but when Madame Rachelle arrived to collect it, Rosabelle was still putting in the finishing stitches and the imperious client was barely able to conceal her impatience.

'I can't wait. I have no time to try it now. My cab is outside. Bring the dress and come with me. You can fit it on me in my rooms. In fact you can sew me into it. I want it to be skin-tight,' she said, rapping her parasol sharply on the floor.

Rosabelle was in confusion. She heard the town clock chiming five from the end of Marygate. 'I'll finish the dress for you, madame,' said Mrs Gibson; but Rachelle ignored that and spoke to Rosabelle, for she wanted only the talented girl to make her dress.

'You can stay the night with me!' she said grandly, but Mrs

Gibson saw the expression of panic on Rosabelle's face at that suggestion.

She said, 'But if I miss my train my mother-in-law will worry about me.'

Mrs Gibson said reassuringly, 'I'll send a message to Eyemouth for your family. Write a note and say you'll be on the later train.'

Rosabelle flushed scarlet. She could sign her name with considerable effort, but writing a note, especially in front of strangers, was beyond her.

Kind Mrs Gibson saw the girl's confusion and in a flash understood the reason, so she said quickly, 'But you're too busy to write notes now. I'll do it for you and send it off with the messenger boy. Who should it be addressed to?'

'To Effie Young, at Jimmy Dip's house. If the boy goes to the Ship Inn on the harbour side, they'll direct him from there,' Rosabelle stammered.

With the dress in her arms she was bustled out of the salon before she had time to think, and driven to Rachelle's rooms on the first floor of an elegant Georgian house further up Hide Hill, nearer the barracks.

The furnishings were very ornate. Swagged curtains framed the windows, gilt-wood chairs with green satin upholstery stood around an oval maple table, and there were china figurines everywhere, gesturing from the chimneypiece, from the top of a bookcase and on every spindle-legged side table. The lighting was flickering wax candles in gilt sconces.

While Rosabelle worked on the dress, Madame Rachelle pouted in front of a round mirror, painting on her maquillage. First of all she cleaned her daytime cosmetics off, and when Rosabelle looked up and caught sight of her at that stage, she was surprised by how ordinary the mystery woman looked. Positively plain, in fact.

After the application of white skin cream, red rouge, black eyebrow pencil, lip salve, eyelash darkener, and face powder splashed generously all over the body from an enormous feathery powder puff, however, a work of art re-emerged and Rachelle, in underskirt and tightly laced corset, turned round on her stool to beam at the dressmaker.

Rosabelle would have died before she took off her clothes

in front of anyone but Dan, but this woman seemed to have no qualms about parading around in hardly anything at all.

'Now for the gown,' Rachelle said, exultantly stretching out her arms.

The red dress fitted like another skin. Two broad straps went over the white shoulders and the bodice plunged into a deep declivity between generous, powdered breasts. Rachelle's waist was already tiny, but Rosabelle was told to pull the client's corset laces tighter, and she wondered how Madame would ever manage to breathe, far less eat anything.

The skirt was draped over her hips into a long fishtail at the back and drawn tight across the legs to the feet, leaving only the tips of black kid dancing pumps peeping out. At last, satisfied, Rosabelle stood back and surveyed her handiwork. The effect was stunning.

'Sew me in. I can't take the risk of any hooks and eyes popping open,' cried Madame Rachelle, pirouetting in delight in front of her mirror.

'But how will you get out of it after the ball?' Rosabelle wanted to know.

Rachelle laughed gaily. 'My dear, that's not a worry. My friend will take it off me, I've no doubt – and he'll enjoy doing it.'

Rosabelle flushed and the other woman, noticing her embarrassment, laughed. 'What a prude you are,' she said mockingly, and began to take mincing steps around the room to make sure she could move in the new gown.

Then she looked back over her shoulder and suddenly, sensing the bleakness that filled the young woman who watched her dancing about so light-heartedly, said gently, 'You're a very clever girl and a very pretty one. Have you ever been to a ball?'

Rosabelle shook her head and said witheringly, 'No.'

'Can you dance?' asked Rachelle, remembering that Eyemouth was a fishing village, and she'd heard that dancing was forbidden in some fishing communities for religious reasons. Did the girl come from one of them?

'Oh yes, I can dance,' said Rosabelle, remembering summer nights when a fiddler played on the quayside and townspeople, young and old, danced to his music. Her skin prickled as she remembered Dan's arms around her, lifting her off her feet, and his white teeth flashing as he laughed down into her face. The awful sadness that filled her was too much to bear and, in spite of her determination not to yield, tears filled her eyes.

'Yes, I can dance, but I haven't done much of it recently. I'm a widow,' she said shortly, turning her face away.

Rachelle stopped dead, taken aback. Shamefacedly, she said, 'Oh, I'm so sorry. I didn't know. But you're too young to be a widow – hardly old enough to be a wife. How old *are* you, for goodness' sake?'

'Twenty-one. My husband was drowned in the fishing disaster.'

As she spoke, Rosabelle realized with dread how much sadness had filled her life since Dan died.

When she saw how the girl trembled, Madame Rachelle's whole manner changed – even her voice became different, less foreign, and more natural. 'Someone I loved was drowned that day too,' she said.

'I know. I saw you at his funeral,' Rosabelle said bleakly.

As if she wanted to hide her face, Rachelle turned away and began fiddling with her earrings, struggling ineffectually to thread their long metal wires through the pierced holes. There were tears in the painted eyes. Putting in earrings was only a diversion. Eventually she succeeded and by that time her composure had returned. The French accent was back too.

'He was a very amusing and special man. I met him in Dieppe and came here to be near him,' she said in a sudden burst of confidence.

'A lot of special men died that day,' Rosabelle agreed bitterly.

There was a bond between them now.

'But life goes on, you know. Don't forget that. You're young; you have a lot of living in front of you. Would you like to start by coming to the ball with me?' asked Rachelle.

Rosabelle was horrified. 'Oh! No, no. I couldn't.'

'Why not? You've never been to a ball and this one is very grand. It's the start of the Christmas season.'

Holding out the skirt of her blue working dress, Rosabelle said, 'Don't mock me. How could I go to a ball dressed like this?'

'I'm not mocking you. We're almost the same height and the same build. You could wear one of my gowns. I have many.' Rachelle was once again looking at herself in the mirror and fastening a sparkling necklace round her neck.

Are those diamonds? Rosabelle wondered as she stared at the glittering stones.

As if she could read her mind, Rachelle laughed: 'Only paste, my dear, but good paste. Did you hear what I said about giving you a dress?'

'Yes, but I don't feel like going to a ball.' Rosabelle wondered if this woman was playing some sort of game with her.

'So you plan to mourn for ever?' The necklace was being adjusted into place so that its large central pendant hung down between the generous breasts.

'Probably.' A short, crisp reply.

'What a shame. You are so lovely. I've been thinking that I could launch you into society. I could make your fortune. Let me dress you up and you will cause a sensation at the ball.'

'*No.*' The tone was stern; Rosabelle found it difficult to stay barely polite, remembering that Madame Rachelle was a good customer of the Gibsons and must be kept sweet. She twisted the plump velvet wrist pad of pins on her arm and said abruptly, 'Are you satisfied with your dress, madame? Can I go now?'

But the client was persistent once she had an idea in her head. 'If your husband truly loved you he wouldn't want you to spend the rest of your life mourning.'

A red tide of colour rose up Rosabelle's neck and over her cheeks. 'You don't know what Dan would want. Or what I want. Please let me go home.'

Suddenly repentant, Rachelle crossed the room and put a hand on the girl's sleeve, saying, 'Forgive me. I've been watching you at the Gibsons' and thought it would be amusing to bring some excitement into your life. It's sad to see you so weighed down with sorrow. At least let me show you the ball – it might sharpen your taste for society.'

Her flow of talk seemed unstoppable and though Rosabelle tried, she could not get in a word.

'If you were ever to leave your little town, you could make your way anywhere, especially with such talent. I could do so much for you. No, don't interrupt. Listen. Accompany me to the ball. Come as my lady's maid to make sure that your wonderful dress is properly arranged before I make my grand entrance. You want it to look its best, don't you? I'll find you a seat on the balcony and you can watch what goes on.'

Rosabelle was shaking her head, but Rachelle still did not give up. 'It'll be better than going to the theatre, believe me. I'll make sure you get home safely. I'll send you back in a carriage, like Cinderella,' she said.

'I've never been to a theatre either and I don't think—' Rosabelle was trying to go on refusing but was stopped by an imperious hand held up in front of her.

'No! I really need you to arrange my skirts. Your work is not finished yet. The cab is outside. We must go now. I'm late already. He'll be furious.'

There was nothing to do but agree. 'Then please make sure I get home tonight,' protested Rosabelle, but she went with Rachelle, intrigued in spite of herself.

The ball was held in the huge assembly hall of the army barracks at the top of Hide Hill. Their cab rumbled through the guarded entrance gate into a vast courtyard that was lit with blazing flambeaux on long poles. Uniformed guards, rifles by their sides, stood ramrod-stiff at the main door.

Guests were milling about – some of the men in ordinary evening clothes but most in brilliant military uniforms with brass buttons and gold or silver braiding. All were accompanied by beautifully dressed women in vast crinoline dresses with skirts that swept the ground and flowers in their hair or tucked into their corsages.

In spite of her anxiety at being whisked into this scene Rosabelle was gratified to see that Madame Rachelle's gown, with its long narrow skirt, was the only one that did not take up a vast area of space; but in spite of that it attracted every female eye.

A choleric-looking grey-haired man in a scarlet uniform with huge gold-fringed epaulettes, a sash and a row of glittering medals on his chest, came hurrying out of the porch when Rachelle's cab rolled up. His irritation melted away when she smiled graciously at him from the cab window, and as they dismounted she whispered to Rosabelle, 'That's my man – Colonel Fairweather, veteran of the Crimea. Will you carry my shawl, please?'

When she spoke to the Colonel, she sounded even more foreign than ever, rolling her words as if they were sweetmeats in her mouth. 'My darleeng, you look magnificent. All day I have been longing to see you,' she said, laying her gloved hand on his arm.

He visibly relaxed. 'Come on, my dear. We must hurry. I have to receive the important guests inside.'

Rachelle took his arm and whispered something in his ear. He raised one white-gloved hand to summon a young officer who was waiting nearby. 'Find madame's maid a seat on the balcony and see that she is well looked after,' he ordered.

Rosabelle, still clutching Rachelle's shawl, watched as the pair swept off through the door and, as it opened, a blast of intoxicating music came through and filled her with a feeling of exhilaration.

The young officer who had been assigned to look after her was impressed by her golden beauty and smiled as he said, 'Come this way, miss. I'll find you a good place.'

She followed. There was nothing else she could do.

He was most attentive as he installed her in a chair beside a line of ladies' maids and chaperons who were all leaning over the balcony rail, discussing the people milling around beneath them. They paid no attention to the newcomer.

When Rachelle appeared out of the antechamber on the arm of her silver-haired escort, there was a concerted in-drawing of breath, and a stern-looking older woman among the watchers said, 'Look at that French hussy! She's got her claws into the Colonel now. His wife only died eighteen months ago.'

'She moves fast, that one,' said another woman, who looked like a genteel lady's maid.

'It was Major Blackshaw last season, but the Colonel has more money, and he's the son of a duke,' added another, as they all leaned further over to get a good view of Rachelle, who obliged them by finding a position in an open space and slowly turning to show herself off. She did indeed look magnificent.

The most genteel lady's maid of all sighed. 'But what a beautiful gown. I've never seen anything so elegant. Where do you think she got it?'

'That wasn't made in Berwick, I'm sure. It probably came from Paris and cost enough to pay all our wages for a year!' snapped the stern woman.

In spite of her fear at being whisked off to the ball, Rosabelle hugged herself in delight and pride. It was wonderful to hear her work being so highly praised.

She was wondering how to make her escape when the attentive officer returned carrying a fluted glass full of sparkling golden liquid. 'From the Colonel's lady for you, miss,' he said, handing it over.

The glass felt very cold in her hand and she looked at it suspiciously. 'What is it?' she asked.

He laughed. 'Champagne. It'll put bubbles in your brain.'

It did. The wine seemed to explode in her mouth and shocked her, but within seconds, it was also making her feel unexpectedly carefree. She leaned on to the padded shelf of the balcony rail and stared down at Rachelle, who smiled slyly back as if she was saying, *I told you so! I'm going to make it my business to change your life.*

That first glass of champagne was followed by another, as the music swelled and resounded from the high roof, filling Rosabelle with the sort of wild wonder and delight that she had not felt for a very long time.

When an attentive waiter in soldier's uniform appeared with a napkin-covered tray of delicious food, the other women stared at her in envy, because they would not be allowed to eat until the important guests had finished at the buffet.

Ignoring their stares, Rosabelle delicately picked at fish, chicken in aspic and little pastry cases with delicious but, to her, unidentifiable fillings. There were slices of ham and beef cut so thin they were transparent, as well as sweets made of tiny fingers of paper-thin pastry covered with chocolate that melted in her mouth.

When the hands of the clock at the end of the hall showed eleven, she began to panic, however, knowing Effie would be distracted with worry about her. She'd never been out so late in her life.

Leaning over the balcony, she saw Rachelle circling the ballroom in the arms of an officer with a bristling black moustache. She had no idea how to escape, but stood up and draped the shawl over the edge of the balcony as a signal she wanted to make her getaway.

Obviously it was spotted, because within a few moments the young captain was back with a message: 'Madame Rachelle has asked me to tell you that a carriage is waiting to take you home, miss. If you will come this way,' he said, holding back the thick velvet curtain that framed the back of the balcony.

A smart hansom, driven by a grizzled-looking soldier, stood at a side door. Rosabelle climbed in, handing Rachelle's shawl to the captain, and within five minutes fell sound asleep, wrapped up in a thick travelling rug that the driver tucked round her.

At midnight, blinking and only half awake, she alighted outside Effie's house.

Since the incident with Anderson, Effie had taken to locking the door, so she had to knock heavily on the wooden panels to wake her up. Effie came to the threshold in her long night-gown, looking furious and obviously considering whether she should box Rosabelle's ears; but in fact relief softened her when she saw the white-faced girl.

'I was afraid that awful man had got hold of you,' she snapped.

'I'm sorry, but I had to finish a ball gown and the woman who ordered it wanted me to go to the ball to make sure it looked right on her,' Rosabelle gasped incoherently. 'Then she sent me home in a carriage.'

'All the way from Berwick!' Effie was astonished, staring out at the man behind the reins, who cheerfully lifted his whip and called, 'Good night, miss!'

As Rosabelle waved back, she felt herself coming back down to earth – back to Eyemouth, back to sorrow and sad memories. The memory of champagne and the wonderful kaleidoscope of the ball already seemed like a dream.

None of them saw a dark figure hiding in the shadow of a house wall at the end of the alley. Steven Anderson had been making his late-night promenade of the town and, as it often did, his route took him past the house where Rosabelle lived.

When he heard the trotting feet of a horse and the rumble of wheels – an unusual thing in the fishing town so late at night – he stepped back into the shadows of an alley. When the woman of his dreams alighted and waved goodbye to a man in soldier's uniform, a bubble of rage exploded in his brain.

She'd found herself a man! He'd convinced himself that she was virtuous and that was the reason she refused him, but now he had proof that she was only a trollop, as bad as the rest of them.

Nineteen

Steven Anderson lost his mind that winter.

His wife's pregnancy was advancing and he dreaded the time when she would be padding through the house, bearing her belly in front of her like a high-pooped Spanish galleon.

Meanwhile she was blooming. *How can the woman look so* fertile*?* he wondered, eyeing her with distaste as if it had nothing to do with him.

When she talked to him, he barely bothered to answer, because he was totally taken up with worry about Rosabelle Scott.

Who was the soldier who brought her home so late? How could such an ordinary man win her – for he was sure that there must be some sexual connection between them – when she disdained him? If he could find the fellow, he would kill him.

Or he might kill her. If he was not to have her, no one else should.

His thoughts darted around like maddened bees. Sometimes he was laying plans to waylay her at night on her way home from Burnmouth and murder her. It would be easy to leave her body in the woods. No one would ever suspect him, because there was no apparent connection between them.

Then, next day, he'd devise a different plan. What he must do was abduct her. Waylay her, certainly, but ride off with her into England or even to France. Once he had her to himself, he'd win her round. Especially if he was able to impress her.

The more he thought about that idea, the more it appealed to him. The only problem was that it required money. In his secret cache there was now about ninety pounds, but if he and Rosabelle were to stay away for ever, he'd need more than that.

So he set himself the task of amassing enough, and decided that he needed at least £300. His financial horizons had widened since he'd been introduced to the disaster fund.

Because his first fake investment scheme was a success, he decided to try it again.

Removing another £100 from his bank account in Edinburgh, he went back to the Eyemouth bank and proudly laid the money on the counter. Beaming, he told the manager, 'Pay that back into the fund. It's interest from the friendly-society investment. Very good, isn't it? My friend is anxious to expand. I think it would be a good idea to invest more, don't you?'

It was almost too easy. When another hundred was paid into his own bank account, he removed fifty, which was earmarked for repayment into the Eyemouth bank after a reasonable lapse of time.

In the meantime, he kept a surreptitious eye on Rosabelle, prowling the alleys of the fishing town at night and peering into Effie's kitchen window, watching the women inside sitting by the fire or cuddling the babies.

Soon he knew every detail of her domestic life: the time she went to bed, where Effie kept their house key, which window was left ajar for the cat, the sort of things they ate and when they went to collect water from the standpipe.

Hester was upset by his habit of nocturnal prowling, but he explained that he suffered from insomnia and a late-night stroll down to the sea was a good way of ensuring a night's sound sleep.

Most times when he got home she was snoring in their big bed, and for that he was grateful, because her pregnant body repelled him.

As he climbed into bed one freezing night, he looked at the mound that was his wife under the bedclothes and thought, *Only another month or six weeks till I'm ready to go. She won't miss me because at least I've given her a baby.*

She was only feigning sleep, however, and as if his thoughts had been transferred to her, she heaved round and asked him, 'Where have you been?'

'You know where I go: down to the harbour to watch the sea. It's high tonight.'

'Have you been hanging around those women down there?'

He spluttered, 'What women?'

'The ones who visit your office and lie down with you on the carpet.'

197

'You're mad, Hester. You're having a fancy. It's because of your condition.'

'I'm not mad. I know about the women who used to come to your office, but if I find out you're still playing around with them, my father will have you run out of town.'

When she turned back and closed her eyes again, he knew she was not making an idle threat.

'But I love you,' he tried, wheedling.

She turned back. 'Do you? You haven't laid a hand on me for two months.'

He put on an outraged look. 'What sort of man do you think I am to take out my – passions – on a pregnant woman? I'm respecting your condition.'

'That's hardly necessary. I'm only five months gone. My friends tell me it's perfectly safe to still have . . . relations.' Both of them were mealy-mouthed and could not bring themselves to be more specific.

Silently he groaned, though making endearing noises, and climbed on top of her to perform a perfunctory coupling; but it quietened her down, and soon they were both asleep.

Unknown to her, Hester's father was watching the deterioration of his daughter's marriage with concern.

His sharp eyes noticed how Anderson barely listened to anything his wife said, and he registered the expressions of distaste on the man's face when he was forced to make gestures of affection to her. Stanhope's worst fears were being realized. His poor deluded daughter had married a fortune hunter.

He'd always found Hester difficult, but she was his child and, worst of all, it irked him that Anderson hoped to step into his hard-earned fortune.

'Goddam,' he swore, 'I'm not going to let the bounder off with it.'

Quietly, and without exciting too much interest, he set about finding out as much as possible about his son-in-law, castigating himself for not having done that before.

It took a little time; during those weeks that followed Anderson repeated his friendly-society scheme again, for another £100 – slow but sure, he'd decided – and his father-in-law was making discreet enquiries about his activities.

198

Because he was not on the relief-fund committee he picked up hints about the finances here and there. From the ministers who were customers at his store he discovered that the fund was in a healthy state because Mr Anderson had done some astute investing.

The new bank manager's brains were easy to pick. Because he wanted to ingratiate himself with such an important customer, he complimented Stanhope on the acumen of his son-in-law. 'Thanks to him, the fund is getting a tremendous rate of interest on some of its investments,' he said.

Stanhope beamed. 'That's good. What rate does the money earn?'

'As much as ten per cent – but not in a year, only in a matter of weeks, really,' boasted the bank man.

'My word, I'll have to get Steven to put me on to that. But I hope that all the money is not being put into one investment. The higher they rise, the lower they fall, remember that,' warned Stanhope, and the warning took root. The bank manager decided that the next time Anderson asked for money to invest with his friend, he would exercise caution and suggest letting things lie for the moment.

There was a frown on Stanhope's face as he left the bank. A few days later he rode out in his carriage to the elegant home of the local MP, and with him he took a large wicker hamper packed with some of the rarest delicacies from his shop, plus a bottle of port and another of fine cognac.

The MP was used to petitioners bearing gifts and was surprised when Stanhope did not seem to have a favour to ask. He looked at the hamper and said, 'How kind of you to give me such a generous gift, Mr Stanhope.'

'I am only repaying your help,' said the old man.

'My help?' Elegant eyebrows were raised and the MP's mind was racked, but he had no memory of doing any such thing.

'You introduced me to Mr Steven Anderson, the disaster-fund administrator, and he is now happily married to my only daughter. I'm very grateful to you for that.'

A splutter and a smile. 'My dear sir, I only asked a friend in Edinburgh for a recommendation so we could find someone to run the fund. How is it going, by the way?'

'Very satisfactorily. He's done well – an inspired choice. How did your friend find him?'

'My friend is on the Edinburgh Council, and Anderson was a junior assistant to his friend, Robert Shaw, the Poor Law Officer there.'

'As I said, you did both Eyemouth and my family a favour,' smiled Stanhope, and made his departure.

His next step was to write to his son Everard and ask him to contact Anderson's previous superior in Edinburgh to find out something of his background. When Everard received his father's letter, he was not surprised because, during his short acquaintance with his new brother-in-law, he had not warmed to the man, and shared his father's reservations.

Everard liked intrigue and set one of his clerks on Anderson's trail but did not explain why he wanted the information.

Within a day the man was back with an address where his quarry had lived while he worked in the city.

Everard frowned: 'Leith Walk? Which part?'

'St James Square,' said the clerk. They looked at each other. The square was a well-known slum.

'In a very poor building,' added the clerk.

'You found the rooms?'

'Yes. In a tenement. An old lady and her daughter live there. The man you're after is the old lady's son.'

Everard wrote to his father with this information, and asked, 'Do you want me to meet with his mother?'

Mr Stanhope thought about this for a while and, at dinner a couple of nights later, deliberately brought the subject round to family. 'Wouldn't it be a good idea to invite your mother and sister to visit us here? They've never met Hester and, now that you are expecting a child, surely it would be good for them to make each other's acquaintance?' he asked his son-in-law.

Anderson never flinched. 'I'm afraid my mother is unable to travel. She is bed-ridden now, and her mind is going too. It's a great grief to me.'

Hester looked up. 'Who takes care of her?' she asked.

'My sister is also an invalid, but devoted to her mama. She never leaves her side. They have a maid, of course, and are quite comfortable in their little house. When the baby comes, Hester and I will be able to go to show it to mother – if she is still alive,' he said in a forlorn tone.

That decided Stanhope. He knew enough about Edinburgh to know that by no stretch of the imagination could a tenement in St James Square be described as 'comfortable' or a 'little house'.

It was necessary to stalk his quarry quietly, however. He let a week pass before he said he was taking a trip to visit his wine supplier in Leith. He did this about twice a year and it aroused no curiosity in his daughter. All she did was fuss around him on the morning of his departure, winding his scarf round his neck and warning him not to catch cold on his way to the train on such a chilly morning.

He was sunk in thought during both his carriage and train trip, and hired a hansom at Waverley Station to drive him the short distance to St James Square.

'You sure you want to go there, sir?' the cabbie asked curiously, eyeing the old man's elegant clothes and shiny silk hat. His walking cane had a chased-silver handle and he looked rich.

'Quite sure,' said Stanhope solemnly. Everard had provided him with the exact address and when they drew up in a rubbish-littered courtyard, Stanhope looked around in disquiet and said, 'Wait here for me, will you?'

The cabbie thought that a good idea, and added, 'If I were you, I'd leave that fine walking stick in the cab too.'

Stanhope allowed himself a wintry smile. 'Is it as bad as that?'

'It's worse,' said the man on the box.

The building he sought was eight storeys high. A ragged crowd of filthy, bare-footed children and a few disreputable-looking men huddled in its open doorway and drew aside reluctantly to let him push his way in. Only the stern eye of the watching cabbie stopped some of the men following the old man.

After he climbed five flights to the room he wanted he was panting and nauseated by the filthy ammonia smell that seeped up the stair like a stomach-turning fog.

A door stood ajar and he rapped on it with his gloved hand. A voice from inside called on him to come in.

The room was dark and gloomy because the window was

tiny and none too clean. Two women were standing in the middle of the floor, staring at him.

'What d'ye want?' the youngest asked in a scared voice. She was about thirty-five, with a whey-coloured face and straggly hair.

'Good morning,' said Stanhope; 'I'm looking for Mrs Anderson.'

'That's me. I'm Mrs Anderson,' said the second woman, who was slightly shorter and older but, as far as he could see, perfectly fit and in her right mind, because her eyes were sharp and curious.

'My name is Robert Stanhope and my daughter Hester is married to your son Steven,' he said, holding out his hand.

The two women stared at him as if he was mad. 'Steven married? To your daughter? That's not possible. He's never said a word about it.'

'When did you last see him?' he asked.

They looked at each other. 'Two weeks ago?' said the daughter, looking at her mother. The answer was a nod: 'Two weeks and three days. He was visiting the bank on fund business, he said.'

She looked at their visitor and told him in a voice full of pride, 'He always comes to see us and gives us money when he comes to Edinburgh on business.'

'He is a good son?' he asked.

'Oh yes, very good! He never forgets us. I was blessed when I was given my son,' said the mother.

To his own surprise, he was suddenly filled with pity for them, in their poor surroundings. 'He asked me to call on you and make your acquaintance. And he gave me this for you,' he said, pulling out his purse and putting two guineas on the top of their table.

The daughter scooped up the money with evident delight. 'I never thought that my brother would turn into such a good provider,' she said in an acid tone.

To spare their feelings, Stanhope pretended that the wedding to Hester was recent and very private, with only her close family present. 'When the weather improves, I'll arrange for you to visit,' he said as he took his leave.

He could hear them exclaiming to each other as he made his way back down the stair.

Twenty

While the winter season, with its balls and concerts, was in full swing, Madame Rachelle's orders to the Gibsons came in thick and fast. Ribbons, laces, rosettes for her dancing shoes, shawls, silk handkerchiefs – there was no end to it.

She embarked on a massive spending spree, continually coaxing the money out of her lover, who, fortunately for him, did not have to exist on his Army pay.

Her demands became even more outrageous when she heard rumours that her Colonel was considering a remarriage, but not to her. He had his eye on a young lady, more than thirty years his junior, whose family were on a social par with his own. This would be a very suitable match, and one which he greatly desired, for not only was the girl rich and good-looking but she came from a family that produced healthy sons – and the Colonel had no children by his first wife.

His brother the Duke was also without an heir, so if the Colonel could produce a son, that child would be in line to inherit the title. His prospective bride's family, however, were known to be very puritanical in their attitudes and it was essential that he present himself to them as a sorrowing widower with no unsuitable attachments.

Rachelle worked this out very quickly and, knowing that her time as the Colonel's lady was running out, coaxed expensive clothes and jewellery out of him. He responded generously because he was afraid that, if he offended her, she would find some way of making her existence known to the other girl's family. He was a timid man at heart and the spectacular rages that Rachelle could display reduced him to jelly.

Every time she entered the Gibsons' salon Rachelle insisted that she was looked after by Rosabelle. 'You're the only person who can make my things exactly as I like them,' she said.

To provide the young dressmaker with inspiration, Rachelle brought in a pile of French fashion magazines, which they studied together. Mrs Gibson and her daughter did not mind that their best customer valued Rosabelle's work more than theirs and it became a matter of pride with them that Rachelle was the leader of local fashion, though she was not accepted in good society. In spite of her notoriety, ladies of title and wives of local dignitaries stared after her in envy as she swept past on the Colonel's arm, and when they found out where her beautiful clothes came from, they too flocked to Hide Hill.

One afternoon, alone in the fitting room with Rosabelle, Rachelle lowered her voice and said, 'I'm thinking of leaving here soon. The regiment is being moved on – to Woolwich. A terrible place! I won't go there. I'll go to London. Why don't you come with me?'

'To London?' Rosabelle felt she'd been asked to go to Africa.

Rachelle laughed. 'Yes. A train goes there from Berwick.'

'I know, but I've a baby and my mother-in-law here and they need me.'

'For money, you mean? I'll pay you three times as much if you'll come. You'd be able to send enough money back to Eyemouth to keep them in comfort.'

Rosabelle stared at the customer's eager face. Rachelle's eyes were glinting, but what with? Was it glee, greed or good will? She'd never thought of going to London but she knew that she was miserably unhappy. All her pent-up discontents, all her brooding unhappiness came into her mind as she considered this strange offer. How she hated Eyemouth! How it tore at her heart to look out to sea and catch sight of the terrible rocks that took Dan from her.

Rachelle knew the girl was interested when she asked, 'What would you want me to do in London?'

The answer was spoken with a laugh. 'When I first saw you at Nisbet's funeral, I thought I could set you up in one kind of career, but when I got to know you, I could see that wouldn't suit you . . . Then I thought you could look after me, dress me, and make me a lady of fashion in Mayfair, because I'm tired of parading in backwaters. I've been up here for three years and that's long enough.

'But now that I've found out about your talent for dressmaking I think that you and I could start up a modiste's business. I've been saving money and I'll buy the best materials from France. You'll make the gowns. We'll call ourselves "Rachelle and Rosabelle". That's a good name for a business, isn't it?'

'But I don't think I can leave my son,' Rosabelle said slowly, shaking her head, though she was tempted.

She loved Aaron but, to be honest, he was more Effie's child than hers. It was to Effie that he held out his arms when he fell over; it was to Effie he went when he was hungry or tired; it was Effie's lap he climbed into for a cuddle. If she could earn a lot of money doing something she enjoyed, his life could be made easier, and he wouldn't really miss her if she went away for a while.

There was no question of taking him with her. The fact that he was so attached to his grandmother, and she to him, meant that it would be cruel to separate them. Effie was not an old woman. She had years of life ahead of her, and having the children to look after gave her a purpose.

Why not try her luck in London? More money would make Effie's life easier; the relief fund was not enough to keep her and the children in the comfort she had enjoyed as Jimmy's wife. But still she hung back and shook her head. London was so far away and, though Rachelle was kind, she was strange and unpredictable. She shook her head and said, 'I don't think so. I can't leave my little boy.'

Rachelle pouted: 'You're being stupid. He'll grow up and leave you, and what will you do then? I'll tell you. You'll either stay here, stitching away for unimaginative women, or you'll go back to your town and marry another fisherman, put on your creel and gather mussels off the shore. Nisbet told me about the lives such women lead. It's horrible.'

Rosabelle stared angrily at her. 'I'll never marry again,' she snapped.

'You say that now, but if you stay here, when you get older, you'll need someone to look after you. Think about what I'm offering you. You are one of the best dressmakers I've ever come across, and I've used many. Don't waste yourself. I'm leaving soon. Come with me.'

'When are you going?'

'Soon.' There was a hard look in Rachelle's eye as she said the word.

Eyemouth in the bitter early spring was a grim place. The herring fleet had gone south again and the remaining boats only went out for cod and haddock when the weather permitted. The men who survived the day of the storm, which was now referred to as 'Black Friday', were more cautious than they used to be, so for many days boats stayed tied up in the harbour while the crews idled about on the decks, smoking and fretting.

What made things worse was that, when they did go out, catches were so bad that few skippers could afford to share their money with the widows and orphans any longer. Only Alex Burgon continued to give handouts, although his generosity was acknowledged with ill grace.

It was hard for bereaved families to live on the basic relief payments, especially since Anderson arbitrarily withheld money from women he considered undeserving. Families that had been prosperous lived in penny-pinching misery. Women who once walked tall bent their backs like crones as they trudged along against cutting winds coming in off the sea. Misery, as bad as the week of the disaster, engulfed the whole town and infected people's minds. 'Will the sun ever shine again?' they asked each other.

Because both Jessie and Rosabelle gave her money for taking care of their children, Effie could still buy coal for her fire and did not have to rely on driftwood. Once a week, almost shamefacedly, she went to the butcher's shop and bought a cheap cut of meat, one of the few local women who could still do so. At least Aaron and Henrietta's clothes were warm and they were plump and rosy-cheeked while many other children were gaunt and pale.

When Rosabelle pushed open Effie's door on the evening that Madame Rachelle made her surprising proposal, the kitchen looked warm and welcoming. Coals were glowing in the range and two happy children played on the hearthrug with a ball between them. A cat slept on a chair and Effie was stirring something that smelt good in a pot swinging over the fire.

Pictures covered the whitewashed walls; some were photographs in wooden frames and others illustrations torn out of magazines, pinned up by Effie, who was a great admirer of Queen Victoria and her family.

It struck the girl that Effie's house was a safe place for her child to grow up in. *If Dan were still alive,* she thought, *I'd have a kitchen like Effie's. I'd stand at the hearth to cook his supper, and smile when he came in from fishing.*

We'd have been so happy, but Dan is dead and my desire for that sort of life died with him. I don't want it now.

The tempting idea Madame Rachelle planted in her head was growing into an overwhelming wish. If she went to London, she would see the world. But how could she reconcile her conscience with leaving?

She walked over to the mantelpiece and picked up a special photograph that Effie kept there. It showed Jimmy Dip and his three sons in their fishing gear, looking very solemn beside their newly painted boat. She stared at their faces and felt the tears rise in her eyes, unaware that Effie, spoon raised over the pot, was watching her.

'He was so handsome. He was beautiful!' Rosabelle sighed.

'Yes, and his son's going to look just like him,' Effie replied.

They both looked down at the little boy on the hearthrug. His hair was tousled over his brow, like Dan's used to be. One day his hands would be big and capable, like Dan's hands, the hands that fruitlessly scrabbled for a hold on the Hurkars.

But he wasn't Dan. Try as she might, his mother couldn't love him as she loved his father.

She put the photograph back up in its high place and said to Effie, 'If I went to London to work for a little while, what would you do?'

A flash of fear crossed Effie's face. 'London! Will you be taking Aaron with you?'

'Not at first, but I'd send money home for him – more than I give you now. I've had an offer to go as a sort of lady's maid with one of our clients, the one I made that ball gown for. It's just a suggestion she put to me. I'm not sure that I want to go really.'

Effie frowned. 'Aaron would be safe enough with me, but

I can't advise you. It depends on the woman you'd be going with. Are you sure she'll treat you right? Will she pay you your wages on time and that sort of thing? People say London's a hard place to be on your own.'

'I've heard that too. Perhaps I'd be safer staying in Berwick,' said Rosabelle, deciding she'd been indulging in a pipe dream.

For the next two weeks the Gibsons' salon was busier than it had ever been and Rosabelle did not have time to worry about whether her decision to refuse Madame Rachelle's offer was the right one.

Rachelle, on the other hand, did not give up trying to entice her to London, continually coaxing whenever they were alone in a fitting room: 'You're so young and pretty. You'll never meet a worthwhile man up here . . .'

'I don't want to meet a man. I've told you that already,' said Rosabelle sharply, resentful at the idea that Rachelle might regard her as another Jessie.

'Oh la, la, what nonsense!' was the blithe reply.

Sometimes Rachelle tried a different tack. 'If you come with me to London, I'll set you up in Mayfair making clothes for rich women. I'm sure we'll succeed. In a few years we'll be rich. You'll be able to pay for your son to enter a good profession – a doctor or a lawyer perhaps,' she said.

The answer was still a shake of the head. 'He'll probably go fishing, like his father,' said Rosabelle sadly.

Rachelle looked genuinely shocked. 'After what happened to his father? Do you really mean that?'

'None of my husband's family for generations have ever done anything else – nor mine, come to that.'

'Then it's time someone broke away. Let your son be the first. Bring him with you to London. Nisbet was a remarkable man who could have done anything he wanted, but he went fishing – and drowned when he was only thirty-one. What a waste. Do you want to waste your son too? Do you want to stand by his grave with your shawl over your head?'

Rosabelle put her hands over her ears and shook her head in despair and pain. She wished Rachelle would leave her alone, because the more she heard, the more she wanted to go south. 'But I have to stay. My life is mapped out for me.

It's impossible to take Aaron away from his grandmother because they're dependent on each other, and losing him would take the heart out of Effie,' she snapped to Rachelle.

'Your mother-in-law might be glad to be free of the responsibility of your child,' suggested Rachelle.

'You don't know her. Family is everything as far as she's concerned. She stopped the Eyemouth people sending their orphans to Quarrier's Home. She'd certainly stop me taking Aaron to London. Stop talking about it. I can't go with you. Please accept my decision,' sobbed Rosabelle in an anguished plea.

With an expressive spread of the hands and a shrug, Rachelle gave in, but still had to have the last word. 'I'm leaving this town in three days' time. I go by the noon train. You know where the station is – if you change your mind, meet me there,' she said.

In Eyemouth, at the same time as the two women were having this discussion, Steven Anderson was reading a letter from his sister:

Dear Brother,

Mother and I have been discussing how to bring up this difficult subject. She wanted to wait till you next came to see us, but I prefer to write and ask you direct. Why did you not tell us that you were getting married? Why did you send your father-in-law to break the news? Are you ashamed of us? Is that it? He was a very well-set-up gentleman, very polite and kind, and I have to thank you for the two guineas he gave us – or were they from him and not from you as he said? You must come here as soon as possible and pacify mother. She is broken-hearted that her beloved son could behave like this to her.

The recriminations in this letter did not upset him as much as the knowledge that Robert Stanhope had tracked his family down. What else had he found out? At lunch he tried to scrutinize the old man's face without seeming to do so, but could detect nothing unusual in his expression. Yet there was something in the air that set his teeth on edge. Trouble was looming. He had to move fast if he was to make his escape.

As soon as Hester retired to bed for her afternoon nap, and

the old man went back to his grocery store, Anderson hurried to his office, where he emptied the cashbox.Then he unlocked his secret drawer and took out his purloined money – £150. The rest was still in his bank account. Not enough to fulfil all his dreams, but better than nothing. All he had to do now was wait for the girl coming home.

Twenty-One

That night Rosabelle worked late and went back by a later train than usual, arriving at the station, with another two miles to walk home, at eight.

The evening was cold and cruel, scourged by rain that drifted in from the sea. Scudding clouds obscured the moon and scrubby trees by the side of the road bent their branches towards the land as an offshore wind battered them. It was very dark and paraffin lamps guttered feebly along the length of the platform when she alighted from the train.

As she stared into the shadows, her heart contracted with fear. The possibility of meeting Anderson terrified her. Since he turned up at the salon she knew he'd not given up following her, and she'd seen him once or twice lingering in the alleys of the fishing town when she walked through them of an evening.

Don't be silly. It's late. He'll be shut up safe at home in Beechwood with his wife long ago, she reassured herself as she walked out of the station gate.

As a present, the kind Gibsons had given her a thickly lined, hooded cloak of dark-brown tweed that reached to her feet. It kept her warm and dry as she headed down the empty road towards home.

It was a horrible journey. All the way her heart beat fast, and every time an animal rustled in a hedgerow or scuttled across her path she bit back a cry. On one dark stretch a large white owl like a ghost flew across the road in front of her, and she screamed aloud in terror.

Breaking into a half-run, she tripped and stumbled along till, at last, she saw the lights of the town below her. Then she began to really sprint, clutching up the cloak and pelting downhill like a harrier.

She flew past the corn mill and on down the hill, past the

boat builders and into the shadow of the fish-gutting sheds. Soon she saw the guttering light on the beacon at the end of the pier.

'I'm safe, I'm safe,' she silently rejoiced as she passed the Ship Inn, and slowed her pace a little as she went along the harbour side. The glow from the lamp in Effie's kitchen was within sight, and she let out her breath in a long shuddering gasp, happy with the idea that the terror that filled her was all in her imagination.

Her pace had slowed almost to a saunter when, from a narrow opening between two houses, Anderson stepped out and stood in front of her.

He was stony-faced and staring-eyed. He looked insane.

Stopping dead, she clutched her cloak around her. 'Let me pass,' she whispered. Her voice seemed to have disappeared.

He did not move, but spread out his arms and blocked her way. 'What are you doing out so late? Where's your soldier?' he asked.

There was no one else around. Most families went to bed at sundown. On her right-hand side the water of the harbour shimmered like oiled snakeskin; on the other ran the long, whitewashed wall of a storage shed.

She managed to say again: 'Let me pass.'

'I asked you, where's your soldier?'

'I don't know what you mean,' she said. Was it better, she wondered, to make him talk, or merely try to get away?

'Your soldier. The one with the hansom. I saw you. I've been wondering whether I should kill you or take you away. Tell me what I should do . . .'

She stared at him, eyes wide with horror, and he delighted in taunting her. 'You nearly bit off my finger. You're a bitch. I'll teach you a lesson when I get you on your own,' he hissed, coming nearer. By this time his feelings about her were a mixture of frustrated lust and rage and he did not know which was uppermost.

Panicked by his menace, she made a mistake and stepped sideways into the shadow of the shed. He seized this opportunity to cut off her escape route and stood between her and safety, penning her into an embrasure in the wall.

'It's nearly nine. Where have you been till this time at night? With another man?' he asked in a hoarse voice.

Facing him, she flattened herself against the rough stones, hoping to slide along them, but he put up an arm to stop her, laying his open palm on the wall above her head, and bringing his face close to hers. Again she smelt his pomade, and it revolted her.

'I'm going to take you away with me. No one else is going to have you,' he told her.

In a horrible flash of understanding she knew he meant what he said.

'You can't make me. I won't go,' she whispered.

'Yes you will go, because I'll knock you out if I have to,' he told her.

Bit by bit he was coming nearer. 'Give me a kiss,' he said. He still had not decided whether he was going to kill her after he raped her or not.

She turned her head away from him, swallowing hard and trying to raise a scream out of her dry throat, but he was too fast for her. His face contorted; he put one hand over her mouth and grabbed her right shoulder with the other, trying to push her back into a narrow alley.

He was very strong, and pressed his mouth down on hers with furious strength. Though she struggled, she could not get free or shout, and felt herself starting to choke.

He's going to kill me! He's going to strangle me! was her overriding certainty. Paralysed with terror, she slid limply down the wall.

Surprised by her sudden capitulation, and half-afraid that he had actually killed her, he relaxed his grip on her neck.

That was all the time she needed. Lying along the bottom of the wall was a broken spar from one of the boats. As she slumped down, her fingers found it, and with a strength she did not know she possessed, she grabbed it, sat up and swung it at his head.

The crunch it made when it connected gave her infinite satisfaction. But, unfortunately, he fell forward, putting his whole weight on to her and flattening her on the ground. It took a second or two before she realized that she had saved herself. The man lying on top of her was unconscious.

When she heaved him off, he slumped on the paving stones like a stuffed dummy.

213

On her knees she crawled out from beneath him and realized someone else was reaching down and trying to help her. It was a scandalized-looking Jessie.

'What's going on? Come on, get up. Let's get out of here. You've knocked him out. I was coming along the road when I saw you whack him. Hurry, before he comes round,' she hissed.

As they ran away, leaving him on the ground, they heard him groaning but did not look back.

If they had looked, they would have seen there was another witness to what had gone on. Old Willie Wake was wakened from his fitful sleep among the nets by the sound of scuffling outside his shed door.

He crawled across the floor and put his head out of the door in time to see Rosabelle fell Anderson, and watch the girls running away.

Like most other people in the town, Willie hated and resented the relief administrator. What did a stranger like him think he was doing, lording it over Eyemouth people? He was asking to be taught a lesson and Rosabelle had done it.

Chuckling to himself, he stepped on to the quay as the man sat up, swaying, with one hand on the side of his head. He was bleeding and a huge lump was rising there.

Aware that someone was standing beside him, he called out, 'Help me up. What happened?'

Willie stood over him like a black wraith. In the darkness, with the woollen hat pulled down to his eyebrows, he looked as if he was masked.

'Help me up!' snapped Anderson, holding up one hand to be pulled to his feet.

The figure looked at the hand and shook its head. Suddenly Anderson felt afraid.

'Who are you?' he asked as he tried to stagger to his feet.

'I'm the deil come to get you!' was the answer.

Gasping and panting, the girls let themselves in at Effie's door, and stood staring at each other in the deserted kitchen.

'I should have hit that bastard with my bottle. When I recognized who it was, I should have let him have it,' said Jessie excitedly.

'What bottle, and what if he's badly hurt?' asked Rosabelle.

'I've got a bottle in my basket. But don't worry: he's not dead. I heard him groaning. Nobody saw you. If you want to make sure of him, we could go back and push him into the water.'

Rosabelle shivered. 'Oh God, no. Let's hope I only stunned him. If he dies, I'll go to prison – or hang. I'm scared.'

Jessie frowned. 'He'll not let on who hit him. He was trying to rape you. I still think we should go back and shove him into the harbour. In this cold he wouldn't last long and they'd think he missed his footing.'

They opened the door again and peeped out. In the light flowing out of the kitchen, the pier side looked deserted.

'He's gone, but I still wish we'd shoved him off,' said Jessie, obviously disappointed.

'No! Leave it be,' cried Rosabelle, closing the door again and leaning against it. Her face was so white she looked like a ghost.

As full realization of what had almost happened hit her, her legs started shaking and she wept, clinging to Jessie, who ineffectually tried to quieten her. The noise she made woke Effie, who appeared in the stairway in her nightgown.

'Are you two drunk? You'll wake the bairns,' she scolded.

Jessie told the story and, when she finished, she lifted her basket off the floor and brought out a dark-coloured bottle with a gold-embossed label. 'It's a good job I didn't hit him with this. I wouldn't want to break it, but I wouldn't care if it cracked his skull,' she said.

'What is it?' asked Effie.

'French brandy. The very best. It's as a present, but let's open it now. Rosabelle needs something to pull herself together,' said Jessie, who seemed unfazed by what had happened.

'Where did you get brandy?' Effie asked suspiciously.

Jessie laughed. 'Somebody gave it to me.'

Effie looked disapproving, because she had fears of Jessie turning into her mother and hanging about bars to pick up disreputable men. 'I hope you know what you're doing, lassie,' she said.

Again Jessie laughed, a cheerful peal. 'Oh I think I do,' she told them.

They each drank a tot of brandy from teacups, and it made

them cough and splutter. When Effie put her cup down, she said, 'Well, if that's French brandy I dinna fancy it.'

However, the spirit gave Rosabelle courage. Putting her arms round Jessie, she said, 'I don't care where you got the brandy, I'm glad you came along when you did. You saved my life. He said he wanted to run away with me but he'd have killed me, I'm sure.'

They all knew there was no question of reporting Anderson to the town policeman, who was always on the side of respectable people and against the fisherfolk. Their story would not have been believed. He'd probably say they attacked him.

Eventually Jessie went home and, exhausted, the others went to bed.

Still unable to break the habit of a lifetime, Effie was awake at five next morning. As the sky lightened, she dressed and went out to fetch a bucket of water from the standpipe that stood on the harbour side.

Minutes later Rosabelle was also wakened by her bedroom door being thrown open. A frightened-looking Effie stood there, crying out: 'Get up! They're dragging a body out of the harbour.'

'Whose?' asked Rosabelle.

'They dinna ken yet. The coastguard saw it floating there early this morning . . .' Her voice trailed off and they stared at each other in horror, neither of them wanting to speak their fears.

'I'll go and find out,' said Rosabelle, jumping from the bed and pulling her cloak off a hook on the back of the door. It was so voluminous she could go out in it without changing from her nightclothes.

A trio of men and a couple of curious women had collected on the pier, staring down into the water. The harbour was quiet and uncrowded. Bobbing about on the black water in the middle between tied-up boats was a scull with three men in it. They were using grappling irons to haul a dripping body in beside them.

'Who is it?' Rosabelle asked the man beside her.

He shrugged. 'He's no' a fisherman anyway. Too fancy clothes.'

216

'Is he dead?'

'He doesnae look very lively to me.'

'So it's a man?'

The other never took his eyes off the scene being enacted on the water as he said, 'It's a man all right. He's got on troosers.'

At last the body was in the scull, and out of sight, while it turned towards the harbour wall, heading for a long iron ladder that ran down the steep side. With one accord, the watchers moved along too and stood where the ladder ended.

The coastguard was first up, but nobody asked him any questions as, grim-faced, he bent down and started to haul up the body. The two other men pushed it up from beneath and eventually managed to get it on dry land, where it was laid out on the worn, flat paving stones. Water ran off it in all directions and its face was turned towards the sky. The eyes were wide open and staring horribly.

The spectators stood round in a circle with Rosabelle at the back. Hysteria was rising in her and she had to fight to stop herself from screaming. The drowned man was her persecutor, Steven Anderson.

Willie Wake appeared and pushed his way through the group. Looking down at the body, he prodded it with his toe and said, 'The deil got him. He'll no' be missed.'

Nobody protested at this cavalier behaviour and all started to speak at once.

'It's the relief man!'

'Do ye think he jumped in?'

'Not him; he was doing too well to jump in. He must've slipped.'

'Aye that's what happened. He slipped. Look at the lump on the side of his head. It must have happened when he hit the harbour wall.'

While they were speculating, Duncan sent a boy off to fetch the doctor, who came hurrying along without his collar and tie and knelt down beside the body to pronounce his verdict: 'He's dead all right. Drowned by the looks of it.'

'See that bump on his heid,' said one of the women, pointing at Anderson's matted hair.

Dr Wilkie's fingers investigated the lump. 'He must have

banged his head on something when he fell,' he said. Then he stood up and dusted down his trouser legs. 'Somebody'll have to go up to Beechwood and tell his wife.'

'I'll gang,' said Willie Wake. Someone in the steadily growing crowd laughed.

'It's all right, Willie. You stay here. I'll go up there with the doctor,' said Mr Duncan.

When the crowd cleared, Willie Wake ran after Rosabelle and caught up with her at Effie's door.

'The relief man's no loss. I saw you gie him a good whack about the heid but I'll no' tell,' he whispered.

White-faced and shaking, Rosabelle managed to get inside the house before she broke down. Gulping and sobbing, she broke the news. 'Anderson's dead. He must have fallen into the water after I hit him. Willie Wake saw me. I murdered him! I murdered him! If we'd gone back to see if he was all right, he wouldn't have fallen in, and he wouldn't have fallen in if he hadn't been knocked out. The policeman'll be after me. I'll go to prison.'

Her cries were so loud that Effie took fright and slapped her hard. 'Be quiet! Hold your tongue or you will go to jail. Nobody but us and Willie Wake knows what happened last night. Nobody believes anything he says, and you must never tell a soul.'

But Rosabelle was beyond reason. She kept on weeping, until, in desperation, Effie poured out another tot of brandy and thrust it into her hand. 'Drink that and shut your mouth. If anyone hears you they'll think you did it.'

The brandy helped a little, but the hysterical girl kept sobbing and shaking, pent-up grief and terror bursting out of her again.

Jessie heard the news when she was on her way to work in Stanhope's shop. As she was running across St Ella's Square, she met another counter assistant, who told her, 'Dinna bother hurrying. There'll be no work today. The shop's closed. Miss Hester's man was found drowned in the harbour early this morning.'

As if she'd been shot, Jessie stopped dead and stared at the woman in horror. 'You mean Anderson the relief man?'

'Aye, Miss Hester's husband. They pulled him out this morning. What everybody's asking is: what was he doing there anyway?'

218

Jessie pulled herself together with an effort. 'When did it happen?' she asked.

'Last night sometime. Apparently he usually took a walk before he went to bed. His wife fell asleep before he got back, and when she woke in the morning he wasnae there. By the time she'd roused her father and sent the servants out to look for him, the doctor was coming up the path to tell her he was dead.'

Jessie shuddered, and the woman noticed her reaction. 'Dinna take on. He was a bad lot, always smoochin' up to the ministers and doin' folk out of their money. Maybe he was helping himself too. It wouldn't surprise me.'

'Helping himself? What to?' Jessie asked in a confused voice.

'The relief money. Folk say it's disappearing like snow off a dyke and it's certainly not been going to the widows and orphans. Maybe he had a guilty conscience and jumped in.'

Jessie had collected her wits now and she managed to say, 'I didn't think he was the jumping-in kind, but you never can tell, can you?'

The other woman laughed: 'Maybe he was pushed. There's plenty of folk would want to do it.'

Jessie blanched. 'That's not very likely either,' she snapped, and turned to run back to Effie's.

She found the household distraught, with Rosabelle still shuddering and incoherent. Effie hauled her indoors and said, 'Help me. She's carrying on something awful and if she doesn't stop, somebody'll hear her.'

Jessie's face hardened as she stood over her friend and took her by the shoulders. *'Pull yourself together!'* she said in a terrible voice.

Rosabelle looked up, saw Jessie and gabbled, 'I killed him. You saw me. I'll go to prison.'

Jessie slapped her and said, 'If you go on acting like this, you might. I've got something to lose as well: I was there; but I'm not going to jail for a bastard like that. If you don't quieten down, you'll be the next one in the water.'

At last Rosabelle began to pay attention. 'I wish I could get away from this awful place. I wish I'd said I'd go to London with Madame Rachelle,' she sobbed.

Jessie looked over her shoulder at Effie and said, 'You can

still go. In fact I think it would be best if you were out of here for a bit. When's she leaving?'

Rosabelle's teeth were chattering, but she managed to say, 'The day after tomorrow, on the twelve o'clock train.'

'Get your bag packed. You'll be on it with her,' said Jessie. The two of them quickly decided that Rosabelle should stay in London till the scandal of Anderson's drowning died down.

'How will you and Effie keep quiet about this if the police come asking questions?' Rosabelle asked Jessie, who shook her head: 'We can control ourselves better than you can. In fact I'm more scared of you than of anything else. There's nothing to link us to Anderson last night. Nobody but Willie Wake saw what happened, or they'd have tried to stop him attacking you. He was alive when we left him. Remember we heard him groaning. If he fell in, he must have slipped on fulzie or something.'

'You don't think it was the whack on the head I gave him that did it?' whispered Rosabelle.

Jessie looked her in the eye. 'What whack? You never laid a hand on him. You imagined it.'

'But . . . !'

'You imagined it. Get that into your head,' said Jessie, staring her out.

Twenty-Two

It was not really necessary for Jessie to make a visit to Beechwood's washhouse after Anderson's body was carried home, but fear and curiosity about how the death would be officially explained made it impossible for her to stay away.

The place was in chaos when she slipped into the kitchen, eager to hear all she could.

The servants were gathered round the big pine table, drinking tea and eyeing the row of bells that hung along the wall. They wished at least one of them would be called upstairs to hear what was going on.

'Aw Jessie,' cried the cook, 'have you heard the news?'

'I was told the shop's closed because Hester's man drowned. What's happening?' was the innocent, wide-eyed reply. Jessie even surprised herself by her acting ability.

'Miss Hester's screeching the place down. The master's telegraphed to Edinburgh for Master Everard. It's a very funny business altogether,' said the cook.

One of the table maids interrupted: 'They think he was trying to run away! The gardener says he hired a horse from the hotel livery stable, and I heard the master telling Hester there was a lot of money in his pockets.'

'In that case he didn'a mean to jump in the harbour. Ye dinna need a horse and pockets fu' of money to kill yourself,' said wee Jean.

Jessie allowed herself a laugh: 'Unless the money was to weigh him doon.'

The second table maid snorted at this bit of black humour, and all the others grinned as well. There was no mourning in the kitchen for Steven Anderson.

Upstairs it was different. Hester lay on the drawing-room

221

sofa, thumping her clenched fists on the upholstered seat and sobbing hysterically.

Her father, grim-faced, looked at the bewildered doctor and asked, 'Can you give her something to quieten her down?'

Dr Wilkie approached the weeping woman and said gently, 'Now, Miss Stanhope, I'm going to give you a draught . . .' She pushed his hand away, spilling the medicine, but he persisted: 'You must take it. Your father is very upset about you . . .'

She glared through swollen eyes and sobbed, 'He never liked poor Steven. He doesn't care. He's been telling me awful things about him, a pack of lies. How can he be so cruel at a time like this?'

The doctor looked over her head at the old man and said, 'I think the best thing to do is to get her upstairs and I'll prepare another draught. It will make her sleep.'

Stanhope grimly crossed the room and pulled the bell. When a maid's face appeared round the door, he said, 'Miss Hester has to be helped upstairs.'

Hester began yelling, 'I'm not going. I want to hear anything you have to say about my husband. I won't have you spreading lies!'

The doctor became stern. 'You must stop this or you will harm your baby.'

It was useless. In spite of the blandishments of the two men and the scared maid, Hester would not move.

'Fetch the others from the kitchen to move her,' snapped Stanhope, who did not think it proper for himself and the doctor to fight with his frantic daughter, whose nightclothes were already slipping off as she struggled. The maid scurried away.

The cook, the other maids, Jean and a delighted Jessie were brought in to form the moving force and, by dint of all taking hold of some kicking, struggling part of Hester, they finally managed to convey her upstairs.

When the cook kicked open the bedroom door and saw a pair of booted feet sticking up from the tumbled sheets, she realized Anderson's corpse was lying on the matrimonial bed.

'Aw my God, we canna put her in here wi' him,' she groaned. 'She'll hae to go in another room,' and they awkwardly backtracked on the landing, dragging a howling Hester with them. Jessie, holding one of Hester's kicking legs, had difficulty in restraining her hysterical mirth.

When they finally dropped their burden on to a high brass bed in a spare room, and the doctor moved in with his draught, the staff filed out. Jessie was last in line and when she passed the grim-faced Robert, she glanced up at him and all her frivolity disappeared, because the tragic look on his face touched her heart.

'I'm sorry for your trouble,' she whispered as she brushed past.

There was a softening of his eyes as he watched her go.

Everard arrived at noon and ran upstairs, taking the steps two at a time. He found his father sitting in the window of his own big bedroom staring out to sea, and ran across the floor to take the old man's hand. 'Tell me what happened,' he said.

'That husband of Hester was found floating in the harbour early this morning. There was a cut and a big bump on his head, but the doctor thinks he drowned. It wouldn't take long, because it was very cold last night.'

'Do you think he jumped?'

The old man shrugged. 'Who knows? If he did, it was a sudden decision, because he'd hired a horse and emptied the fund cashbox. As well as his purse, he also had almost two hundred pounds in cash. I pulled it out of his pocket myself. Maybe he had a sudden attack of conscience.'

'Do you think he knew we've been checking up on him?' asked Everard.

'Yes, he knew. There was a letter from Edinburgh for him yesterday morning. He said it was from his sister when he saw the envelope, but he read it at the breakfast table and I could see how it angered him. He never said what was in it and I've looked through his papers but can't find any trace of the letter. He probably burned it.'

'Does Hester know anything about our suspicions?' asked young Stanhope.

His father sighed: 'I'm afraid she does. She heard me telling Dr Wilkie about the money. I was surprised that he was carrying so much, and I'm afraid my tongue ran away with me . . .'

'What did you say?'

'Something about hoping he hadn't been fiddling the fund

. . . She heard me and went off into hysterics. The doctor gave her a good strong draught that's put her to sleep.'

When Hester woke from a drugged sleep, she found her brother sitting by the bedside. When he rose to kiss her cheek, she turned her head away, asking, 'Are you with Father? Do you think bad things about my poor Steven? Father is wicked, wicked and cruel. I will never, ever forgive him!' and she went off into another storm of weeping.

Everard grimaced and said, 'Hester, you really must pull yourself together.'

'Why should I? The love of my life is dead and my father is spreading ugly rumours about him before he's even cold!'

Her brother rose from his chair and walked across to the window. This room too had a view of the sea, which today was steel-grey and heaving with white-topped waves. The memory of the fishing disaster came into his mind and he mentally compared the intemperate behaviour of his sister with the stoical fisherwomen who lost their husbands.

'Have some dignity, Hester,' he said sharply over his shoulder.

'*Dignity!*' she screamed. 'Father's the one who should have dignity – talking about my husband the way he did with the doctor. The story will be all over the town by now. Mrs Wilkie can't keep control of her tongue.'

Everard walked back towards the bed and said sternly, 'I suspect that the story was round the town before father even opened his mouth. The men who found him searched his pockets. It's to their credit that the money was returned untouched.'

'Money! That's all Father cares about. I hate him. I swear I'll never speak another word to him as long as I live.'

Everard's patience snapped. 'Poor Father has only been concerned for you and your reputation. He's been making enquiries about your saintly husband for weeks now. I'm sorry, but the man was a total fraud, and now we know he was a swindler as well. You are well rid of him, Hester!'

Her mouth dropped open and she stared at him. 'You too! You hated Steven as well. Were you jealous because he was so big and strong while you're a fat weakling?'

'He was big and strong perhaps, but he was also a fool and a liar. He told you his mother was too ill to travel to your

224

wedding, but that was a lie. I'll invite his relatives to attend his funeral and then you'll meet them. If you have any sense, you'll put as good a face as possible on this and calm down. Father will try to squash the rumours as much as possible for your sake.' Everard was cold and angry.

There was fear in her eyes as she looked at him, though she did not want him to know how frightened she was. Her social position was more important to her than anything else – even her professed devotion to her husband.

'I don't care what Father does. I will never address a direct word to him again,' she hissed, more quietly this time.

'Please yourself, but count yourself lucky that he won't be as vindictive to you as you are to him,' her brother told her.

From Beechwood to Effie's house Jessie ran all the way, bursting with news and reassurance that no suspicions were being entertained about murder. To her disappointment she was received with little enthusiasm, because both Effie and Rosabelle were in tears.

'You're not greetin' for that bastard, are you?' she asked them as she burst through the door, and Effie shook her head.

'No, we're greetin' because nothing'll ever be the same again if Rosabelle goes away. Is it really the right thing to do?'

Jessie spoke with determination, 'It *is* the best thing. It's the *only* thing. There'll be trouble if she stays here because she can't keep the secret to herself. She'll blab and I don't want us all to be hauled up in the police court, so I'm going to make damned sure she's on that train to London tomorrow.'

The weeping women stared at her in awe and did not protest.

Remembering how Rosabelle's mother lost her mind after Black Friday, Effie began to fear for her too and tried to shake her out of apathy by putting Aaron on her lap; but, scared by his mother's tension, he started to cry. Rosabelle stared at him without smiling and handed him back to his grandmother.

'Keep him, Effie,' she said. 'He's more yours than he is mine anyway.'

Tears came into Effie's eyes and she said, 'I'll take good care of him for you, lass. When you're ready, come back for him.'

* * *

225

Next morning she and Rosabelle walked without speaking to Burnmouth in drifting rain. Rosabelle wore her big cloak but Jessie only had her shawl, and when she saw her friend shivering in the bitter wind, the tall girl silently held out the wide cloak and they shared it, huddling together and walking in step with Rosabelle's bulging carpet bag between them.

As the station came into sight, Rosabelle was the first to speak. 'I'll miss you, Jessie. I'll miss you more than anybody,' she said.

Jessie's pert face was sad when she asked, 'More than Aaron?'

'Yes.'

'That's sad.'

'I can't help it. He's so like Dan already. It hurts me to look at him . . .'

I could never leave Henrietta, thought Jessie, but she squeezed her friend's arm and said, 'I'll miss you too.'

They stood on the empty platform as the Berwick train pulled in, and Rosabelle said, 'Go home now, please.' But Jessie shook her head. 'I'm going on to Berwick with you. I'll not be content till I see you on that train to London,' she said, for she was still afraid that Rosabelle might change her mind at the last minute.

Berwick station was crowded when they arrived at fifteen minutes before twelve. At the sight of people milling around on the down platform, Rosabelle quailed and hung back, but Jessie kept her hand on her taller friend's elbow, firmly pushing her along. When she glanced up to reassure the other girl, she was struck by Rosabelle's fixed expression. She looked as if she was in a trance. Her eyes stared sightlessly in front of her, and her feet were going forward automatically like the feet of a clockwork doll.

'Where is that Frenchwoman? What if she's changed her mind and isn't here?' Jessie worried. Pulling Rosabelle along, she scrutinized people as she passed, but there was no sign of Madame Rachelle and the hands of the big station clock were creeping nearer and nearer to noon, which was the time the London train was due to leave.

Suddenly there was a piercing whistle and the crowd began surging towards the edge of the platform. *Where is she?* Jessie thought desperately.

'Are you sure she's leaving today?' she asked Rosabelle, who nodded and murmured, 'That's what she said.'

At the moment the train rolled up to the platform, the door of the First Class Ladies' Waiting Room opened and a vision in mauve silk and grey fur stepped out. Jessie ran towards Rachelle and flung out her arms in an embrace, so great was her relief.

'Thank God you're here. I've brought Rosabelle. She'll go to London with you,' she cried.

Madame Rachelle raised her eyebrows in surprise. 'So she changed her mind after all?' She was obviously pleased, but when she looked at Rosabelle, she wondered if the girl knew what was going on. Perhaps she was drunk. She certainly looked blank enough. She turned back to the little dark-haired companion and asked, 'Has she got a ticket?'

That had never entered Jessie's mind, and anyway she had no money to buy one. She shook her head, but Rachelle rapidly scrabbled in her reticule, pulled out a satin purse and ordered, 'Run and buy one – first class. One way.'

The gigantic locomotive was breathing steam beside them. The boiler of its engine was glossy black, banded with strips of gleaming brass, and a ruddy-faced driver hung out of the cab like a victorious charioteer; but Rosabelle looked at it without registering anything.

A porter appeared with a huge trolley heaped up with trunks and boxes, all of which turned out to belong to Madame Rachelle, and they were stowed in the guard's van while she hustled Rosabelle on to the train, for she too was now afraid that the girl might attempt a getaway at the last moment.

Jessie ran along the platform to the booking office and by the time she came pelting back with the little bit of cardboard in her hand, the train's pistons were moving and huge puffs of smoke were rising out of its funnel.

Rosabelle and Rachelle were aboard, and Rachelle reached her hand out of the carriage window to take the ticket and her purse. 'I'll look after her. Goodbye,' she told Jessie in a matter-of-fact tone, as if she was a governess taking over a helpless child.

'You'd better, or you'll have me to answer to,' was the sharp reply.

For the first time Rachelle smiled. 'How terrifying,' she said.

Jessie, with her dark shawl pulled back over her head, stood on the platform watching as the train pulled out, but there was no sign of Rosabelle, who stayed huddled in her seat and never even waved goodbye.

First class. One way . . . were the words that kept running through Jessie's head. For her, having to leave her home town would be a tragedy and she mourned for her friend. Would they ever see each other again? she wondered.

Though she rarely wept, hot tears slid down her cheeks as she turned to make her way back to Eyemouth.

Twenty-Three

What am I doing? The question kept running through Rosabelle's head as the train rumbled along.

She sat with her bare head back against the deeply upholstered seat and kept her eyes closed because she did not want to open them and face reality. Every now and again she heard Rachelle's skirts rustling as she moved and smelt the spicy perfume she always wore.

What am I doing going to London with this strange woman? Rosabelle was not so naive that she did not know Rachelle was a woman of mystery with a doubtful past and an undisclosed identity.

Lifting her eyelids a little, she scrutinized her travelling companion from under the dark lashes. As always, Rachelle was immaculately dressed, with grey fur framing her made-up face and gold glinting on her fingers, round her neck and in her ears. Money was obviously no problem for her – but where exactly did it come from?

How foolish to cast in my lot with an adventuress, thought Rosabelle. *Will I ever see my home again?* Apart from her wedding trip to Edinburgh, she'd never been further than Berwick. Nor had any other woman in her family except Clara, who'd only gone to Yarmouth once a year with the herring gutters before she'd taken off for America.

The slowing down of the train as it drew into Newcastle station made her sit bolt upright and open her eyes. Rachelle stiffened to attention opposite her.

'I think I'll get off here,' Rosabelle said.

Rachelle sighed and sat back. 'If that's what you want . . .'

'You don't mind?'

'Not really. I'm not forcing you to do anything. Make up your mind. Either come with me or go back now.'

But going back meant facing a furious Jessie, and worse, it meant living in fear of discovery of her involvement in the relief man's death. If that came out, she might even hang! Her skin prickled in terror at the thought and, in a sudden movement, she put a hand on to her bare neck as if to tear away a noose.

Nothing was lost on Rachelle. She noticed the movement, sensed the fear, and wondered what had happened to change the girl's mind about going to London, because it was obviously a reckless and unpremeditated decision. This was not the time to start probing, however. She opened her reticule and said, 'I'll give you the money for your ticket back.'

Rosabelle dithered. Should she take the money? Should she go back and face the music?

Then she remembered how much she hated Eyemouth. How she mourned Dan there. How every face she saw, every glimpse of the sea, brought back memories of him and his terrible death. If she was ever to come out of the bleak misery that engulfed her, she had to get out of that town, no matter if it meant leaving everything – including her son – behind.

Am I brave enough, though? she wondered. 'Perhaps my dressmaking isn't good enough for people in London?' she said.

On the seat opposite, Madame Rachelle began drawing the long steel pins out of her large hat, and laughed: 'Oh, you're good enough, believe me. I wouldn't be investing in you if I wasn't certain.'

As her hat was removed, a shaft of winter sunlight came through the window and illuminated her face. She looked tired and drawn, and for the first time Rosabelle realized she was much older than she looked. In fact she was probably almost as old as Effie, and certainly as old as Rosabelle's own mother had been when she died.

Painted and dressed up at a ball she could pass for thirty, but in the hard light she looked at least forty-five.

She needs me, and I need her, Rosabelle thought, and felt a sudden sense of security. Rachelle was like a substitute mother – not as comforting or caring, but somehow, in spite of her apparent indifference, trustworthy. This gave her strength.

As if she sensed the girl's thoughts Rachelle smiled and said, 'We can help each other. We'll make a good combination.'

Rosabelle silently nodded her head. She knew she was at the point of no return.

'You don't talk much, do you?' Rachelle asked after a long silence.

Rosabelle had never talked a lot except to Dan, or Jessie.

'Are you upset about leaving? Are you afraid you'll be homesick?' Rachelle persisted.

Rosabelle shuddered, 'Homesick? *No*. Certainly not! I hate Eyemouth now. I hate that sea. It's always there, day and night, roaring or sighing . . . I'll miss my baby and my mother-in-law, of course. And I'll miss Jessie.'

The mention of the baby was not one that Rachelle was eager to pursue, so she asked, 'Was Jessie the girl who saw you off? She is *formidable*, as the French say.'

'Formidable?' Rosabelle pronounced it in the English style.

Rachelle nodded. 'When she is old, she will sweep all before her!'

Rosabelle managed a smile but thought that Rachelle was not a very good judge of character.

'What made you decide to come with me after all? – it must have been a spur-of-the-moment decision,' was Rachelle's next question.

The girl's face clouded again. She wished she could tell the real reason she was running away, but feared to trust anyone with such a momentous secret. Jessie's grim warning about keeping quiet dominated her mind.

'My mother-in-law persuaded me. She thought it was an opportunity for me, and she knows how sad I've been since . . . She'll look after my baby till I return and he'll be safe with her. But London's very far away and I've never been south of Berwick in my life,' she said.

Rachelle smiled. 'Oh, you'll like the city. It'll change you. It changes everybody.'

She reached into her reticule again and brought out a flat tortoiseshell case, which she opened and held out, saying, 'Try to calm down. One of these will help. Have a cigarette.'

The reply was an astonished shake of the head. Some of

the old fisherwives in Eyemouth smoked clay pipes, or took snuff in copious quantities, but never touched cigarettes, which were only smoked by women considered disreputable.

Rachelle shrugged at the refusal, struck a vesta match against the edge of her case, and lit a narrow cigarette, which soon filled the air with an exotic, aromatic smell like nothing Rosabelle had ever smelt before.

'I hope you don't mind Turkish. I smoke them a lot,' said Rachelle, blowing a waft of smoke in the girl's direction.

The smell was actually delicious and, emboldened by the other woman's air of relaxation, Rosabelle leaned forward to ask earnestly, 'Tell me something . . . Is Rachelle de Roquefort your real name?'

'Why do you want to know?'

'Because it sounds unreal . . .'

'Rosabelle sounds unreal too, come to that.'

'Does it? I was called after my grandfather's fishing boat.'

'And I called myself after a cheese,' Madame Rachelle laughed merrily; but seeing that Rosabelle was still worried, she became serious again and told her, 'Don't worry. I used to be an actress and Rachelle de Roquefort was my stage name. I use it all the time now. You can call yourself anything you like, you know. After all, you were married to a man called Dan Maltman, so legally you're Mrs Maltman, but you call yourself Rosabelle Scott.'

'All fishermen's wives in Eyemouth keep their maiden names,' Rosabelle said defensively.

'All actresses keep any name they fancy,' was Rachelle's retort; but she didn't tell her real name.

Rosabelle furrowed her brow, for she was still worried. 'Tell me exactly what I'll have to do in London.'

'I've told you: make gowns.'

'But I'm not a society dressmaker. I don't know anything about high fashion.'

'Maybe not yet, but I do, and you're an artist. I've seen how you can look at a length of cloth and turn it into a garment in your head. There's not many people able to do that.'

'I've always liked pretty things,' Rosabelle demurred.

'Pretty things? Don't underrate yourself. What I want you to do is come with me to buy the best materials and then you'll design the gowns they can be made into. I'll find women to do the basic stitching, and you'll only have to add the finishing touches. You won't be in any sweatshop. It'll be easier for you than making the dress I wore at the military ball.'

'That *was* easy. I looked at you and I looked at the cloth and saw what it ought to look like.' Rosabelle did not think it had been any great problem.

'Exactly! You have a wonderful gift. I don't know what it's going to need to keep your magical faculty alive, but whatever it is, I'll give it to you. I'll give you anything you want.'

The girl stared, suddenly excited, but still diffident. 'I want to tell you something. I'm not very clever. I can't read or write . . .'

This was her secret and it made her very ashamed.

Rachelle was not a bit surprised and only said, 'So? I'll read and write for both of us. As soon as I put on that red dress I knew we'd make an unbeatable partnership. Rachelle and Rosabelle, dressmakers to the nobility. I even designed a business card for us . . .' She reached into her bag and pulled out a folded square of paper.

'Look . . .' she said, holding it out, pointing at the words it contained.

Rosabelle flushed scarlet and sat back, thinking she was being taunted. 'I told you I can't read.'

'Oh, sorry, I forgot. I'll read it to you . . . It says: "Rachelle and Rosabelle, Dressmakers to the Gentry and Ladies of Fashion".'

'Were you so sure that I'd come with you that you designed our card?' Rosabelle asked suspiciously.

'My dear, I hoped,' Rachelle replied, and smiled. It was the smile that really won Rosabelle round, because, for the first time, Rachelle looked genuinely open and uncalculating. On that smile they founded their partnership. On that smile they were to build their fortune.

On the day after Rosabelle arrived in London, Steven Anderson was buried. His funeral cortège was one of the most impressive the town had ever seen – Hester would have no less. His silver-handled coffin was carried downhill from

233

Beechwood on a huge ebony-coloured hearse with engraved-glass windows, solemnly drawn by four black horses bearing black plumes on their heads. The harness was covered with black velvet and the horses bent their necks and mouthed their silver bits as they paced along.

Effie and Jessie, clutching the hands of the well-wrapped-up children, were among the crowd of sceptical bystanders who watched the cortège go by. They had spent the time since Rosabelle's departure shut up at home in deep depression, occasionally weeping and asking each other when she'd be able to come home, and if they thought she would be safe with the mysterious Rachelle.

Going to watch a funeral was almost a relief for them. Standing together, with their shawls drawn up over their heads, they whispered sharp comments to one another.

'They've put on an awfy grand show for him,' said Effie, eyeing the flowers heaped around the coffin. 'They say the more a woman is relieved to be rid of a man, the more show of mourning she puts on. From this parade I'd guess Miss Hester is pleased to be free of Anderson.'

Jessie laughed. 'I don't know about her, but the old man certainly is glad.'

'How do you know that?'

'Listening and looking,' was the reply.

Hester, riding in the first carriage, looked thunderous, as she sat encased in total black with a tear-soaked handkerchief crunched up in her hand. Her father, at her side, seemed ill at ease and tried not to notice that she was refusing to exchange a word with him. In the second carriage with Everard sat two dejected-looking, shabby women, who, the crowd of watchers whispered, were Anderson's mother and sister. Hester had refused to allow them to ride with her, and for their part the grandeur of her home and manner intimidated them so completely that they had almost lost the power of speech.

After the cortège passed, the townspeople visibly relaxed and started talking animatedly among themselves. Most of them believed that Anderson had done away with himself, driven by guilt because he'd been helping himself to the disaster fund. A small minority were of the opinion that he had fallen into the harbour by accident; but there was a third, vociferous faction who said that he'd been pushed, though none of them had any idea of who pushed him, or why.

Effie and Jessie listened and nodded, but never voiced any opinions themselves, only occasionally glancing at one another when some gossip speculated that Miss Hester wouldn't leave a stone unturned to find out what had really happened to her husband.

After the interment in the town's burying ground people began to drift away, and Effie warned Jessie, 'Let's go hame. That wind's snell. The bairns must nae catch the cold,' she warned.

As they hurried up the alley towards the fishing people's houses, they met Willie Wake, who was sitting on the ground with his back against a high wall. He was shivering and his lips were blue with cold.

'Aw Willie,' said kind-hearted Effie, 'you should get in oot o' the cauld. Come wi' us and I'll gie you a wee whisky.'

He looked up with rheumy, red-rimmed eyes. 'You've a' been a kind-hearted wimman. Yer mither was the same and so was yer granny.'

Jessie leaned down and held out a hand to the old man. 'Come on, Willie,' she said.

He staggered to his feet and held on to her arm as she led him to Effie's house where a fire was blazing merrily in the hearth. He sank into Jimmy Dip's chair and held out his skinny hands to its heat. Neither of them knew how old he was, and he smelt rank, but he wakened their pity because his daughter-in-law treated him like a stray cur now that his son was dead.

Effie poured out a stiff whisky and handed it to him, saying, 'Drink that up, Willie. You look as if you need it.'

He downed it in one and held out the glass for another. They knew he could become obstreperous in drink, but he looked so pathetic that Effie gave in and poured a second. It had an immediate effect on the old man.

'I'm gonna gie you a wee sang, yin I wrote myself,' he announced, standing up and rocking on his heels in front of the fire.

Jessie laughed: 'All right, Willie, sing away.' But her smile froze when he started . . .

235

'When the deil came oot on a cold black night,
He saw a man and woman fight.
The lass was bonny with lang yellow hair,
It'd hae been better if she was never there.
The man was oot to do her wrang
But she was swift and she was strong.
Ae push was all it took,
Ae push put him in the drook.
The deil thocht the man was better deid
So he pushed him aff the auld pier heid.'

The women in the kitchen stared at each other in horror. For a moment Effie wondered if Willie was trying to blackmail them, but decided against that, because he'd always been her friend. He wasn't used to whisky and he was drunk, that was all. But he'd seen what happened between Rosabelle and Anderson – that was only too obvious.

Jessie knew that too. Her face was flaming red as she stood up and pushed the old man in the chest. 'I dinna like yer song, Willie. I think you should sing something else,' she told him.

He stopped singing at once. 'Dinna worry, Jess, dinna worry,' he said, and made for the door. Neither of them tried to stop him.

As the door banged behind him, they stared at each other.

'He knows, and he's daft as a brush. We canna be sure he'll keep his mouth shut,' said Jessie.

Effie shook her head. 'I dinna think he's as daft as he makes out and he didnae like Anderson any more than we did. We'll just have to trust him, but poor Rosabelle'll no' be able to come home as long as he's alive.'